I PLACED THE C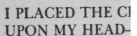
UPON MY HEAD—
and suddenly I was no longer gazing into a
fire on a circular granite altar. Instead I was
pinned in the light of a supernatural gaze, and
the vivid, raw reality of it staggered me.

I knew beyond doubting that if I reached out
in power, into the heart of the flame, I could
break through the skin of everyday life and
pass into the mythic country underneath.
The Sun lived there not as a warm orb in the
sky, not even as the kindly wish-giver my
people petitioned every day, but as something
real. The Crown and the fire were the keys
to the door. I was the king of the Shan, the
wearer of the Crystal Crown. I called myself the
Son of the Sun. Did I dare to meet him now?

THE REALM
BENEATH

B.W. Clough
has written these novels of Averidan:

THE CRYSTAL CROWN
THE DRAGON OF MISHBIL
THE REALM BENEATH

THE REALM BENEATH

B.W. CLOUGH

DAW BOOKS, INC.
DONALD A. WOLLHEIM, PUBLISHER

1633 Broadway, New York, NY 10019

Copyright © 1986 by B.W. Clough.

All Rights Reserved.

Cover art by Walter Velez.

DAW Collectors Book No. 676.

First Printing, June 1986

1 2 3 4 5 6 7 8 9

PRINTED IN U.S.A.

To my parents

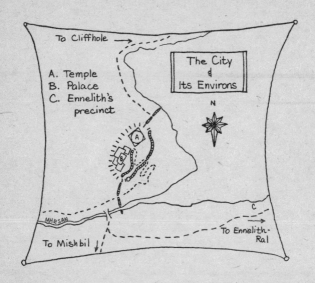

To Cliffhole

A. Temple
B. Palace
C. Ennelith's
   precinct

The City
&
Its Environs

N

A

B

MHESAN

To Mishbil

C

To Ennelith-Ral

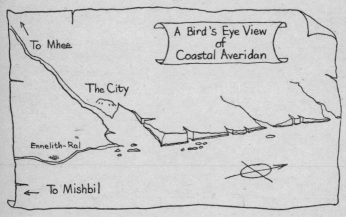

To Mhee

The City

A Bird's Eye View
of
Coastal Averidan

Ennelith-Ral

To Mishbil

PART 1

PART 1

Show me a hero and I'll write you a tragedy.
—F. Scott Fitzgerald.

CHAPTER 1:

A Person of No Importance

It was a dream. The sleeper knew it to be a dream. But another I, the dreamer, held smooth leather reins between the fingers of one hand. The partly trained colt under my thighs pretended to shy at the water a vendor sprinkled on the dusty hot road. Expertly I restrained the beast, patting the gleaming chestnut neck. "Which way shall we ride today, Liras?" my elder brother Zofal-ven called.

"East," I said. The sleeper could remember that this morning Zofal had been very witty about my ill-disguised preference. Melayne had gone that way. She had conceived last year, after my return from Ieor, but the summer heats of Averidan wear hard on foreigners, and she had miscarried. Was she now pregnant again? In bed, my head on the pillows and the covers under my chin, I knew. But in the dream I was anxious yet unwilling to admit it.

This time we rode east in silence. White powdery lime rose in clouds from the road, baked dry after the long summer. The wind of our speed blew it back in gauzy raveling wings from the horses' hooves. Very soon we saw what I knew we would see—a six-bearer sedan chair, brave with gilded wood and inlaid ivory. A red-brown head like no other in Averidan emerged from between the dust-curtains even before the bearers set the chair down—Melayne's. Her smile of triumph told me the news, and happiness like heady wine seemed to burble through my veins.

But as I leaped off my horse the dream slipped

11

around a corner and became nightmare. The wind rose, and the dust with it. With an inarticulate shout of dismay Zofal was buffeted away in the gale. My own mount squealed with terror and broke from my grasp. The eucalyptus trees beside the road swayed and snapped, offering long crumbly leaves to the moaning wind, and the pallid lime dust clawed at my throat and nose. Only the sedan chair was left, perched on its four legs carved like leopard paws.

I jingled the light curtains on their rings. "Let me in, Melayne, before I choke," I shouted. With a sweeping gesture someone rattled the curtain back. My jaw dropped, letting in the dust. Someone was in the car with my wife. I blinked watering eyes and shielded my head in my wide sleeve, trying to make out the face.

Because it was a dream the dust politely avoided the interior of the car. So the other was plain to see—it was I. Dark hair, dark eyes, the faint scar on my cheek, even the summer-weight green leather riding boots—but his were clean. As when I first donned the Crystal Crown, my own face and form stood before me. Or, more correctly, it lounged indolently on the padded yellow linen seat, one possessive arm draped around Melayne's shoulders. "Be off with you, messir," my double said. "If you have a petition to lay before the Shan King you must go through channels."

"Now wait a minute," I blustered. "This juvenile stunt is not going to work twice. *I'm* the Shan King, not you."

My double smiled, remote yet kind, revealing white even teeth. Without thinking, I ran my tongue over my own. Was my smile really that reptilian? "You are mistaken," said he. "I am indeed the Shan King and native to this realm. You are merely Liras-ven Tsormelezok—a worthy individual, I doubt not, but of no importance."

With another rattle of silver rings the curtain closed. An imperious tap on the car's inlaid roof signaled the bearers, who had stood patiently through dust and storm, to move off. "Wait a minute," I called, foolishly. "That's my wife you've got there. Melayne, tell him who I am!"

Of course there was no reply. The tramp of a dozen feet was quickly swallowed up by mournful wind and rustling leaves. The dust had lessened somewhat, but when I rubbed the grit out of my eyes I saw I was no longer on the east road. Barren and pale, the desert stretched to either side of me, and the light was going.

I knew who was responsible. That other I, the Shan King, had stripped me of everything of value. These were the leavings, suitable to one "of no importance." For the Kings of the Shan are not born but made, chosen from among the people of Averidan. After my enforced accession I had painfully grown into my rank, learning courage and kingship with clumsy doggedness, helped only by occasional mental dialogues with the Crystal Crown. But now all this was taken from me. Just as in the old days, I began to run, aimlessly and in panic. And to my horror the sands clutched at my feet. I fell, and with inexorable tenacity they drew me down and down, into the hot close dark.

"Liras, wake up!" Cool hands brushed the sweaty covers back from my face. A thick tumble of sweet-smelling hair curtained me, and Melayne said, "That was a nasty one, from the sound of it. I told you that second lobster would make you sick."

I clutched at her, and then relaxed with a gasp. The night-lamp had gone out, and from the stars outside the window I could tell it was nearly morning. "I dreamed—" But she could not understand my terror, though I tried to tell her. "There's only one of you in your head," I explained, more to myself than her.

Melayne has learned to ignore my more confused statements. "You're so worrisome," she said. "A babe will be the ruin of you. Your nightmares should at least reflect real terrors. I wish I *had* gone by sedan chair. That barge trip was a horror."

I could not help smiling at her injured tone. Truly, her expression had been anything but triumphant when she had returned this afternoon. Though the river crossing to the goddess Ennelith's local Sodality had been extremely brief, the day calm and clear, Melayne had been violently seasick. After her pregnancy had been confirmed she had refused to return by water, and forced the bearers to carry her in the sedan chair in a wide circle, up the southern river bank and over the bridge to the City again.

Through the thin silk night robe I felt her solid familiar warmth. "There isn't anything here," I said, stroking the flat belly. "Are the priestesses sure?"

"Feel again." She untied the garment and slid out of it.

I caught her fingers as they tugged at my robe. "Are expectant mothers allowed to do this?" I asked uncertainly. "Isn't it, ah, bad for the child?"

"Right now the child's too young to notice," Melayne said with authority. "Don't start fussing, you have at least five months, perhaps six, to work yourself up to fatherhood."

It was too dark to see her expression, but her tone brooked no argument. "I can't sleep anymore," I said.

"You will," she predicted, smugly.

That was in Arnep, the last month in the season of Summer. The two months following the autumn equinox were unusually placid, marked only by seasonal affairs. My klimflowers bloomed again, cloaking the walls and arbors of the Palace in living purple. The second planting of barley came up, and the grapes were picked. The year's wine flowed, ruby or pink, gold or white, into waiting clay jars. Plums of every color, so abundant that their branches bent down to kiss the earth, were brought in. A traveler in the countryside would walk in and out of great clouds of fruity steam that surrounded local distilleries. The villagers were laying in their stocks of plum brandy.

This time last year I had been miserable. Autumn is a golden season for food-lovers, a class that includes just about all Shan. Minor lordlings—I was one once—spend the long mellow days supervising the harvest. But though the Shan King receives his share of the bounty, protocol forces him to keep high and remote state. Last year had been the first harvest-time I could no longer ride around the estate, sampling plums, tasting and evaluating new wine, or helping to dispose of brandy that overflowed the bottles. I had sulked like a child left out of a party.

The further districts send their portions in midwinter, when viceroys and local lords come to account for their stewardships. But farmers near the City bring the grain or fruit or wine right up the winding road to the Palace. The carts had always been unloaded in a courtyard before, and the produce carried directly to storerooms. I had seen only the tallies and scrolls.

This year I was wiser. All the duties were brought right in with the farmers to the wide audience hall. This took more time and effort, but meant I could see and feel—and sample—the harvest. A boring and onerous royal duty was transformed into a continuous flow of delightful presents.

The farmers were agreeable too, once word spread that my main interest was tasting the tithes. Everyone sympathized with that, while they would have grumbled at mere interference. My cat Sahai pretended to supervise, scrabbling in the baskets with a dainty gray paw in case a mouse was hiding with the wine jars. Only the chamberlains were unhappy over the dust and indignity of the proceedings. When the Shan King condescended to unseal wine jars or pick over apples Palace etiquette got dented.

An old neighbor of my mother's brought some nectarines one afternoon, and I sent for Melayne. "I know the fruit is very nutritious," I told Hoob. "You know the Lady is expecting."

Hoob grinned with pleasure, revealing the gap where his front teeth had been. I had known the lean old man, and his fruit, ever since I could walk. "The very bees fly out of the orchard fatter than they went in," he boasted. "Have another, young sir—or no, they're not mine anymore, is that right, Your Majesty?"

"Don't worry about it," I said, cutting off the Director of Protocol's whispered rebuke. The mouth-watering perfume of the ripe fruit made the air sweeter than the most costly incense. With malicious generosity I pressed a particularly luscious specimen into the Director's hand. "Try one, my lord, they're very good." Then I pretended not to watch the struggle between his appetite and his dignity.

When Melayne appeared she was impressed; no such fruit grows in Cayd. "And last year's harvest was just as big," she marveled, licking sticky fingers. "No wonder your folk can afford five meals a day."

"You ought to eat more," I said incautiously. As a matter of principle my wife discouraged any vestige of overworry on my part. This time she threw the stone of her fruit at me, but not with serious force. Discreetly the Director laid a handkerchief over the fallen pit, before Sahai could bat it across the tile floor.

"No, Lady, we have our lean years." Hoob nodded sagely, like an old tortoise. "The year this lad was born, now, or was it the year before? There was unseasonable cold. Froze the blossoms right off the trees. And only fifteen years ago, the year of the flood in Mishbil, it was dry. Terrible dry."

"All in all, though," I put in, "the land is blessed. We're descendants of the Sun, so the god favors us."

Melayne chose another nectarine. "Is that just what rhetors say in their plaiv, or is it really true?"

"It's genuine fact," I told her.

"And there's proof, too," Hoob told her with a

cackle of glee. "You carry it in your belly. What will you wager, the child will look just like her sire?"

Melayne raised downy eyebrows. Though the Caydish way is salacious talk but conservative behavior, our more decorous manners had rubbed off on her. But she said only, "I'm counting on a boy, myself."

"Don't accept the bet," I cautioned her. "For sure, whatever the sex, it will have dark eyes and dark hair, just like all the Shan. That's the legacy of Viris our foremother. You'll still be the only carrot-head in town."

She scowled at me, for it was a libel. Rather, her hair was the deep rich color of the new buds in spring, bursting-full with life to come. But before she could finish her nectarine, and so free a new missile, the door swung wide. The chamberlain opened his mouth to announce a caller. Behind him, however, a red-hatted head bobbed as its owner jumped up and down. "All right," I said, dismissing the chamberlain with a wave, and Xalan danced in.

"You'll never guess what the Sardonyx Council just accepted—on your behalf," he announced. Though his narrow face was composed, the merry glint in his dark eye betrayed him.

"This is how he informed me I was getting married," I told Melayne, laughing.

"This doesn't have that comic potential," Xalan said. "It's just odd." And he held out a little knife with a red stone haft and a stone blade, broken a short way from the hilt.

For a moment I didn't recognize it. Then Melayne gasped, "It's the war token. They're declaring war."

"Is it truly?" Xalan stared with interest. No one in Averidan knew of the little knife's previous history so he did not recognize it. "Why declare war? And why now? One doesn't begin war in autumn, with winter coming on. Are you sure you aren't mistaken?"

"She's quite right," I cut in, before Melayne could

become indignant. "Did the messenger have any other word?"

"No, he left straightaway," said Xalan.

"A pity," Melayne said. "I might have recognized him, been able to learn more for you."

I looked at her. "You don't feel you'd be betraying your kin?" For in Averidan relatives stick together like leeches; the only socially acceptable crimes are those of nepotism.

Now she did throw her fruit pit, with a hard expert flick of her wrist. It bounced off my middle, leaving a wet stain on my green sash, before I could dodge. "I'm your *wife*," she said firmly. She planted one fist to either side of her waist and glared at me. "And wars are bad for children."

My mouth opened as the realization hit me. My first-born might enter a world of disorder, even danger. The relative importance of my responsibilities suddenly and violently re-ordered themselves; the happiness of a tiny being I wouldn't even set eyes on for another season became vital.

"We must mobilize," I decided, "but we'll also send out an envoy. The task will be to find out what the Cayd want. If it's at all reasonable we'll give it to them, so we won't have to wage a war."

"If you say so," Xalan said a little doubtfully.

Melayne interrupted. "That's not the way to do it," she declared with impatience. "You must fight and win!"

"No." I turned to Xalan again. "Have the Council send an envoy the Cayd will like. How about that rhetor?"

"Bochas-hel," Xalan remembered. "We'll see." He bowed to Melayne and withdrew. Hoob, who had listened to all this high-flown talk with true Shan curiosity, also scurried away to spread the news.

"You know we respect strength," Melayne began to scold as soon as the door shut. "Compromise and King Mor will think you're weak!"

I sat on the dais and drew Melayne down beside

me. She was short enough to lean comfortably back against me, with her head under my chin. "You can't be displeased that I'm reluctant to kill your brothers," I said reasonably. "We'd win a war, and then I'd be bound to order their execution. Wouldn't you rather know them to be alive and going about their affairs in Cayd?"

She turned to hug me, her strong little arms making my ribs creak. "You are the nicest man, Liras," she exclaimed softly. I kissed the braid-wound top of her head, between the silver hair-rods that pinned the mass up, and was just congratulating myself on my diplomacy when she added, "You wouldn't survive a year in Cayd!"

When the Shan consider war, it's inevitably in the lurid images supplied by plaiv. Those oral legends are long on forlorn last stands, unlikely double-crosses, and amazing battlefield revelations of long-concealed blood-ties. Mundane realities like tactics or supply are studied only by commanders. So the initial preparations for conflict were leisurely, impractical, and conducted through a haze of unreality.

The work was further complicated by habits acquired in that favorite Viridese pastime, social feuding. Our quarrel with Cayd had begun the way any family's might have done, with disagreements at a joint function—in this case, the minor war a year before last. Now that hostilities were formally opened everyone instinctively expected a year, or perhaps two, of exchanging veiled insults. We never dash into things.

All this explains, but does not excuse us. The City worked itself into a froth of pleasurable excitement. I had a bath, supper, and a night's sleep before helping the Sardonyx Council draft a letter to King Mor of Cayd. We had a sumptuous luncheon afterward, to ensure an amiable frame of mind: green seaweed soup from tureens shaped like broody hens, redfish wrapped in sage leaves, and the barley, steamed, tinted, and arranged almost grain by grain into a fantastic sculpture representing a water-lily blossom the size of a draft dog.

By the time all these good things were consumed, my royal missive had summoned Bochas-hel, the rhetor who had been so admired in Cayd. My authority canceled all his other plans, and he left that day on his errand west.

That afternoon I did justice. One of the last genuinely hot days of the season blazed outside. Though the mosaic floors and high ceilings were meant to be cool, the tall triple-arched windows to trap every breeze, the heat made everyone in the Hall of Justice sleepy. Only the first group of disputants were alert as ruffled geese, glaring and whispering invective at each other from either side of the room.

I arranged my ornate sleeves and draperies comfortably around the tall throne and nodded at the chamberlain to begin. The first disputant, a lean farmer in painfully clean clothes, stepped forward.

"Your Majesty, my name is Orn. My neighbor Melic is cheating me."

"I am not," Melic hissed. The chamberlain hushed him.

Orn gave him a triumphant glance and continued, "I am the owner of a good bull, sire to many strong oxen in my village. Shortly after Your Majesty's accession I made agreement with Melic concerning the bull's services. The bull would serve Melic's cow twice. The first calf was to be his, and the second mine."

The generous luncheon weighed in my middle, and I thought longingly of a nap. "That sounds fair," I said, clenching my jaw to hide a yawn.

"Imagine my dismay," Orn said, warming to his subject, "when Melic refused to deliver over the second calf! The whole summer I've been after him about it, and at last I appealed to Lord Zener-lis, who brought the decision to you."

I fixed the elderly Lord with a disapproving eye. If this dispute had taken place in Mhee or Ennelith-

Ral Zener would have had to decide on his own. But since his domain was local, Zener could shuffle even the most petty problems off onto me. However, before I could call him to task the farmer Melic had to have his say.

He bounced forward, plump and indignant. "Your Majesty, this skinny sack of mendacity is spinning a plaiv for you. No such agreement was made at all. The first calf was sired by his bull, it is true. But only because Orm refused, from laziness or parsimony, to keep the bull's pen in repair. The poor frustrated beast broke through, onto *my* property, and lured my Blossom into congress."

"It was you!" Orn almost sputtered in his rage. "Tethering a cow in heat on the other side!"

"The second calf," Melic said loudly, "was sired by a piebald bull owned by my wife's brother-in-law's second cousin. All you need do is view the calf to discern its parentage—its hide is black and white."

"We brought the calf for Your Majesty's inspection," Lord Zener volunteered. My chamberlain visibly paled at the thought of cowpats on the tile.

"Why didn't you make the judgment yourself, my lord Zener?" I asked. "You can judge a calf's color as well as I."

With a portentous frown that wrinkled up his forehead past the former hairline, Zener said, "Well, Your Majesty, unfortunately the bull in question is also piebald—Orn's, that is. Most of the cattle in my district are. Perhaps Your Majesty's special insight could discover the calf's ancestry?"

I rubbed my forehead and sighed, wondering if all monarchs dealt in such idiotic disputes. At least in Averidan the Crystal Crown helped me render swift decisions. I gestured for Xalan to bring it forward. With a start—he had been nodding in his seat against a pillar—he rose.

It had been against custom when I named Xalan Bearer of the Crystal Crown. He is a magus, a geomant, and in theory has more important things to do than carry valuable relics around for me. And the office requires no skill, for no one but myself or my Bearer would dare touch the thing. The tiger's teeth need no guardian. But the convenience of having a friend in so intimate a post was irresistible, and anyway Xalan's interests are so diverse his magian talents get diffused. Now he winked sympathetically as he bowed and held out the gold-plated wooden casket.

I held the Crown on my knee for a moment before putting it on. Lately, for my private amusement, I would make my own assessments before using the Crown to learn the truth. It was gratifying to find I rarely guessed wrong. Now, with a long glance at each disputant, I surmised there were lies on either side. The Viridese habit of shutting away unpleasant truths would enable both parties to enjoy the pleasures of righteous anger.

The white, crystalline substance of the Crown clasped my head snugly from brow to nape. As it warmed, my awareness grew, extending up and out across the room. Behind Xalan's mischievous facade I could now discern his intelligent and loyal heart. Lord Zener, on the other hand, showed even more foolish and indecisive than before. Yet all this I knew already. I was learning my trade both with the Crown and without it. Perhaps that was why bit by bit it had ceased "conversing" with me inside my head, as it had when I first became King.

I surveyed the two farmers and smiled. It was easy now to sift truth from lie, as easy as picking out the mushrooms floating in an oyster stew. "Both your accounts are correct," I mused. "The bull did indeed break into Melic's pature. It was then that the agreement Orn mentions was struck. So the second calf does indeed belong to him. My lord Zener, you will see to the animal's delivery."

With almost the same voice all three of them exclaimed, "I told you so!" Before more arguments could begin I signaled the chamberlain to show them out. The next group immediately perked up, with the expression of cats when fish are cleaned. When a guardsman pushed through to the head of the queue he received peevish glances and muttered imprecations.

"There are dreadful tidings, Your Majesty," the guardsman announced in a loud voice. Everyone hushed, to hear better. "The Caydish have invaded Averidan. The outpost at the Tambors was burned four days ago."

For a moment no one said anything. Everyone stood or sat, silent, in their traditional spot, King on throne, disputants on their benches along the walls, chamberlains herding them along. Our petty histrionics now seemed like the play of children; our vehement and narrow conflicts stood stark in all their foolishness. It was as if I had passed the Crown among the crowd, so that everyone could see the truth with merciless clarity.

Xalan recovered first. "When was this?"

The guardsman didn't know. "But it's, what? a day only, since we received their declaration of war," Xalan calculated. "They must have moved against the Tambors almost immediately after issuing it."

I took the Crown off. The hearts of the Shan are open to the King, but it would be discourteous to probe their dismay any more. "My people," I announced, "there will be no more judgments today." Stepping down from the dais, I returned the Crown to Xalan and hurried from the room. From shock, the chamberlains were slow to close the tall doors behind me, and the stunned murmurs of my sheltered subjects followed me down the wide hall.

Like everyone, I had muttered often at our cumbersome customs. But I had never before discovered actual fault. Now a terrible lack in our governing was laid bare. Only one war had ever been waged on Viridese soil—eight hundred years ago. Then, we had lost—the Tsorish outlanders had ruled, married

in, and at last become one with us. We now had
elderly generals leading a part-time soldiery. It would
take days to mobilize.

Grimly, I began. That very hour General Horfal-yu,
premier veteran of the Ieor campaign, was deputed
to muster the Army. He had to be called away from
a complicated tabletop battle he was waging with
wooden blocks and reeds on maps, and grumbled
that autumn was too busy a season for war. Of far
more help to my peace of mind was the renowned
warrior Sisterhood of Mir-hel. Commander Silverhand
immediately sent reliable squads of cunning women
west to harry the Cayds, but stayed herself to assist
me.

And the magi spied on the foe from afar with
their mirrors. A preliminary hydromantic scry revealed looting, robbery, and rape, but oddly enough
none of the wholesale slaughter I feared. "Then it
can't be just a raid," I worried. I had not forgotten
the previous Warlord's interest in our country. Suppose his death had not been deterrent enough?

"Be grateful for what we've got," Xalan said. "They
can turn vicious any time."

But the Commander agreed with me. "Scrying
won't plumb their purposes," she declared, "and knowing the purpose of your opponent is half the way to
beating him. We'll be off-balance until it's discovered."

"Let the magi scry over the pass into Cayd," I
suggested. "If they really intend to stay, the women-
folk will be packing up and preparing to follow."

But this last turned out to be impossible. "Our
mirrors reveal nothing of speculi or lands beyond
Averidan's borders," the Master Magus explained.
Then he yawned terribly, smothering it politely behind a long pale hand freckled with age-spots. The
Council had worked all night, and now we all waited
in an anteroom of the Sun Temple. Just then the
priestess signaled that all was ready.

It was still night in the valley of the Mhesan, but
here on the hill the first morning sunshine enriched

the gilding on the Temple's dome. Quickly I put on the Crystal Crown. We took our places in the procession, the magi last, then me. Silverhand paced just before me, slim and tanned, the very image of a woman warrior with her hair knotted back below a gilded helmet. The General's grizzled head bulked over her. I picked up my sacrifice. The Lord of Life dislikes gifts that smell of death. But such a pass demanded a valuable offering, and of course it must be combustible. So after some thought I had sent for a large flask of vintage plum brandy. Knowledgeable General Horfal-yu winced at the sight but could not protest the appalling waste.

The round green glass jug was full and heavy, and awkward to hold. But it would be improper for anyone else to carry it. For this was not a personal wish-sacrifice. We, the descendants of the Sun, were as a nation asking a favor of the god. As Lord of the Shan I had to represent my people. The frantic urgency of our plight notwithstanding, I had had to dress to the teeth so that the god should not mistake me. My chief fear, what with my sleepiness, the slick glass jug, my ornate trailing silk sleeves, and uncomfortable emerald-sewn shoes, was that I would trip. Xalan helped by unobtrusively poking my sleeves back with his magic wand.

The deep boom of copper gongs announced the opening of the rite. The tidings had spread throughout the City, and a deep reverential murmur met us as we paced through the crowded courtyard into the sanctuary. Instinctively I skimmed the emotions that surged around us.

A little fear, mostly from folk with relatives living near the border. Optimism—the Shan King would take care of it as he took care of everything. And, to my annoyance, a remnant of the old pleasurable excitement. We all adore incident, and no one really believed our pleasant way of life was in genuine peril. Not for the first time, I reflected that we were getting softer than an over-ripe peach. When would the fruit slip from the stem?

Singing, the white-clad priestesses led the way from the bright autumn morning outside through the gold-sheathed doors into the Temple's familiar dimness. We followed behind, and then came as many of the folk waiting outside that could be accommodated. The flicker of the altar fire made my eyes heavier than ever. But I had no space in me to remember the long night now.

The shimmering white line stood motionless in its circle round the fire, while the priestesses immersed themselves in their melody. With a pitter-pat like the pulse of a startled heart, one and then another of the long wandlike drums underscored the rhythm with their high solemn note. Then the handfast circle began to turn, slow and stately, four steps forward, one back, then three more forward and two back, faster and faster. In this oldest dance of all, we earth-born children of the Sun reach up, like trees or vines, to join hands with our brother-stars and sister-planets, take our place in the turning celestial spheres.

And we also took up the song and the step. The General held up the hem of his full white and green cloak; I set my jug down near the altar and girded up my sleeves and hems; the Commander lay down her buckler and the Magus his wand. We made up the smallest and slowest circle, round and round the altar, not touching hands but spinning separately like comets. The many other worshippers formed the third, rotating out near the wall.

For a moment we were one, a single heart abeat in the core of Averidan, a sole mind brimming with a united song. But nothing unalloyed can be long maintained, here so far below the sky. Too soon the High Priestess stepped out from among her sisters. We halted, panting a little, to take up our belongings again, and the outer ring slowed also. But the spinning white circle continued to turn, deliberate as the cycle of seasons. Though the dance is ordinarily made only once a year, on Mid-Summer Day, they did not tire or falter.

But now I became aware of something new. Here in its long home, in the warmth of the fire that forged it and the pulse of my heat from the dance, the Crystal Crown almost hummed with arcane power. An intolerable flash of arctic light burst from it, startling everyone including me. The columns, the golden dome arching high above us, every strand of the Magus' long white mustaches, stood out in the glare.

A little shaken, the High Priestess began the prayer of invocation. I did not take it in. Never before had I occasion to wear the Crystal Crown here. Now I felt the hand of the deity pressing on my mind, heavier than a hundred men. They called me the Son of the Sun. Was that just a royal epithet?

When I made no move to hand over the jug the priestess gently took it from my nerveless fingers. She unstoppered it and splashed the liquor onto the altar slowly, so as not to quench the flames. The fire roared eagerly at this new fuel, blooming into joyful red and gold tongues. A plummy wave of sweet intoxicating heat scorched our faces. The priestess paused and looked at me. "Your wish, Majesty?"

My mouth opened but nothing came out. The wording of this all-important wish had been hotly debated, the General favoring "overwhelming victory in battle" while the Magus wanted "a miraculous Caydish defeat without a fight." In the end we had agreed I should wish "for a swift and glorious victory over our foes" and so leave the deity room to manipulate events. Now in the presence of the god I felt the presumption of this wish. We called ourselves the Children of the Sun. Could we not trust him to take care of us?

The Crown seemed to pulse on my head from the heat of the sacrificial fire, and the shrill song of the priestesses rang in my ears. With a sidewise mental skip into irrelevance I wondered how the god put up with all the silly wishes people begged of him day after day. A new variety of pear, the recovery of a sick cat, a black foal rather than a gray one—the frivolous requests I myself had made here over the years flitted through my mind. What a waste of divine attention!

Then, so clearly that I could not tell whether it was the Crystal Crown itself that spoke, I was certain the god listened to and considered every wish. When Melayne gave birth I would give ear to the whims, however foolish, of our child. Parents love their children. The heat that smote my brow was a furnace of paternal love. I no longer looked into a fire on a circular granite altar. Instead I was pinned in the light of a supernatural gaze that stared out at me with a jealously devoted regard. Of course everyone knows the god takes care of his children. But this vivid, raw reality staggered me. It was unheard of.

Suddenly I knew that if I reached out in power, into the heart of the flame, I could break through the skin of everyday life and pass into the mythic country underneath. The Sun lived there not as a warm orb in the sky, not even as the kindly wish-giver we petitioned every day, but as something real. The Crown and the fire were the keys to the door. I called myself the Son of the Sun; did I now dare meet him?

As soon as the invitation became clear in my mind, I realized I wanted no part of it. The most terrifying aspect of becoming Shan King was the nearness of this other world, the realm beneath yet more truly real than ours, where plaiv becomes reality. And the last deity I wanted to meet was our forefather. The scars from years of inadequacy ached at the very idea. No doubt the god had a great deal of criticism to offer about the way I was managing his realm. To meet his disappointment face to face, fumble out excuses, blush under that burning eye, was impossible. By now my long delay had drawn everyone's attention. Silverhand, who stood behind me, quietly prompted, "The wish, Liras?"

"The wish, yes," I mumbled through dry lips. I dared not go forward, into that searing reality. Yet presenting our untrusting request to this searing fountain of affection was beyond me. Slowly I said, "I wish—for what is best, in the god's judgment, for us all, in these circumstances."

The Magus covered his eyes in frustration. Xalan grimaced consolingly at me. The priestess poured out the rest of the liquor and stared attentively at the flames to divine the god's answer. I watched too, and it came to me that I had wished rightly.

And indeed, after a long moment, the priestess turned to us with the serene smile proper to the delivery of glad news. "The god regards your wish with favor," she said.

The General puffed like a grampus with relief, and Silverhand discreetly patted my back. The ring of dancers scattered, seemingly flung in all directions by the force of their circling. Everyone relaxed, and the Magus said with resignation, "I suppose I should have written that wish down for you."

"It slipped my mind," I apologized. There seemed no point in discussing my complicated experiences; I needed to think them over. Better to be thought foolish. And now I considered further there was nothing to worry about. Such a furious love would hardly be balked. All would be well.

"Specific wishes are better, though," Xalan said, "if you want straight yes-or-no answers. The whole point of the exercise was to learn what would happen. Now what do we do?"

"We fight them," the General said with great conviction. "And we'll win. What could be better?"

"When we do," I said, "we must have a thank-offering." For at that moment I felt cheerfully pious.

CHAPTER 2:

The Honor of the Tsormelezoks

Our messenger had taken two days to reach the City by horse. The Caydish force could not, we surmised, travel so fast. They were afoot, and had to subdue an increasingly sullen and uncooperative peasantry. The unarmed woodsmen and farmers could do little more than hide their goods, scuttle the bridges, and then hide. The sparsely settled western terrain is a gift to those who know it. Scrying magi reported more complicated annoyances: fouled wells, strangled Caydish scouts, and sudden forest fires. These could no doubt be credited to the Sisterhood.

For our part in four days we were ready. The General laid out a series of supremely complex battle plans, each with its appropriate map. We resolved to march to Mhee, a day's journey upriver. The battle could be fought just west of it, thus saving the town from sack and giving us a convenient base for supplies.

The evening before we marched was the only one I could spare for my family. Only my older sister Siril was foolish enough to pout about the neglect. "You haven't invited us to dinner in weeks, Lirasven," she complained, helping herself to a generous ladleful of spicy octopus soup.

As the eldest sib, Zofal felt bound to come to my defense. "That's right," he said to her, his brown forelock jerking with annoyance. "What's the good of being Shan King if you don't perpetually entertain a wide circle of your relatives?"

In a lifetime with my sister, Zofal had never grasped her utter immunity to sarcasm. "I think that's only right," Siril replied with a serious nod. The effect was impressive. To please my relatives I had ordered the meal laid in one of the grander dining halls. A many-curved ceiling stuck with gold foil was supported by pillars cast of glass, a gigantic jewel-box to suggest that the Shan King's meals were costly as gems. For the occasion Siril had piled her dark hair elaborately atop her head, and further heightened the structure with a tasseled silver ornament. "All these clever cooks, the gorgeous vegetables Liras raises, why shouldn't he share with us? Don't you think so, dear?"

Her husband Dasan-hel was far too diplomatic to criticize me. "You must remember, wife, your brother has many other social obligations." He smiled toothily in my direction to be sure I appreciated the tact, and smoothed back his thinning hair. Despite all the talk of it my brother-in-law is the only relative who still hopes to derive substantial advantage from me.

In her annoyance Mother let her porcelain spoon fall back into her bowl. As she dabbed at the soup-splash on her expensive amethyst robe she exclaimed, "How did I ever birth such a feather-headed brood? Only Liras-ven grasps the peril we're in. We could lose the war. Do you foolish children realize what that means? Do you never listen to the plaiv of sacked cities and defeated nations?"

"There aren't many, you know," Yibor-soo sniffed, wrinkling her button nose. "Unpleasant plaiv spoil the appetite."

"And I don't see why Liras-ven gets any credit," her son Rosil chimed in. He had rapidly absorbed his soup and was now peeling a peach. "It's his duty to be concerned about Averidan."

"So that we don't have to be?" Mother turned to me. "What do you say, Liras dear?"

Once, as the youngest of an argumentative family, I had kept my mouth shut to stay out of trouble. Though I was no less quiet now, I had decided it was from royal dignity. My kin accepted this valuation so readily it surprised me. Thus appealed to, I pointed out, "Every Viridese has to do his part; the Shan King can't carry a dead weight. Surely in any real crisis the *chun-hei*, the impractical honor in our folk will rise to the surface."

Mother cast a chilly glance up and down the sumptuous table, but said nothing. Since I had become King I appreciated more and more how wise Mother was. Though her manner was frail and high-bred, her face as delicately painted as a peony, this was deceptive. She had ruled the Tsormelezoks, body and soul, for years, for my sire had left her a widow early. Her raven hair, sparse but still untouched by frost, was combed simply back, to reveal massive pearl earrings. I had traveled far to acquire grit and mental toughness, but all this time Mother had possessed them.

Melayne had no patience with our argumentative ways. Her growing bulk made her restless, and though under my anxious eye she had eaten heartily of the scorpionfish baked in clay, the radishes and turnips carved into flowers, and the pan-fried duck, she had skipped the soup course that closes formal Viridese repasts. Now she came in through the triple-arched terrace doors, saying, "Is there a festival tonight, Liras?"

"I haven't ordered one," I said, "but there's nothing to prevent private parties."

"No, it's not private," she said. "I can see the fireworks."

I frowned and rose from my place. The magi, who occasionally supply fireworks for official functions, had no time to waste now on such frivolity. The wide doors gave onto the terrace that surrounds the Palace complex, and Melayne pointed to the night sky, past the bright windows of her own rooms. "There, to the west, you see the lights?"

The cliff is more than sheer to the north and west, down to the river valley. Below, the fields are flat, criss-crossed with canals; one can see for leagues. A reddish glow glimmered below the horizon, waxing and then dimming again, staining the sky and back-lighting a single tree, tiny and black with the distance. "I suppose they're fireworks," I said doubtfully. "I've never seen the like."

"I have." Mother had followed us outside. Her still-unwrinkled face was like bronze in the lamplight streaming from the windows. She stood so still her earrings did not flicker. "It's fire. Something big is burning."

"Ah, Viris!" I cried. "It's Mhee! They've sacked the city!" The wood-built town would burn unchecked, once set alight.

Siril burst into dramatic tears as she stood in the doorway. I pushed past her, shouting for the chamberlain. Yibor, who was still at table dissecting a pomegranate with a knife and pudgy fingers, remarked, "The standard of royal manners has gone down terribly, I must say, since my late brother's reign."

With more perception, Rosil said, "No, there's something wrong." Mother came in and in low tones broke the news.

"Send to the magi," I instructed the chamberlain. "They must descry Mhee. Get General Horfal-yu to assemble his men, and send word to the Sisterhood. We march immediately." Before, the Caydish had always surprised us; I had had enough.

Siril's sniffs echoed weirdly from the arched ceiling. Zofal came up as the chamberlain hurried away. "Can we help, brother?"

I turned to face him; Rosil stood behind his shoulder with a nervous yet determined expression on his face. In the way of most leisured Viridese, both my brother and half-nephew had learnt some minimal handling of spear and sword. They had no experience whatever in war, but I hesitated to decline their help. The Shan custom is to argue furiously only over trivialities; in major crises we pull together. I felt strongly now that any appearance of this quality, this *chun-hei*, should be encouraged.

"We can use every hand," I decided. "If you can be ready by morning, come along and welcome."

Mother's lips thinned tensely; she had already lost me to the Kingship. But it was Yibor who threw down her fruit-knife and squealed, "No, Rosil, I forbid it! You're my only child."

I sighed. But rank does have privileges. To Rosil I said, "You deal with it. I have work to do." As I banged the door and hurried down the hall I regretted momentarily that Mother and Yibor-soo were too old for military service. I would back them against the Cayds any day.

Dawn broke over a City that seethed like a trampled anthill. The magi confirmed Mhee's sack; the news swept through town like corrosive acid. Soldiers who lived in town had followed my example and spent the evening with their families; others made merry at the local taverns and food-stalls. All were displeased to hear the alarm-gongs, trundled through the streets on a dog-cart so that all could hear and know.

The Director of Protocol wrung his hands at the disorder. "You're not scheduled to leave today," he wailed. "It's very unlucky, for the Shan King's forces to march without a parade."

"This is an emergency," I said. I clasped the heavy lamellar coat and accepted my sword and shield from the armorer. "Xalan, are the magi ready?"

"If we arrive at the field of battle early enough to set up the weather magery," said Xalan, "the Cayd will have a tornado to contend with."

"That I'd like to see," Rosil said with a sort of grim glee. He sat on one of the wardrobe room's many clothes benches, awkwardly balancing his late father's javelins against his metalled shoulder. His lamellar jacket was an heirloom, so antique the bronze plaques rattled loose in their lacings.

"It'll take some of the fight out of them," I predicted, "but not all. You know Melayne is a Cayd—imagine an entire army of stubborn red-headed firecrackers."

Xalan shook his head as he uncovered the mirror. "That's why magi don't marry," he said.

I cast only a perfunctory glance at myself in the glass before setting the Crystal Crown on my head. Its white-faceted helm shape covered my dark hair completely. "Now the cloak," I directed, and a heavy deep green one was draped and pinned on. Mirrors are magic in Averidan; it was easy to look at this stranger in the glass, grim and competent—the hero-king riding out to save his people—and separate him from myself.

Zofal had taken Mother and Yibor-soo home to the family estate, and returned with mounts. When we clattered out to the Palace courtyard he was there, stroking the necks of several horses. "Try not to get Sorrel killed," he cautioned, holding out the reins of the red stallion. "He's the tallest beast we've ever raised, and we haven't bred him yet. To lose his bloodline would be a disaster."

"It's good to have the relative importance of these things clear," I replied with a straight face. Since there was to be no parade we simply rode out when all was ready. The General and the Army were to meet us just outside the City, in the marketplace. The Sisters were all ready—about two hundred tough, slim women in businesslike brown linen and light bronze armor. But the magi were tardy, straggling from their towers in ones and twos as if they had worked on their individual magian studies to the very last minute.

"I'm too old for this," the Magus grumbled. "You're sure that thing is well-trained? I don't want it to dash off and start biting Caydish axemen."

"She's tame as a dog, and I'll lead her myself," Zofal said peevishly. He hated criticism from non-horsemen, who were nearly everyone in Averidan.

"You rode one before and had no difficulty. If you'd rather walk to the fight—"

"Grand-uncle is over eighty," Xalan interrupted. "To expect an old man to walk all morning and then direct a magian attack is cruel."

Zofal made a brushing gesture, as if at an annoying fly. Then he boosted the Magus aboard a plump white pony. The Magus rearranged his long red robes and did his best to look dignified as Zofal mounted his own tall bay. Everyone else would walk. Horses are still an oddity in Averidan and so have no protocol attached to their use. I had introduced them into official commerce by buying them for a discount from my brother.

The single narrow stepped road of the Upper City winds from the Palace downhill, below the Sun Temple and through the warren of tiny whitewashed houses that are the oldest settlement of the Shan. In the early blue light the yellow or orange doors and windowsills looked sickly pale, the green good-luck emblems painted under the eaves impotent. We had to pause at the bronze gate that closes off the Upper City. As the keepers strained at the wheels that turn the bolts, Xalan rapped on my metalled shin. "Look, you forgot someone," he said, and pointed back.

"Forget me if you want to," Melayne declared as she came up. Her growing belly gave a hint of a roll to her stride, and she held a wicker basket on one arm. "But you can't omit saying good-bye to Sahai."

"I had meant to let you sleep," I said. "We won't be gone long, or very far either." I bent low on Sorrel's shoulder to kiss her, glad to see she had dressed warm in a quilted yellow jacket. It is perilously easy to read the heart of anyone I touch when wearing the Crystal Crown, and it is impossible to lie to the Shan King. Now I could not help reading her fear for me under her light words. I would far rather not have known. To address it overtly would upset her, and perhaps sap her courage. I could only ignore what I had learned. "Let's see Sahai, too. I'll bet she's furious, she hates baskets."

Like all cats Sahai knew when something was afoot. Sulky and limp, she glared at me through blazing emerald eyes as I lifted her out of the basket, and clawed fruitlessly at my armor. "She'll shed on your cloak," Melayne said, "and gray hairs show so terribly on that color." So I let her take the cat again.

We peered awkwardly at each other in the gloomy shadow of the gate, holding hands. The words we could not say to each other—the fears unvoiced, injunctions swallowed, advice aborted—charged the air between us. When the gates were opened and wedged into place it was time to go. I was glad Sahai refused to be put back into her basket. The last moments were filled with our struggle to force the cat back in. By the time Melayne slammed the lid down over Sahai's bitter protests I could wave her a final cheerful kiss, and ride away.

The citadel wall was so thick that the dog-leg outside the Upper Gate was nearly a tunnel. I was at the end of the procession. When I emerged blinking into the new day I was surprised and touched to see how many people had risen early to see us off. There had been no time to prepare the foliage, real or fake, that properly carpets a Shan King's departure. With the Crystal Crown I could sense a slight disappointment in the minds around me that such an important event looked so ordinary.

Outside the main gate the wide cobblestone marketplace was bustling with sleepy soldiers sorting themselves into their fists of fifty. Long bronze-tipped spears and curved rectangular shields were being distributed from the armorers' oxcarts. It was far too early for any of the booths and shops to be open, but some meat-pastry vendors were doing a brisk trade. One cheeky fellow with a pushcart even offered me one: "No charge, Your Majesty. I'm a patriot."

I sighed, sensing mummery somewhere, as I took the piping-hot fold of bread. "And how much," I asked conversationally, "are you charging my soldiers?"

He considered a fib, but then came out with the truth. "Three coppers."

"And the usual cost is one copper." I hadn't patronized a pastry-vendor in years, but it was easy to pick the correct figure out of his head. "I will pay you two coppers for this pastry. Then you will sell to my men at two coppers also."

He didn't like it, but there are advantages to being an absolute monarch. Then he cheered up. "I'll undercut everyone else," he grinned, and held out a horny hand for the money.

Unfortunately armor has no pockets. "Xalan, give him two coppers, will you?" I asked, and smothered my embarrassment in a bite of pastry.

"Is it good?" Xalan asked, watching me with narrowed eyes. My mouth full, I nodded; the filling was minced pork, clams, and onions. Xalan sighed and fished out two more coins. "Give me one too."

There were no ceremonies when all was ready. So I took off the Crown, for convenience while traveling. One by one the fists marched off. We had nearly a dozen, in addition to two hundred Sisters. General Horfal-yu fell in beside me. Though he had a habit of losing warhorses, the General felt a mount was due his rank. We walked our horses, knee to knee, and he spread a map out between us.

"I've chosen the field of battle, Your Majesty," he announced proudly. "Right here."

He dabbed a thick finger at a spot a little more than midway between the City and Mhee. I searched my memory. "Barley fields and pear orchards—one of Yibor-soo's cousins is lord there," I recalled. "Nothing there of note."

"Not so!" Tactics, at least on paper, were the General's great love. "Look at this nice deep canal, here. There's flat fields on either side of it, and the road going up the middle."

"If we fight it there someone will surely get wet," I observed.

"*They'll* get wet. They'll walk right into it," the General chortled. "Xantallon has developed a truly duplicitous magery, or rather his assistant has. Xorlev, that's the one—"

In his enthusiasm the General suddenly spurred his horse and galloped up the grassy verge of the road, passing the fists until he came to the magi. He paused there, presumably to extract this Xorlev. I let Sorrel proceed at a walk, while I wrestled with the unsupported map. By the time it was rolled up I had come up to them. I pulled my horse over, out of the line of march, and let the rest of the army pass behind me.

Xorlev was neither an administrator, like the Magus, nor a lightweight like Xalan. His gentle abstraction, even on the way to a battle, the way his red magian robe was allowed to trail in the white dust, all marked him as a dreamer. Though he must have been over forty, his vague gaze was that of one younger than I, younger even than Xalan. His bow as the General presented him to me was awkward. "Show His Majesty your trick," the General urged, eager as a child. "Here's a good canal, try it here." He climbed off his horse and seemed prepared to drag the skinny magus over the reedy soft bank into the nearest channel.

I asked, "What does your magery involve, Xorlev?"

With thinly disguised relief Xorlev began, "It's a form of transmogrification, Your Majesty. Your Majesty has seen the Master Magus give milk the appearance of wine."

"Ale," I corrected. "Milk to look like ale."

"The plaiv say wine." When I looked blank he added, "You remember—in the valley of golden-fleeced sheep, after the battle, where you and the Master Magus were beset by robbers?"

Xorlev's nervous tones were not much like the rhetors' deep trained voices, but I recognized the high-flown imagery. "It wasn't like that at all," I said. Things seemed to be wandering somewhat from the point. "You're a geomant," I prompted, noting the tall black stone wand.

He nodded. "I've developed a similar glamor for solids," he said. "But I must say I've never done it for serious business—only in experiments."

"Now's your big chance!" the General congratulated him. To me he said, "You mustn't look now, Your Majesty, while he sets it up."

So I stared obediently the other way, at the passing army, while the magus and the General argued, splashed, and (from the sound of it) tore up weeds behind me. "All right, Your Majesty, you can look," the General called.

With knees and reins I turned my horse again. The grassy verge, the greenish water of the canal, the rustling reeds, the clear, pale autumn sky—all looked the same. But knowing there was magery I peered around closely. There was something odd about the canal. A section of it had been filled in, level with the grass. Yet water flowed on both sides of the block. Curious, I nudged Sorrel closer.

"Don't let it step there!" Xorlev yelped, so suddenly that my horse shied violently and made as if to bolt.

"You must not shriek like that," the General scolded. "Horses aren't donkeys, they have nervous, delicate temperaments."

"Both of you, silence!" I ordered, wrestling the horse's head around. When he was a little calmer, I said, "How is it done?"

"The magery?" Xorlev returned to the present. "Oh, there has to be some sort of surface—we bent the reeds over on either side. I haven't yet got it to be as convincing as fluid transmogrification, though."

"So I can see." When I bent and looked more carefully I could see, under the grassy illusion, broken reeds criss-crossing over green water.

"But the Cayd won't be expecting geomancy,"

the General was saying with great excitement. "All they've seen is a little weather-working. Now you see why that field is best. We cover over the canal with weeds and branches. We wait, on the other side. The Cayd advance, yelling and screaming and blind with excitement. And then, when they fall in—"

"We strike," I finished for him before he could go into detail. "Perfect—I don't see how we can lose." The fists had quite passed us by, and if we did not hurry they would be out of sight. "Let's catch up with the army, shall we? General—" I was going to have him take Xorlev up on his horse, so that the magus should not have to trot up the dusty road alone. But years of good living showed in the General's hamlike thighs and round trunk. "I'll give you a ride, Xorlev," I offered.

"If Your Majesty insists," Xorlev said doubtfully.

"On campaign, etiquette is loosened." At my direction he put his toe on mine and clambered on behind me. I was careful to hold Sorrel to a walk, but the magus clutched my belt tightly anyway, and slid to the ground as soon as we caught up with the tail of the column.

The day was clear as water. After its brutal summer force the sunshine was pleasantly mild now. Silver-green canals divided barley fields into innumerable rectangles and triangles. By noon we reached the one the General had chosen. The road arched itself over a wide canal, one of the major arteries of the water system hereabouts. To our left the young barley rippled down to the river bank. On the other side the grain field ran for about an arrow-shot before ending at a lane bordered by plane-trees. Already the fists were wading through the knee-high grain, trampling it down, spreading out cloaks and unslinging packs.

"We'll have lunch," the General announced, "and then set things up. Xorlev will prepare his geomancy, while the hydromants descry the Cayd to see when they leave Mhee. We may have to wait until tomorrow for them to finish looting the town."

Xalan approved. "I've about digested that pastry," said he. "Did Your Majesty say they raise pears around here?"

"Yes," I said. "My half-sister-in-law's cousin—"

My words were drowned in a dreadful brazen clamor. In their traveling-racks the gongs were swaying in frantic alarm as the lookout swung his sticks. A plume of white dust rose from the western road. "This can't be happening," I gasped. "They can't be early!"

And indeed it was more like a nightmare than any waking experience. Each of us behaved as the dreamer does, and clung to our wonted behavior. The General panted across the field, almost weeping from frustration as he tried to arrange a battle line. Down near the river I could just make out Xorlev's red hat as it bobbed among the grain; with dogged determination the magus was bending reeds and arranging branches. The white glitter in the ranks showed the Sisters were unsheathing their deadly special weapons. "There's no cover," Silverhand ran up to tell me, "but at your word a suicide patrol will blunt the edge of their advance." I shook my head. In this pass the Sisters might be our only chance to salvage anything from the wreck.

Things seemed to be happening very slowly. I signaled Xalan for the Crown as if there were no peril at all, as if we sat at our leisure beside the lily-pools in my own garden. For this was why the Lord of the Shan was again risking himself in war. Only I could wield the power of the Crown, and so read the ultimate intent of our foe.

The Cayd saw us the moment we saw them. A hoarse shout of cheerfully bloodthirsty enthusiasm rose from the first of them, and the noon Sun gleamed on oddly made bronze armor and bronze battle axes.

"Shields up, everybody!" the General cried. Our soldiery was trained to fight in neat lines, rectangu-

lar shields overlapping and spears abristle. My worst
fears had not led me to envision that we might not
have time to prepare. The line of shields was uneven
and broken, not properly regular as a string of pearls.
We were badly off balance. It was only a slight consolation to notice the Cayd were even less organized. They straggled, every man where he pleased,
in an uneven crowd.

"We must get Your Majesty and the Crown to
safety," Silverhand insisted.

"A moment," I said distantly, and reached out in
power toward the oncoming Cayds. I had never used
it on redheaded King Mor, and doubted I could
"recognize" his mind among so many. But his brother
Musenor, the new Warlord, had felt my power once.
Though I could not strike at him until he attacked
me personally, I could seek out and ransack his
mind. I skimmed the surface of the attackers before
us, found my man, and dived.

The heat. The real I was vaguely surprised; the
weather was actually pleasantly cool. But Warlord
Prince Musenor flicked the sweat from under his
straw-blond bangs and scratched under his royal copper necklet. There were no battle maneuvers at all in
his brain. The proper Caydish way to fight is to run
screaming at the foe. His men were already doing
that; the clash of bronze on bronze and shouts were
rising from the field. I pressed past these surface
concerns. What did he intend here in Averidan?
Only loot and revenge?

My cheeks tingled as the shock of discovery chased
the blood from them. The Cayd had no intention
of going home. They had in fact no home to go to.
The Tiyalor had invaded Cayd, pressed out of their
land near the Tiyalene Sea by folk from farther
west. Lanach had fallen a few weeks ago. Now they
meant to take Averidan from us.

Quickly I babbled this discovery to Xalan and Commander Silverhand. "They can't do that," Xalan protested feebly. "It's not right, it's against custom."

"In Cayd you have a right to what you have the strength to take." Silverhand's voice was hard and cool as marble. "We may not win this battle, Your Majesty. But we must not lose the war here as well. A fighting retreat, not a rout. Too many die in a rout. And you, above all, must survive."

Reluctantly I agreed. Already our men were being forced back and back, toward us. Worse, there were gaps in the line. The soft earth was seeping red, the mash of barley stalks growing slippery with gore—ours. "Save as many as you can," I pleaded.

"To fight another day," said indomitable Silverhand. "You have a horse. Ride for the City. Now."

She whirled and vanished into the melee. As I took off the Crown, Xalan held out its casket for me. "Tie this on behind your saddle," he said.

"Sorrel can carry us both," I said. "You come too."

As he helped me with the thongs, I glimpsed the fantastic face he made at me over the saddle. "You, and this, are vital," he said ruefully. He knotted the cords once more, and with a final wave rose like a bird into the sky. The magi had taken to the winds for safety but maintained their own offenses. With their black wands the geomants coaxed rocks into skull-cracking leaps, and a swirling herognomic wind threw dust into the faces of the enemy.

Sorrel tugged at the reins, hungry for battle. When I swung into the saddle and turned him east I could almost feel his equine contempt. I had too recently learned to shut out fear. Now though prudence commanded retreat my young courage cried out for resistance. Uneasily, I scrutinized my emotions, trying to decide if I was secretly glad not to fight.

The road was already crowded with panicky men in retreat. I rode wide, through the standing grain riverward, to keep clear of the press. Some Caydish arrows hissed past me, but at this range, I hoped, the archers would have to be crack shots indeed. Abruptly Sorrel twisted to one side under me, so that I nearly lost my seat. I leaped off, fearing he had been shot after all, and tripped over what the horse had been clever enough to sidestep—a body.

Gently I turned it over. Though he was dead he had not stiffened yet. The arrow had taken him high on the shoulder where it joins the neck. Hair, skin, lamellar and cloak, all were gluey with blood. He had been shot before retreating here to die. The face was masked with earth over streaky gore. I recognized him by the faithless loose-jointed armor that had let in his doom—Rosil-eir.

I sat back on my heels, stunned. My first foolish reaction was chagrin. Not since my childhood, when Rosil's father, my half-brother, died had any family member perished untimely. Whatever should I say to Yibor-soo? Though Rosil had been five years my elder, in the count of Shan generations I was the senior—he was my half-nephew.

Then my own loss overwhelmed me. All my life Rosil had been there, to plague and tease me, and to be a victim of pranks in return. When our respective mothers had quarreled we would either quarrel also or unite against them. Only lately, in the past year or so, had mutual respect and cordiality become a habit between us. Now they were lost again, forever.

Shivering, I wiped sticky hands on my cloak and tottered to my feet. It was good to lean for a moment on my horse's neck, to feel the warm moving life under my cheek. An arrow thumped into the trampled earth beyond me. It was not safe to stay.

Then a faint yelping noise intruded on my misery. I looked up and around. Three Caydish axemen were splashing along the canal to my right, slipping on the muddy shore and swearing. They were chasing a magus, I could see the red robe as its wearer darted in and out of the reeds.

Something seemed to snap inside me. I vaulted into the saddle and kicked Sorrel into a gallop. Almost of its own will my sword leaped out of its scabbard into my hand. Hot with their chase no one noticed my flank approach. The thunder of hooves warned the rearmost Cayds too late. With a long arching leap Sorrel sprang between them right over the canal.

With a shout I brought my blade down on a leather helm as we passed, and the bronze came back wet and red. As my mount turned, the second Cayd whirled, slipped on the slimy moss and fell flat into the turbid water. Quickly I urged the horse forward again. The hooves took him right in the back, trampling my foe into the muck at the bottom of the canal. Sorrel's weight, plus my own, was more than enough to crush bones. Only a thick marshy odor arose as we waded away.

The third axeman grinned at me from the bank and raised his weapon. I had used up my surprise edge and, while Sorrel stood belly-deep in the canal, could not take the horseman's advantage of height. The Cayd stood well back, ready to close and chop at belly or hooves when the horse scrambled up the soft bank. Hastily I rummaged through my stock of Caydish oaths and insults. Coaching from Melayne had vastly increased my vocabulary this past year. "Sheep-buggerer," I offered in that tongue. Then with more confidence I amplified, "Your amatory powers are inadequate even for goats!"

The results were even better than I hoped. Even at this distance the pale Caydish skin showed my foe crimsoning with rage. I reined Sorrel a little back, as if in dismay, as he strode forward.

At my signal Sorrel's head flicked out like a striking snake's. Horse teeth the size and color of ivory spoons took the axeman in the thigh just above the leather legging. Yelling with pain he brought the axe whistling down. But my shield was there to guard the horse's neck. With an unmusical clang the axe sheared through gilding, bronze plate, and wicker, to stick fast.

For a moment we tugged and glared at each other like children disputing a toy. Then Sorrel thrashed up out of the water onto the spongy verge of the canal. The axe-handle wrenched out of my opponent's grasp when Sorrel kicked him in the gut. A backhanded chop down with my sword, and it was over.

"It's safe, you can come out," I called in Viridese. A red hat peeped cautiously out of the tall grain. Xorlev had hidden in the barley. "What are you doing here," I said, panting a little. "You should have lifted, joined the other magi."

Mild innocent eyes stared at me from his mud-striped face. "But Your Majesty, what about my geomancy?" Xorlev demanded. "Aren't I going to get a chance to field-test it?"

I sighed. "Wipe this on that grass, will you?"

Awkwardly Xorlev took the wide blade I handed down. "Is this blood?"

"What do you think?" I returned crossly. Now my hand was free I could work the axe out of my shield. "Here, this is for you." I gave Xorlev the axe and took back my sword, sheathing it. "This is a royal order, now—take the axe, lift to join your fellows, and drop it on a Cayd."

Xorlev assented reluctantly, with the formula, "My powers in your service, Majesty. But what will you do? Do you need assistance?"

He had to shout the last question up at me. A knot of our spearmen had rallied only a few dozen paces away, shouting encouragements to each other. But they were too few. Beyond them bronze axes flashed up and down, and deep Caydish voices shouted, "Outflank them! Get under that shield!" The tide of the battle had turned inexorably against us. No longer was it a question of maintaining an orderly fighting retreat. My people stood an excellent chance now of being completely overrun. We battled not an army but an invasion force, the entire fighting population of Cayd.

I stared at the seething line but did not see it. Rather, I envisioned the main gate of the City, when the rout arrived there—the marketplace noisy with the cries of peddlers, the yawning gatekeepers, the laden barges drifting majestically through the river gate down to the harbor. No one would take the first stragglers seriously. Had not the god promised that all would be well? I imagined our foes' arrival, and shivered. Would anyone think to close the gates and barricade the river?

I reined Sorrel around so suddenly he reared in protest. "Go, obey me," I shouted to Xorlev. "I go to warn the City." Sorrel thundered away as though a demon were in the saddle. Indeed, I felt utterly estranged from myself now. The minor nobleman's worries over his bravery and repute melted into insignificance as the Shan King took over.

CHAPTER 3:

The Gates of the City

When the first stragglers appeared, we were as ready as anyone could be on such short notice. The booths and shops were forlorn and empty in the market-place. All their contents had been loaded onto carts and brought within. The river gates were stuck open. It seemed the bronze gears and counterweights inside the great square forts on either side of the Mhesan had not been cleaned or repaired in decades. But a boom of chain and scuttled boats had been hastily stretched across the gap, just beneath the surface of the water.

The enormous portals of the main City gate were, for a wonder, in perfect order. But the gates could not be shut and sealed until our Army—or what was left of it—returned. The timing decision was too delicate to trust to anyone else. I took up watch myself outside the gatehouse with the gatekeepers. The bronze doors were ten feet high, and thick as a man's body, opening outwards to foil battering rams. The oxen were yoked ready to drag them shut. In a discomfort induced by awe the gatekeepers left me ample room on their stone bench outside the gate.

Though the day was cool the westering Sun warmed the wall nicely. I leaned my head back and stared up along the wall. The Upper City was fortified in the time of Shan Vir-yan himself, but these walls were by our standards relatively new. Tṣantelekor Sea-Reaver built them to consolidate his conquest of Averidan. They were much less fine than the upper walls, being erected Tsorish-fashion out of fired brick under massive granite facing blocks. Later the Tsorish learned Shan sophistication, and applied a veneer of green and white ceramic tile.

My furious energy chilled as I looked at the wall with new eyes. It was four stories high, and impregnable—straight and sheer. But over the years illicit houses and shops had accumulated at its foot. The tiles were loose and worn. Some of the lower gray facing blocks had been pried off for use in other projects, leaving raw sores of crumbling reddish brick. Bushes and clinging plants furred the cracks; here and there stubborn trees had won a toehold. The entire effect was green and domestic, even friendly, but not likely to intimidate invaders.

"If we get through this I'll clear this up, repair the walls and gates." So I prayed, to any deity in hearing. But though the last time I promised to reform I had been miraculously rescued by a foreigner named Sandcomber, this time I felt the words fall, leaden and spiritless, rather than rise.

The first forerunners of the storm to come were the fugitives. Rumor leads an independent life in Averidan; the tidings of disaster had spread swifter than a horse could run. Carven sedan chairs laden with nervous lordlings chipped enamel from each other as they jostled through the gate. Behind them came dog-carts heaped with household goods and valuables. Farmers goaded fat oxen that hauled wainloads of grain or fruit. Their wives led donkeys so overburdened they resembled four-footed bales of clothing and bedding-rolls, with a few screaming children perched on top.

The crowd was too anxious to recognize me—I had taken care to borrow a gatekeeper's white-and-green cloak. Nor did I come forward when the first remnant of our soldiery trudged up. Thirsty and weaponless, the stragglers made straight for the fountain. Many were wounded; I would deal with that later. They were quickly besieged by worried bystanders. But by my order the City guardsmen stepped

up to bring them in and question them. It was vital
to get an early estimate of the survivors; the memory
of Silverhand's grim words— "too many die in a
rout" —made me twitch with fear. I sat back and
watched over the newcomers jealously, like a miser
counting incoming coins.

But from pity I had to stand up when General
Horfal-yu appeared. The Shan have no tolerance for
failures; the crowd stared and stepped back so that
he came up to the gate alone in a sort of miasma of
distrust. The General felt it more than anyone. He
drooped with more than his wounds. Seeing me, he
lurched down on one knee. In a shadow of his old
hearty tones he said, "Too long have I lived, Your
Majesty. Order my lapidation."

No Crown was necessary to assay the temper of
those within hearing distance. The people would
assent to his death. But in prudence I had to answer,
"Later, perhaps. For now, consider other ploys against
the foe. We shall need every man, and there is no
time to judge the case properly now."

Too crushed to argue, the General shuffled inside.
No one would contravene my given word. The least
I could give this old man—he looked at least ten
years older than he had this morning—was justice.

The Sun was low and orange in the west when
they came, so that our enemies seemed to be striding
out of his hot living core. Suddenly our troops were
pouring into the square: shamed, silent men drained
from the long retreat. "This isn't the way war is in
plaiv," the nearest gatekeeper observed in hurt tones.

"You're young," I said. Though he looked my age
I felt weathered and gray with responsibility. We
clambered onto our benches to see over the crowd.
Only about a dozen more wagons were waiting to
pass in. Sullenly, the troops joined the press.

Emboldened by my notice the gatekeeper continued, "If this were plaiv the rhetor would surely put
in a final gallant stand."

"Preferably on a bridge, a parapet, or a cliff," I

agreed dryly. In my anxiety I was cruel. "You should take care in your wishes, though. Not a magus nor a Sister do I see. Perhaps there was a final gallant stand, after all."

The gatekeeper gulped and stared around, as if he hoped to see red robes or brown linen tunics in the press. A ripple passed through the crowd as the first of the Cayds appeared at the far end of the marketplace. It was easy to pick them out. Cayds are tall—Melayne is reckoned nearly a midget in her homeland—and they wear leather helms, not bronze like ours. The first arrivals pointed and gestured at the sight of us cowering at the gate, and I fancied I could hear their laughter over the noise. But nearly all the wains were safely through the gate, and the soldiers could speed in. "Get the ox-drivers ready," I commanded. "The gates must close without a hitch."

Then disaster struck. The very last wagon, heaped high with sacks of hulled barley, tried to edge ahead. One copper-bound wooden wheel wedged behind that of the wagon before it. Before any of us could point out the mistake to the driver, he tapped the fat piebald rumps below him with the goad. With a muffled crunch the wheel popped off its axle. The victimized wagon lurched and foundered sideways, spilling its load—bolts of undyed linen—into the gateway.

"You thief!" the linen-driver shrilled. "You criminal! Ennelith shrivel your generative organs to the size and color of raisins!" But the grain-driver only turned his oxen to pass, and trundled blithely over the tumbled cloth to safety.

"No more of that!" I snapped. "Quickly, messirs, haul that wagon clear." For the gates could not swing shut now. Dozens of hands lifted the axle, and balanced the wagon on its one remaining wheel. The phlegmatic oxen dragged it in.

But the slight delay agitated the worried crowd to fever pitch. "They're closing the gate," shrieked a short-sighted old lady with a basket of pullets. "The

Cayd will kill us!" Suddenly I was slammed back against the worn tile by a tide of hysterical people. They clogged up the gateway, clawing past each other, catching their feet on the cloth and falling.

With a whoop the Cayds began to run, seeing their chance to storm the gate. I snatched at the nearest soldier's arm. "You have armor, and your spear," I said. "Gather some of your fellows, go down and engage the foe for a few moments."

The fellow shook off my hand. "You are no soldier," he rasped.

"You are wrong," I said, dragging off my borrowed garment to reveal lamellar and a royal green cloak. "I am the Lord of the Shan, and command your obedience."

Everyone in hearing gaped. But I kept my eye on the soldier. So much that once was solid had crumbled; suppose my folk no longer acknowledged my authority? With a pang I thought of the Crystal Crown, the badge of my power. I had left it under my bench.

But my fears were groundless. The soldier gave me the royal salute, spear-shaft to forehead. I pointed at the other soldiers in the press, saying, "Gather your fellows quickly, and come."

The awed crowd parted to let us through. I paused only to take the Crystal Crown out of its casket. In my left hand, behind my shield, it was nearly invisible. I made a swift tally. There were scarcely a hundred soldiers here fit to fight. Even counting those already inside, and the wounded, our losses had been appalling. It would be a gallant last stand indeed. Oddly enough I felt no fear whatever. Only one tiny part of me stood to one side, and admired the boundless *chun-hei* of the Shan King.

So deeply was I King that I stared blankly at the soldier who blocked my way. "Liras, have you lost your mind?" he demanded.

I felt like a donkey whose cart rolls into a pothole. Blinking, I said, "Zofal?"

"Say you're glad to see me," my brother said with the sarcasm of relief. "Or no, say you didn't get your horse killed under you. I did. I'm never going to forgive the Cayds for this." He wiped sweat and dust off his forehead, flicking his hair back.

"Sorrel's at the Palace," I said, hugging him with my free arm. "And you, you're lucky to be unhurt."

"I'm fine. Doesn't fighting from horseback give one a tremendous edge? I was right, we must breed more big animals. I'll just go up and check Sorrel over—"

Gently I interrupted his enthusiasm. "No, Zofal, you can't do that." It was a curious sensation, to feel the King take the reins from me. "I need every fighter here, the odds are ludicrous enough as it is."

Zofal gulped. "It's sure death," he pointed out. "They say the White Queen doesn't approve of too many immigrants a day."

I smiled. "They say, also, that it is death to defy the Shan King."

For a moment Zofal stared as if he couldn't believe it. Then he shrugged. "Well, if we're going to the Deadlands anyway—"

"We might as well go together." And all of a sudden I was the younger brother again, anxious for his approval.

Zofal seemed to understand. He clapped me on the shoulder and then exclaimed, "Ouch, you're too well-armored to punch."

When the Cayd saw we meant to make a stand they came on more warily. I drew our line up as far across the marketplace as I dared, so they could not easily get round us. If the Cayd on their part had chosen an arrow-shaped formation we would be done for. But their armies are organized not by rank or family, but in loose coteries of mutual trust, to leave scope for feuds. So they dashed at us helter-skelter, shouting uncouth defiances that fortunately only I could understand: "Limaot with us!" "Mince them fine, and we'll have them for breakfast tomorrow!"

"Dibs on the one with the shield!" I smiled at that; of course everyone else had lost theirs in the retreat. I had deliberately chosen a prominent position in the front rank.

Glum but faithful, Zofal was just behind me. "You can have this," I told him, sliding the shield off my arm.

He frowned. "You don't need it?"

"No." He stepped back as I held up the Crystal Crown. The Caydish were quite close; a badly cast javelin clattered along the cobbles between us. "Have you ever heard the Cayd term 'witch' before, brother?"

"Of course not, you're the family linguist. What does it mean?"

"I'm not all that sure," I admitted. "But I can supply a demonstration." The foremost Cayd was only five paces away, axe already raised and aimed at me. Lifting the Crystal Crown I set it on my head.

The effect was all anyone could ask. The axeman's eyes bulged with horror and he stopped in his tracks. The axe slipped from his nerveless hands as the warrior behind collided with him. "Witch!" the two of them yelled, almost together. "The Witch-King!"

Their reaction was so funny I almost laughed aloud. The entire Caydish line halted, and showed distinct signs of wanting to hide behind one another. My men took heart at this inexplicable faltering, and threw javelins into our massed foes. To everyone's delight the Cayd actually retreated a bit. "What on earth is a Witch-King?" Zofal whispered in my ear.

"Someone very dangerous," I said. "Me. Remember, I killed Warlord Prince Melbras of Cayd? I hoped the story would have spread."

"You should have done this before—perhaps they would have gone home."

"Oh, they'll get over the fright fast," I predicted. "All I'm fishing for now is time. Look back, has everyone gone through the gate yet?"

"No. And they'll have to gather up that cloth, too, otherwise the bolts won't act."

"Too true." From somewhere farther back I could hear Musenor cursing his men. The two brothers' heads, the blond and the red, were just barely visible above the others, as they repeated what sounded like old arguments—that the evil Shan King had to be dealt with sooner or later, that my witchery had never yet prevailed over cold bronze, that Limaot would ward them.

In Musenor's place I would have offered a prize, gold for my death. But in Cayd things are done differently. Pushing through to the front ranks, Musenor shook his axe in my general direction. "By my brother's beard I vow, I'll kill him myself! That'll show you rabbit-hearted turds!"

With that he began to run straight at me. Shamed, his men followed. I smiled, flexing my mental muscles. The Crystal Crown can kill as well as save, but only if its wearer is attacked. Cayds are barbered only for very great occasions indeed; Musenor's hair had grown out since his brother's coronation so that it now stuck out all around. With the westering light behind it looked like his blond hair and beard were afire. "An odd effect," I remarked cheerfully, "but I can top it."

It's a simple trick, to make the Crown glow, and very impressive. The sizzle of blue-white light momentarily banished twilight, sucked all color from our foes. They exclaimed it was lighting. It was really unfair, I reflected, as I prepared to stop Musenor's heartbeat—like charming a fish to its death with music. Musenor could not help faltering practically at my feet.

But behind me Zofal grunted as he thrust with his long spear. The Warlord was not quite in range, and the point took him high on the arm, above the edge of his jeweled arm-ring. As Zofal wrenched the spearpoint out I gasped at the pain and clutched at my arm. There was nothing there. Then I staggered, darkness washing over my eyes, as Musenor sunk the axe in his good hand into the skull of a spearman beside me. Dozens of agonies plucked at me, dragging me this way and that. I crouched, ducking behind Zofal's knees, and with unsteady hands ripped the Crown off my head. Its power was a two-edged weapon; nowhere could the careless wearer destroy himself faster than on a field of battle.

I fell to my hands and knees, breathing deep lest I faint and then be trampled. To my surprise the men actually forced the Cayd back farther. I found myself kneeling on blood-spattered cobbles behind the swaying line. The Crown was my first charge; I reeled to the gate, shut the Crown in its box and thrust it into the hands of a gatekeeper. "Take this inside," I gasped.

"We're ready to shut the gate," he told me. "At your command."

"Not yet," I said. I clutched my aching head. The enemy would certainly give us no chance to retreat to safety. I could accept the loss of everyone still outside, and shut the gate. Or I could guide our men back, step by step through the gate, and hope the Cayd could not overrun us, jam the gates open, and sack the City. "This is not fair," I muttered. "No one can make this kind of decision."

Then a familiar shrill whistle echoed among the warehouses and docks to my left. A slim armored woman darted out from behind a booth, whirling a unique razor-sharp blade on a long rope. For one fatal moment the Cayds on that side were too startled to react. The bladed rope blurred in its spin and spattered a grisly circle of blood, leather and bone into the faces of the foe. Those cut shrieked, and clutched at their spilling intestines before they died.

"The Sisters of Mir-hel!" I shouted. Drawing my sword I ran to join the men. "Quickly, while the Sisters hold their attention!"

The Cayds wavered under this vicious flank assault. More Sisters appeared, keeping well apart so their ropes should not tangle. A withering rain of arrows forced the Caydish back. For our part the men were not slow about hurrying through the gate. The fallen might have been abandoned in their haste. Just as I was ordering the living at least to be brought along, Commander Silverhand herself dashed up to me. "In Mir's name, what are you doing here?" she shouted. "You're supposed to be *safe!*"

Her face was streaked with Cayd blood, in which setting her eyes scorched out wild as a cat's. In the most soothing tones I could muster I said, "We can discuss it later, Commander. Suppose for now you get your Sisters inside, and we'll shut the gate."

She stuck two fingers into her mouth and whistled another complicated signal. But already the Cayd were advancing again. Their advantage of numbers could not be offset even by the Sisters' ferocity. Swiftly we were hemmed in. It was almost night, and the mill was too dizzy to allow for elegant swordplay. I hacked at every bare arm or leg that whirled by in the dimness—my own folk were sleeved and trousered. Our backs were to the gateway. The Caydish intent was clear—they would push us through, and not allow us any gap in which to close it.

Silverhand grasped the situation instantly. "We're trained for this," she said grimly. "I'll choose a dozen Sisters to hold them, while we shut the gate."

Remembering the Sisters' vow of virginity I felt impelled to say, "Perhaps men would be better for this; what if a Sister is captured?"

"Do you think us fools?" she demanded. "There are many roads to the Deadlands today."

"I don't doubt it," I assented unhappily.

Very slowly the open bronze doors enfolded us. We were being forced through the gate. Suddenly someone tugged at my cloak from behind. "Your Majesty," the gatekeeper hissed, "order everyone to stop fighting and come in—now!"

"I can't," I began, when a noise like an exploding pottery kiln made everyone jump. I could hardly credit what I saw. Someone had hauled a wagon up onto the City wall and then pushed it off into the marketplace. Wood and wheels crashed directly before the gateway, just missing the foremost Cayds and crushing a number of those in the second rank. From the wreck yellow flames leaped up hungrily. In an eye-blink the whole mass was roaring, blotting out the new stars.

"Come, Majesty, quickly!" the gatekeeper pleaded, and indeed the scorching heat drove us all back. Everyone crowded through the gate. The Caydish army howled at our escape but could not pass the burning wagon quickly enough. With quiet dispatch the Sisters knifed the few who followed us in.

"Close the gate!" I ordered. The great bronze doors swung slowly in as the oxen hauled at the cables. Orange and yellow flame walled the narrowing gap. At the last moment a Caydish arm and leg thrust into the opening, but with javelins we forced them back. With a boom like thunder the doors slammed home, and the gatekeepers threw themselves on the wheels that work the bolts.

"Viris be thanked," Silverhand gasped. "Your Majesty, are you all right?"

"Surely," said I, wiping my forehead. "Who was it who thought of the wagon? He saved us all."

The gatekeepers grinned at each other proudly. The boldest piped up, "We helped, Your Majesty. It was the linen-dyer's wagon, you remember. We hauled it up the stairs, packed the linen back in, and soaked the whole with oil. But it was the General conceived the idea."

He pointed, and I looked up. And there was General Horfal-yu, leaning from a high gatehouse window. "And jars of linseed oil balanced on top," he fussily reminded them. "They were very important."

"I don't think we'll execute you just yet, General," I said, smiling. "Come down and take charge of these men again."

Demanding the Crystal Crown, I found it safe in

the gatekeeper's room. When I emerged the men were moving off. Though the herbals and bonesetters had been carrying the wounded to sickhouses, those hurt in the final rush still lay here and there on the cobbles. The bonesetter in charge suggested, "Perhaps Your Majesty should rest?"

I smiled but offered no arguments. Kings, I had learned, never do. As I put on the Crown it came to me why I rarely heard the Crown's beautiful wise voice anymore. The ancient presence no longer inhabited the Crown. Slowly, over the past year or so, it had transferred its residence—to my own head.

Once the idea would have terrified me. Now it seemed obvious, hardly notable at all. The Shan King fears nothing. With brisk efficiency I went from soldier to soldier—closing cuts, joining bones, pulling partly severed limbs back together—all with the touch of my hand. So long as I could do something about them the cacophony of pains was bearable. The bonesetters gave over carting the wounded away, since I was so rapidly stealing their trade, and lit my way through the dusk with pine-resin torches. The herbals still had plenty of work left, however, among those concussions and stunnings that I had no power over.

I did not recognize Zofal until his face came into shape under my hands—one side had been hacked open and broken bits of jawbone gleamed at me through the gap. Thus I had no time for pain, but only delight at his surprised expression. "You'll be fine now, brother," I said cheerfully. "I told you the Crystal Crown would be of use to the family some day."

Zofal sat up, retching. The bruising which remained swelled his face like a baked apple, and his brown forelock was matted and black with his own blood. "Better not," I said, and gently pushed him back.

"No—Liras!" He coughed, and clung to my wrist. "Are the gates shut?"

"Oh yes," I said with offhand pride.

"What about Mother?"

The blood turned to ice in my veins. In the excitement I had completely forgotten. She and Yibor-soo were still at home—outside the walls. When I did not reply, Zofal insisted, "You sent and fetched her, didn't you, earlier this afternoon?"

"Well, no, Zofal," I said weakly. "I've been rather busy."

"How could you forget?" I cringed at the horror and outrage in his glare. "You're supposed to take care of us all! What if she's killed?"

"She and Yibor probably arrived quietly this afternoon." I interrupted in a speedy gabble, hardly listening to my own words. "They're probably sitting on the Palace terrace right now, sipping tea and wondering why we're not back for supper. Why don't you go up and see? I'll just finish up here and follow you."

Without waiting for his answer I rose and scurried away, sick with guilt. In vain I told myself the Shan King had had too many calls on his time today. I had never felt less royal. A terrible weariness dragged at me. I stumbled up to a wounded Sister and tried to close up her cuts. Of course nothing happened. For the Shan King had that power, but not Liras Tsormelezok.

CHAPTER 4:

Family Affairs

So we were besieged. After a few days of frantic anxiety life in the City went on with surprisingly little change. The harvests had been got in, so we did not hunger. And winter was closing the roads, the yellow leaves swirling off the trees in the chilly wind while rain tapped on travelers' hats.

Another consolation was that the seas were still ours. The Cayd could besiege us from landwards, but from the harbor and fleets would flow food, supplies, and eventually troops. "This is a temporary setback," people told each other. "We'll beat them off yet." In Averidan the proper way to do anything is slowly. No one doubted there was time.

The City was brim-full. Country kinfolk moved in with town-dwellers, inns and taverns bedded lodgers under their tables in shifts, and the Sun Temple reported a new trend in all-night worship. Though it was like loaning out pieces of my own flesh I allowed shelters to be built in the ornamental gardens, to house Palace servants and clerks. Their old quarters, in the tiny white houses of the Old Town below the Palace, were given over to those too grand to camp in gardens or taverns—lords and viceroys fleeing the Caydish.

Siril-ven was of course too lofty even for this. She and Dasan had always yearned to live with me in the Palace, and now I could no longer put them off. They agreed with Zofal that I had been criminally absentminded. To allay my own anxiety I ordered a scouting expedition the very next day to the family estates. And for the sake of family peace I had to give Zofal permission to go along, when they left that night.

"But for the love of Viris herself, obey Pardia," I begged him at the harbor that evening. "The Sisters have no equal in devious warfare."

"I don't actually plan to hail any and every Cayd we see," Zofal retorted crossly. "Hold this, will you?"

I spread the sticky length of greased linen while Zofal fastened one end to his sword and began to roll it. They were to swim the Mhesan below the river-gate before moonrise. The weapons and armor would be floated across on a raft of flotsam, and so needed protection from the damp. I glanced apprehensively past the dock into the dark, dirty water. The night shadows made the river look oily and dangerous, and it was very wide hereabouts, near the bay.

"Don't fear, Your Majesty," Pardia comforted me. She was Silverhand's second, a short dark woman of about thirty, and tough as rawhide. "We'll keep him out of trouble."

"And if he can't keep up," Silverhand directed, "find a safe nook and stash him to pick up on your way back."

"So now I'm a cripple as well as a fool," Zofal growled.

"You had better not be rude," said Silverhand with deceptive mildness. "The Sisterhood never brings raw novices on campaign. It's only by His Majesty's special request we allow this at all."

"Yes, otherwise we'll duck you in midstream." Pardia's grin gleamed white in the twilight.

It was a cold evening. Silverhand and I were wrapped up well, but the scouting party wore only dark brown linen to swim in. Their warm cloaks would be floated across. Pardia and the other three Sisters dived in without hesitation—the noise of shipping concealed the splash—but Zofal shivered on the pier, rubbing one pale goose-pimply foot against the other, before jumping in feet first. The gloomy water swallowed him utterly, and I almost choked with fright. Then his head bobbed up sleek above the surface. "Sun above, but it's cold," he spluttered, throwing his long front hair back. "Good-bye, little brother, see you in two days."

"Good-bye, Zofal. We'll be watching for your return. And *be careful!*"

We stood in the chill and strained our ears for the sound of any Caydish alarms. The night was black as velvet, moonless and overcast. A fishing-trawler sailed by, with a clank-clank from the stern and prow bells. Its pinpoints of light—the crew, playing Thumbprint on the deck—made the ship look like a constellation touring the lower realms. A dull mutter of thunder made me start; then a fine steady rain began to fall. "Perfect weather for a little espionage," I remarked, pulling my hood up.

Silverhand noded, her hands deep in her sleeves for warmth. "I asked the Magus to get the hero-gnomers to call up some rain."

"Why didn't I know?" I asked, a little hurt.

"You would surely have told your brother," she said blandly. "And why make him miserable before he needs to be? Now he can curse the weather, not the magi or you."

Her smile, happy and conniving, made me laugh. My anxiety did not dissolve, but no longer choked my throat so. "Well, I suppose they've landed safely," I said. "Let's go home."

The Lady's rooms, with their long view north and west over the cliff, were taken over by the Sisterhood. They made an incongruous sight in the luxurious pink and peach-hung suite, but needed quarters because their monastery was outside the walls, north of the City. Melayne moved into my suite. Though the magian scries revealed far more detail, no one could resist peering out over the cliff. Silverhand often unlatched the frame to lean out, searching for signs of her Sisters' work. I, of course, watched for Zofal or Mother or Yibor-soo, not that there was any possibility of recognizing them from three hundred feet up. The Magus visited daily to scan the earth and sky. The rains in these parts do not ordinarily arrive until winter; this year the herognomers were warping the climate to annoy the Cayd and favor our cause. It was blustery and cold for days on end. "But we must be careful," the Magus told me. "We certainly don't want to cause a flood by accident." To him floods were still the ultimate catastrophe.

The Cayd gave over pounding on the main gate after General Horfal-yu pelted them with a succession of unpleasant missiles—rocks, boiling water, and scalded bran. Soon they found the smaller North Gate. Silverhand, who was in charge of its defense that day, directed the narrow, low wicket gate should be wedged temptingly ajar. I did not believe her report of the number of Cayds foolhardy enough to clamber through—and be quietly strangled—until she showed me the bodies. Dozens of them were laid in tidy rows in the street. The curbs were crowded with my curious subjects, getting their first close look at the foe. "They're not tacticians, but they're brave," I admitted.

"Rather, I would say stupid," said Silverhand.

We both started as a horn sounded from outside. "What's that?" I exclaimed.

"A parley, I suppose," Silverhand said. "How fortunate you're here. Let's go up." The North Gate was similar to the main one, but on a smaller scale. We climbed the stairs and peeped cautiously from between the battlements. Sure enough a Caydish herald stood in the road below, waving a green bough in token of truce. "Bring up your leaders," Silverhand called, "and we shall inform the Shan King." Turning to me, she asked in an undertone, "Unless you'd rather not? After all, we already know their real intent."

"Oh, let's hear what they have to say. Besides, one always parleys, it's in all the plaiv."

From our height Musenor's face was hard to recognize, but his barrel chest and blond hair marked him. Beside him a slimmer warrior nearly as tall sported a glorious mane in a familiar red-brown tint. This must be Mor, King of Cayd and the eldest of Melayne's many brothers—a mighty man of at least forty who had waited all his life for his crown. Both warriors wore the crude bronze armor unsophisticated Caydish metallers forge, and jingly copper or brass jewelry on wrist and arm and finger.

In a deep voice Musenor shouted, "Is the Witch-King there?"

I bellowed back in Caydish, "Here I am, Warlord." A Viridese quarrel would properly involve oblique yet razor-edged insults—flaying, not stabbing—or at least not yet. But I knew such finesse would be wasted on our foes, and in any case the forthright Caydish tongue has no room for such subtlety. "I don't recall inviting you to visit Averidan."

The blond beard split in an unwilling grin. "Knowing your hospitality, we couldn't resist surprising you," he called back.

"Save the chatter," Silverhand murmured, "and ask them their business. This is a war, not a pleasure party."

Apparently King Mor was also displeased at the tone of the parley thus far. Elbowing his Warlord back, Mor yelled, "Surrender, you demon's slave! We have you surrounded!"

I laughed loudly so that Mor could hear. "Why don't *you* give up and run along home? The City will stand against you forever. This is our land, our gods gave it to us. You have no right to it."

"Your gods haven't been very helpful so far," Mor taunted. "*Our* deity told us to throw you out."

"Could that be true?" I asked Silverhand.

She shook her head. "I'm no priestess. Their Limaot

is a herdsman's god. Perhaps he's warring with Ennelith and the Sun, even as we fight the Cayds?"

It did not sound unlikely. But Mor was continuing, "Surrender now, and save your town from sack."

"And then what, eh?"

Musenor broke in, "We'll promise you a clean death—strangulation—and a decent funeral, return your body to your kin."

"Resist," Mor added, "make yourself a pest, and I promise you a prolonged and grisly fate." His smile, though superficially similar to Musenor's, sent a shiver down my back.

"The brass-balled nerve of them," Silverhand muttered. "They must really believe they can prevail."

I leaned far out over the battlement, squeezing my shoulders past the stones, to yell, "If I were as gullible as you, Mor, I should consider your offer. As it is, we'll be happy to sweep you and your army out of the country. Too bad we'll have to wash everything down afterwards with lye soap!"

Mor began to sputter some profanities, but his brother grabbed his arm and they marched away. "Very courageous and fiery," Silverhand approved. "Impugn both their intelligence and their cleanliness."

It was not, however, really courage. The truth was that no one, least of all I, could imagine defeat.

A steady stream of refugees—and news—began to arrive, mostly by water. The Mhesan is not navigable west of Mhee, so the Cayds know little of boats. Our people found it easy to elude them on the water, and floated, swam, or sailed down or across.

The tidings were not good, but could have been worse. It appeared the Cayd planned to step into the slippers of the landed lords. Everyone of leisured status was beheaded without exception or judgment. There would have been a bloodbath if the Cayd had possessed some touchstone of truth like the Crystal Crown. But the lords and ladies threw off their trappings of rank and took refuge in forges, pigsties, and grain-houses, and the Shan peasantry kept them safe. Truth is the prerogative of the Shan King; mendacity for us is an art, almost wasted on these unpleasant invaders. They didn't even speak Viridese properly; it was like catching a potted lobster.

I could easily envision Mother and Yibor-soo, meandering up the road to the City behind a laden bullock-cart, humble hats pulled down over their noses and hands, with their smooth uncallused skin, hidden in sleeves. But five days passed without any word. And Zofal and the Sisters seemed to have vanished. They, at least, should have come back. "What can have happened?" I demanded in frustration.

"A moment," the Magus asked. He slid his thick round mirror out of its bronze case. "Now, your family estates are south and west of the City?"

"Yes." Anxiety made me terse, and I paced up and down the green and white salon's ornate tile floor. "You scried there before for me."

"There was no one home then," the Magus agreed mildly, "but perhaps your kin have returned. Don't flit back and forth like that; you disturb my concentration. I'm not as young as I was."

I plumped down onto a brocade floor cushion beside Xalan. On my other side Siril-ven whispered, "If they're killed how will the Magus know?"

"Unless he can descry the Cayd in the very act, there's no way ever to find out by mirror," Xalan said in a low voice. "We can only see what is, not what was. And it's a real handicap, not to be able to touch things. A corpse that's face down is unidentifiable."

"Will you cease this morbid conversation!" I exclaimed.

"Sorry," Xalan said, embarrassed.

"Are you there yet?" Siril asked the Magus.

"No, I'm not," he said, sitting sharply up and tugging at his mustache in annoyance. "Every time you interrupt me the image slides back toward us."

"There are exercises the apprentices learn for that," remarked Xalan, whose apprentice days were not long past. His grand-uncle shot him a quelling glare.

We sat silent as the Magus bent once more over his glass. "Wait!" he exclaimed. "Here is Pardia!"

"Where?" "What's she doing?" "You don't see Zofal?" we cried.

The Magus held up a long knobbly hand. "She's crouched on the roof of a warehouse just across the river," he reported. "I see no one with her, but I doubt she's alone—she looks to be on watch."

"You don't see Zofal," I repeated.

"He could be concealed anywhere," Xalan comforted.

The Magus stood up. "At least a term is set to Your Majesty's suspense," said he. "They probably plan to swim the strait as soon as possible."

"Tonight," I said feverishly. At the time it was late afternoon. I blinked at the pale, cool sunlight that poured through the high windows. "We must have an overcast tonight, Magister—or fog. Can you arrange it?"

"It's terribly short notice," the Magus sighed, but hurried away to alert the herognomers.

So it was that Siril and I spent that evening lurking among the docks, like thieves. Commander Silverhand had other duties; instead, an unhappy pair of Palace guardsmen followed us about to signal handkerchief-snatchers and cutpurses we were unsuitable prey.

"What a horrible fog," Siril complained as she sat down on a bale. "I can't see a thing."

"The Cayd can't either," I said. The weather-wizards had obeyed magnificently. A thick weepy fog trammeled the night harbor. Behind us ships swung blind at their slips, and lame for want of wind. We were farther east than before, at the south-ernmost edge of the harbor, near one of the best places where a swimmer could land. A deep sloping bank of silt and tide-borne trash extended from our disused dock to the water. Somewhere not very far away some fish were achieving a redolent old age.

I crouched miserably on the planking beside my sister, arms around my knees for warmth. "Even if she's alive, Mother will never forgive me," I predicted gloomily.

Siril took pity on me, and scratched the top of my head as she used to when we were children. "Look on the brighter side," she said encouragingly. "Imagine what Yibor-soo will say when Zofal tells her to hop into the water."

In spite of myself I grinned at the picture. Siril had a kindly heart, though too often it was hidden by her thoughtlessness. In a way it was a pity I had been named Shan King, to so become a perpetual lure of possible advancement. Left alone, Siril might actually have begun to think of subjects other than clothing and status.

Then I jerked my head from under her fingers. "Listen! Did you hear that?"

The sound of a stealthy splash drifted to us through the fog. We leaped up and peered into the murky darkness. For a moment all was quiet. Then another splash, and another. "They're coming!" I exclaimed in a strangled undertone, and jumped off the dock into the mudbank.

To my astonishment a tall black shadow, taller than any Shan, loomed up in the mist. With a splash and a wallow a leggy brown colt appeared, blowing and dripping. Without thinking I caught the halter and stroked the wet shoulder. As I did so a plump gray mare materialized, shaking water out of her mane. I caught her too, and led both horses up toward the dock. "These are *our* horses, from the farm," I called softly to Siril.

"They all look alike to me," she said, bewildered. "How did they get here?"

"I don't know. Here, hold these, there are more coming."

I undid my sash, and knotted it through the halters. Siril took the loop. The fog was bursting with horses. Another splashed up onto the bank, and yet another. I recognized them all. Our entire breeding and riding stock seemed to be swimming across the strait. The homey smell of steaming horse surrounded me. I pushed through the stamping, snorting herd, knee deep into the chilly water. For now human figures were emerging from the void.

"Zofal!" I reached out and grasped my brother's cold hands.

Zofal floundered onto firmer ground and gasped, "Wonderful, I'm glad you're here. Are the horses all right?"

"I think so. And what of you?"

"I'm freezing, is there anything to drink?"

I shouldered back through the horses to the dock. Though it was not really proper, I was certain one or the other of the guardsmen had brought a flask along. "Do either of you have some brandy?" I demanded, and sure enough, one reluctantly produced a stoneware flask. I took it and turned, but Zofal had followed me.

"Siril, you look quite out of place here. Ah, that's what I need now." His throat pulsed as he took a long warming nip.

"What about Mother?" Siril asked. "And Yibor?"

"There was no trace of Mother," Zofal replied sadly. "She went downriver that morning to the precinct of Ennelith, and before she returned the Caydish came. Let's hope she stayed in their sanctuary." Then, more cheerfully, he added, "We did bring Yibor-soo."

We stared, deprived of speech, as a crude flotsam raft floated into view. It was towed by Pardia and two other Sisters, who swore quietly as they hauled it up the bank. Trailing behind, clinging to the cloaks and weaponry, was Yibor-soo. Though the water there was less than knee-deep, she did not seem to realize landfall had been achieved, and lay half in, half out of the water like a jellyfish washed up in a storm.

"You're terribly wet, half-sister-in-law," Siril observed at last. "Why don't you come out?"

We could barely hear her whimpered reply. "My poor joints!"

"Oh, come along, old mother," Pardia said with weary sympathy. They hoisted Yibor up as if she were a tuna, and laid her out on the dock to dry.

"Why did you bring all the horses?" I asked, more in wonder than in ire. "We are, after all, under siege, or had you forgotten? People we can feed, but horses?"

"You didn't think I'd leave them for the Cayds," Zofal said indignantly. "I thought we could sneak them north, to the sea-marshes, and let them run wild there for the time being. These animals are so rare, so unique in Averidan—"

"Enough!" I interrupted. "I've heard all this before." I glanced at Pardia. "I wouldn't have thought you Sisters would get sucked into an enterprise so—so full of *chun-hei*."

Pardia wrung out her trouser-leg and stared thoughtfully at the milling herd. "I didn't forget we were besieged," she said. "There's a lot of good meat on the hoof there."

Zofal would have been less shocked if she had proposed cannibalism. "You can't mean to *eat* them," he cried. "We should *preserve* horses, they're so expensive."

"We could pickle them," Siril began to giggle. "I'll bet they'd be delicious."

"Over my dead body!"

Pardia stared at Zofal with disfavor. "That can be arranged," she snapped.

"Let's not discuss it here and now," I interposed. "I'm sure you're all wanting baths and a meal."

Yibor refused to rise, so I sent for a sedan chair. With some difficulty we coaxed the horses up onto the dock. "We can keep them in your gardens," Zofal said, "until they can be smuggled out." The whites of his eyes glittered as he glanced sideways at me. "You won't really order them to be butchered, Liras, will you?"

"It's not at all necessary," I soothed him. "The boats go fishing every day, and we receive food shipments from downcountry."

"Viris be thanked," he sighed with relief.

"Just get them out of town fast," I warned him, "in case I have to change my mind."

Even to my inexperienced military eye it was plain the situation was unstable. As a whole the City was never meant to withstand long siege—only the Upper City was a citadel. Either we would quickly drive the invaders away, or they would storm the gates, swim the rivers, and overrun us.

So I sent for men. In ships from Mishbil in the south came rangy, talkative, yet indolent young men with faces narrow and sharp as knives. Both Xalan and the Magus were of that kindred; it was strange to see so many leaves from the same tree. They even favored mustaches like the Magus', though not as long because of their youth.

Ennelith-Ral on the coast sent many solid, well-grown lads, biddable and soft-spoken. I looked them over without much enthusiasm. As the last stronghold of matriarchy the holy city is renowned for competent women-folk. But Ennelith-Ral was in imminent danger of invasion also. I could not blame them for reserving the more spirited inhabitants for their own defenses.

A motley assortment of fishermen and woodsmen trickled in from the northern sea-marshes and forests. That realm is empty and peaceful, the domain of birds and antelope. I chose out several young men from the shore districts to help Zofal move the horses there. Only Sorrel was left to tenant the once-bustling royal horse-stable— "a mount for your triumphal parade," my brother prophesied.

Thus there were plenty of troops, though not perhaps of the doughtiest quality. The terrible lack was armament. The royal armory held only the weapons and armor of the guardsmen. And the metalworkers and smelters of Mhee were all lost now. Though the Shan King has great store of metal, we could hardly throw ingots at the Cayds.

Even after privately held weapons were contributed there were not enough. I called on the populace, to search attics and storerooms for antiques or mementoes. The morning after this appeal had been made, the eldest chamberlain recalled, "Shan Norlen-yu had the armaments from his pirate campaigns stored away in the cellar."

"Shan Norlen? My great-grandfather?" I was delighted—and curious. History is odd in Averidan. Plaiv and chronicle tug it this way and that, in the endless battle between fact and myth. As a result I knew little about my heroic ancestor, the only Tsormelezok to precede me on the throne, and that little was unreliable. "Show me," I commanded, and with only one doubtful glance—properly, I should have waited on my throne for the contents of the store to be displayed before me—the chamberlain led me there.

Armed with lighted lamps we descended into the bowels of the Palace complex—cramped, twisty staircases apparently built for exhaustion-proof legs, debouching into a low narrow corridor hewn out of the living rock. He pointed to our right. "That way, Your Majesty, to the dungeons," he informed me. I was not interested; the dungeons see little use because execution is so much cheaper. We turned left. Soot left by thousands of passing lamps smudged the upper walls and ceilings, and came away greasy on our sleeves—or more exactly onto *my* sleeves, since I was the taller. The silence and stony loneliness pressed around my ears. It occurred to me that everywhere in the Palace, save only here, there were people—chamberlains, officials, servers, or at the very least a humble lamp-filler on his ceaseless rounds with a long-spouted oil canister. As we paced along my light revealed and then hid side chambers lined with massive pottery jars taller than a man. Painted emblems of Ennelith and the Shan King blinked at us like limpid eyes, blue and green. The long-handled ladles hanging from each rim looked like skinny arms and clenched hands. And between them other eyes glowed, living ones of vigilant yellow or slit-pupiled green. No mouse dared steal from the jars while the cats kept their watch. "Grain-stores," the chamberlain murmured over his shoulder. "The jars go all the way back."

"That's a comfort to behold," I said.

We halted at a thick bronze door, green and pitted with age. Here, where the Sun of life never came, the cold seemed to gnaw our bones. The chamberlain fumbled with chilly hands at the lock, and at last turned the key. He and I leaned on the door, pressing a creak of anguish from a corroded hinge. A musty metallic smell rolled out of the darkness to greet us.

"Is this all?" I said in disappointment.

"All the armor and weaponry left from the campaigns of Your Majesty's great-grandfather," said the chamberlain, lifting his lamp high. "No monarch since then commanded further additions to the store."

Gingerly I took a wide leaf-shaped sword from the shelf and slid off its mouldering leather sheath. The blade was still sound, but the wire-bound ebony handle wobbled loose. There was enough here to arm at least two fists of men.

"A hundred." I sighed, more to myself than my companion. "Perhaps you've heard the plaiv of my great-grandfather's campaigns against the pirate Gorlis and his band: the battles on land and sea, the sword of fire on Cliffhole rock. Those plaiv were the reason I wanted to become a hero."

When I fell silent the chamberlain politely ventured, "After all, they're only plaiv."

"Still—to learn only a scant two fists were involved!"
"I wondered if all the grandiose legends of our past had been erected on so slight a foundation. Why had my great-grandfather caused these weapons, espe-

cially, to be set apart? The proper place for weaponry was in the armory. "Let this storeroom be cleared out," I said at last, "the contents carried up to the armory for repair."

The General and I formed up fists, and drilled them every day. The weather was vile, as it is at this time of year—leaden skies dripping cold rain mixed with sleet. "It's winter," I complained. "Don't they feel it at all?"

Melayne laughed at me. "You've visited the western lands. A Cayd wouldn't call this winter at all—a brisk day in spring, perhaps." And I had to own she was right.

After her night swim Yibor-soo caught a heavy cold. Zofal, Siril, and I waited apprehensively for her to recover enough strength to see visitors. "For certain she'll blame Rosil's death on our side of the family," Zofal worried, as I led the way down the hall. "She still remembers that time Rosil spent in the dungeons, on suspicion of doing away with you, Liras. And after all, you are Shan King." He did not speak in reproach, but I flinched anyway. I had never looked forward less to meeting Yibor. I felt almost ill with guilt—that I had not managed things better, that I let Rosil join us, that I had not at the very least contrived to rescue his body for a proper funeral. Zofal continued, "Would the Crystal Crown be able to help her cold?"

I shook my head. "Its healing powers are circumscribed. I can do nothing for diseases and illnesses. More and more I think we don't use the Crown properly. All the little tricks I do with it are—" I groped for the word—"peripheral."

"Now that Mother's gone, I ought to stand up to Yibor," Siril announced.

Startled, I glanced over my shoulder at Zofal, and caught him with the same expression of stupefaction I knew I wore. "I wouldn't think you'd have time, Siril," I said tactfully. "Dasan-hel has so many projects you help him with."

Zofal was far more blunt. "Mother's irreplaceable," he said. "We're going to need a strong woman to head the clan."

Fortunately we arrived at Yibor's room before a real quarrel could begin. Remorse had driven me to allot her excellent quarters, on the ground floor of a magus's tower—Xalan's as a matter of fact. Since Xalan spent so little time on magian researches there was plenty of room. I had even directed the Palace staff to care for her, a real concession now that the Upper City was swarming with high-born refugees clamoring for service.

The chamberlain waited for us outside her door, at the head of a retinue of servers. A magnificent luncheon, I had thought, would start our sick-call on a soothing note. An oily, mouth-watering aroma of fried bonito with mushrooms followed us into the chamber.

Yibor-soo lay propped on a couch carved of cherrywood. Like most plump folk she seemed to deflate and sag when she ailed, and her nose was bright red. "How are you, Yibor?" I asked.

She snuffled and cried, "Liras, you made that wish. How *can* this be best for us, in the god's judgment?"

I winced at the pain in her voice. "I don't know, sister-in-law," I muttered. "I'm only a king."

With more wisdom Zofal put in, "You'll feel much better after a meal, Yibor. See, we brought lunch. It would be a shame to let the food get cold."

That argument never loses its force in Averidan. Yibor allowed herself to be helped to the table, and the servers loaded our plates with blackbird grilled with lotus roots. No serious talk is allowed to interfere with digestion, but for the first time we were hard put to find a safe topic. The war, Mother's quarrels with Yibor, Rosil's doings—even Siril recognized these all were impossible. So we ate in glum silence, and as a result far too quickly. The servers scurried back and forth to the sound of clinking porcelain and steady chewing.

When the last course was cleared Yibor said, "I do feel better. Perhaps it was the oyster soup." For oysters are thought especially healthful, being the first of all life created. She looked at me and snuffled mournfully again, saying, "It's hard to believe Rosil will never eat another."

I had taken advantage of the abnormal quiet to think hard. There were only three conceivable possibilities. The deity could have lied. This I did not believe; the Sun has always pronounced truly. And the Crystal Crown, our touchstone of veracity, had shown me the deity's true affection for us. Of course some other being could have thwarted the god's kindly intent toward us. I could not imagine who. The fiend Ixfel was littl more than a name to me. But everyone knew his malevolence was tied to a locality, somewhere far away.

So with genuine conviction I said, "I'm certain in the end everything will work out for the best, Yibor. That's the only plausible answer."

I doubt she heard me. A tear rolled down her chubby cheek as she whispered, "Dosal and Eisen and now Rosil. And Lady Zilez, too." With a slight shock I recognized Mother's given name. Of course she and Yibor had been alike in both age and temperament; our family conflicts had in fact stemmed from the rivalry between two natural leaders. "All gone. Only you are left me, half-sibs of my late spouse. We must not quarrel any more."

Tears in her eyes, Siril squeezed the plump hand that Yibor held out. Zofal cleared his throat in sympathy. Once I too would have dissolved in the sentiment of reconciliation. Annoyingly now, in one corner of my head, the Shan King's cool assessment was that family accord would collapse the instant the tragedy was past. There was, however, no point in saying so.

CHAPTER 5:

A Luncheon with Liver

With her knowledge of her relatives' ways of war Melayne was able to predict the next assault for us. "They'll roam around the countryside for a week or two, in smallish groups," she informed us. "When they tire of robbing peasants and exploring they'll gather together again, outside the City, and work themselves up with stories for a fortnight or so about the wealth within—everyone knows the Shan are rich. Then, be ready."

"Would it be better to wait for their attack, or to make a sortie now?" I wanted to know, and indeed that was the question. General Horfal-yu pointed out that despite their poor condition the walls were still unbreached. The most sensible tactic might be to let the Cayds beat themselves silly against the fortifications, and then march out and mop up the leftovers. He illustrated his argument with many examples from past campaigns.

Commander Silverhand's advice was less positive, but on the whole tallied with the General's. "Scotching a widely scattered force is like battling mist," said she. "I ought to know. If the Cayds will oblige us by massing together to be eliminated, we should take advantage of it. That's presuming," she added, "that we can beat them in pitched fight."

"We couldn't before," I noted.

"But they caught us by surprise!" the General cried. "It wasn't fair! But this time they'll have to fight on *our* terms."

With very mixed feelings we watched from the

walls as the invaders began to gather again, after nearly a month of fairly placid siege. Mysteriously, they had commandeered bullocks and oxen from the entire district round, and brought the livestock with them. Herognomy was good for veiling our actions, but not a very useful offensive weapon, for the Cayd were a hardy folk. Nor could the geomants call up an earthquake from so great a distance. Instead they occasionally made bricks hop like fleas, breaking bones and cracking heads of whoever was visible. The bolder young magi would stroll off the wall and across the marketplace at night, four stories in midair, and drop boulders, old furniture, and the contents of chamber-pots onto the Cayds.

"We don't kill many," Xalan admitted with modest pride after one of these midnight excursions. "But I venture to promise we annoy everybody."

"Just stay high out of arrowshot," I said testily. Xalan could afford to be lighthearted; he had no real responsibilities.

He grinned, mischievous as a monkey and too intelligent not to know my thought. "Come with us, one of these nights. Eight magi could manage both a passenger and a missile. Yesterday Xarvet found a lovely old ballast-stone in the harbor; we thought we'd send it, as a present, to Musenor himself."

I was tempted. An icy melon slice of moon glittered low in the west. The night sky was cold yet inviting, like virgin snow. It cried out for creative action—sculpted caricatures or dished up with fruit syrup. Magi don't really fly; they use basic herognomy to literally walk on air. I had always envied them, but it's a magian art, and I was too old to learn—and too valuable to try. "A King can't risk it," I said regretfully. "Suppose you by accident let me fall."

"Unimportant," Xalan said very positively. "The Crystal Crown could stay at home. So Averidan wouldn't really be imperiled." I had to look twice, in the watery moonlight, to catch the twinkle in his eye.

Our foes must have known they could no longer

hope to surprise us. Otherwise they would not have thrown a party. From the walls we could watch them trundling kegs of wine and jugs of brandy into one of the more distant warehouses. Since the magi had taken to nocturnal wind-walking the number of goat-skin tents had noticeably decreased; shops, boathouses, and warehouses were used in their place.

"Don't they fear we'll dash out," I asked Melayne one day, "and put them to the sword while they're drunk?"

Melayne's healthy Caydish appetite had not les-sened during pregnancy. She nibbled not much, but constantly. Now she sniffed deeply as with a flourish and a deep bow the cook lifted the lid off a deep porcelain cauldron. Creators of innovative dishes properly have the honor of presenting and serving their inventions. I watched therefore with particular interest as the cook accepted a warmed plate from the folds of a white linen towel held by the server, and dipped up savory slips of meat in a thick brown sauce, fragrant with spices and colorful with vegeta-bles. With an elegantly careless gesture, like a prince dangling some bauble worth a province, he offered the dish to Melayne. She smiled, allowing him to set the plate before her on the round green-glass table. Another server proffered, on bended knee, a cruet of sea-salt and a silver porringer holding crisp-fried bread crumbs. A third hovered behind with a basket of rolls. Certainly Melayne had learned well the Shan philosophy of eating as an art.

There was complete silence as Melayne raised a steaming spoonful to her lips. Her expression re-mained gravely judicial as she chewed, thoroughly, and swallowed. Then she smiled again in delight. "One of your greatest successes," she pronounced.

The cook bowed, graceful as a cat on a windowsill. A most glorious steam, redolent with cunning spices, permeated every corner of Melayne's frescoed dining hall. Unable to resist any longer, I asked, "What is it?"

"Have some," she invited. "It's a new departure for Shan cookery—stewed pig's liver."

The cook hastened to serve me a portion. I prodded it carefully with my ceramic spoon. "I'll taste it," I allowed, "but you realize swine guts are usually fed to draft-dogs."

"The Lady asked especially for it," the cook spoke up, answering my implied criticism.

"It's good for babes in Cayd," Melayne argued, "so why not here? And the rest of the pig's flesh is a perfectly allowable viand."

I sucked a single bite-sized slice of liver into my mouth. It was delicious, spicy and tender. But all I said was, "Let's hope the child doesn't bark at birth."

She scowled. "They don't in Cayd."

"Don't get upset," I said hastily. "I was joking. You must eat whatever you fancy. I entirely approve." To demonstrate, I took a second bite. Attracted by the toothsome aroma, Sahai crept onto my lap and purred in a hinting sort of way. Certainly, the dish was superb, rich yet subtle, and I took yet another bite.

Melayne laughed at me, her mouth full. "As to my kinsmen," she said after swallowing, "the theory is one fights better drunk. The only difficulty with the idea was we hardly ever had liquor enough for the whole army." With solemn satisfaction she sipped from her wine cup. The server refilled it the moment she set it down.

"How odd," I said. Then another thought occurred to me, and I turned again to the cook. "Where did you purchase this liver? The dogs' meat dealer?"

"I took charge myself, of butchering one of Your Majesty's pigs," the cook assured me. "And the beast was maintained in luxury, on wine-sprinkled barley, acorns, and cabbage leaves."

A pig destined to become sausage and dog-food would not have been fed so well. Satisfied, I inquired, "And what did the other cooks make of your radical experiments?"

Like all artists the cook was only too pleased to

converse about his craft. "*We* were delighted, Your Majesty," he said, "but opinion was divided in the rest of the servants' wing. Most of them hold with your Lady, that we're wasting a good viand on the canines. But some would have it that only Cayds would serve up offal."

A bit of stewed carrot nearly went down the wrong way, and I choked and coughed. "How dare they!" I angrily exclaimed as soon as I could.

But to my surprise Melayne was not at all offended. "That's a knife that cuts both ways," she said placidly, wiping her bowl clean with a bread crust. "Do you know what creatures in Cayd eat raw mussels, as you do?"

"No," I said, still simmering. "What?"

"Crows and rats. Certainly not human beings."

I could not help laughing at that. All up and down the river mussels are a plentiful delicacy. It was just like the ignorant Cayds to suffer famine while surrounded by them. "Crows aren't edible," the cook said thoughtfully, "but rooks are delicious, in pastry."

Melayne allowed him to refill her plate, and I pushed mine forward too. "It would be even better with calf liver," she said. "Is there really none in Averidan? Can you find me some?"

"I'll give it some thought," I promised her. I rolled a spoonful on my tongue and glanced at the cook. "Did they change their minds after tasting this masterwork?"

He shrugged. "There are those who will never trust a Caydish idea. After all, they are our foes."

"But not Melayne," I insisted. "How can they think evil of her, she's my wife."

The cook put the lid on the cauldron and eyed me with some nervousness. But the Shan King is enjoined to rule justly, and I had a reputation for clemency. Furthermore, cooks can afford to be freespoken. They are welcome anywhere in Averidan, and are successfully lapidated only for the most heinous crimes. So he came out with it: "There are them that wonders. Everyone knows the Lady's brothers are out there, and their blood might speak louder than the marriage tie."

All of a sudden I lost my appetite. A whole tangle of knotty difficulties had me in the toils. I wondered how I had failed to realize that Melayne might be hated. "Something must be done," I said to her, distracted. "I won't have it. You could be poisoned by some misguided patriot."

Seeing her opportunity in my inattention, Sahai insinuated her front paws onto the table, and then poked her head up to plate level. Melayne flicked a half-eaten roll at her. "Don't take on so," she soothed me. "Something has."

I was unconvinced. "What?"

"Look at me," she commanded. "No, not my face or my form, look at my dress."

I did. Only I could don the true deep royal green, so her gown was of a bluer tint, like sunlit ocean depths. The wide garment, trailing at sleeves and hem, was starred nearly all over with silvery embroidered lily blossoms, presumably to look well with the wall-paintings that depicted water-gardens complete with lilies, dragonflies, and a long-legged heron. The gown was lovely, but Melayne has hundreds of lovely gowns. "Is it new?"

"That doesn't matter," she said. "What matters is that it's Viridese."

"How should that weigh against the prejudices of fools," I said impatiently.

"Your Majesty might be surprised," the cook suggested respectfully. "It's hard for cooks, at least, to deplore any patron, let alone one of appreciation and taste."

His words, and Melayne's, clicked a piece of the puzzle into place. "Taste? You know the Cayds stole all the local oxen?" I asked. "They must be slaughtering them!"

"The magi descried them in an abandoned garden," Melayne remembered. "Someone was theoriz-

ing the invaders were planning a takeover of the
farm economy."

"That made sense," I said. "Oxen turn water wheels,
haul wagons, drag ploughs. But this makes more.
Remember, Melayne, that dinner in Lanach? They
must have served up two or three roast bullocks,
plus any number of lambs and goats." An idiotic
vision popped into my mind, of myself politely calling on King Mor to borrow some beef liver for
nourishing his unborn nephew.

"You don't have to tell me," Melayne said. "But
here it's wrong! There are so many delicious things
to consume in Averidan. And if they eat our draft
animals the farmers will perish."

The cook nodded at me approvingly. "You see?
That's the right way to talk," said he.

I fished in the sauce at the bottom of the cauldron
for any last bits of meat. It awed me to realize that in
Melayne's reckoning I was worth more than all her
kinsmen. Even when one considered that Cayds as a
people take their familial ties more lightly, it was
impressive. And how clever she was, outflanking my
insular subjects like that! Clearly she had things well
in hand. The story has it that foreigners in our land
soon merge in with us, their lesser lights overwhelmed
by our fiery god-descended life. I had always thought
this referred to their half-bred children, dark-haired
and dark-eyed no matter how strange their parent.

"Certainly I must disapprove," I said slowly. "But
they are foreigners, so how can we expect them to be
like us? I can understand."

"I can't," Melayne said without a scrap of sympathy. "This is a different land; they should try to fit
in."

"Nor I," the cook muttered. "Who knows what the
barbarians will do next?"

What they did next was, of course, to assault the
walls. The entire City listened with fascination as the
noises of merriment—which lasted three days—grew

imperceptibly more and more bellicose. At last, very early one morning, my chamberlain roused me. "Good morning, Your Majesty," he said politely. "I am given to understand the Cayd are attacking."

Sahai hissed at him from her nest in the quilts at the foot of the bed. I opened one eye and demanded, "Who says?"

The chamberlain pointed to the door, where a nervous yet curious recruit peered in. "General Horfal-yu sent a messenger."

With a yawn I sat up, shivering in the night chill. The chamberlain lit a taper at the brazier and set about kindling the lamps, so I should not slide back into sleep. The Master of Wardrobe appeared, leading a train of assistants who each carried a piece of armor. By the time I was armed the commotion had woken Melayne. I dropped a farewell kiss onto her cheek, saying, "Don't start worrying, this may take a few days." A warm, sweet smell rose fom the quilts as she reached up to hug me.

The full moon loitered on the pellucid western horizon as we tramped downhill, but clouds were rolling in from the sea. The gongs had roused the City. There was no point in forming up the fists, since there would be no pitched battle yet. But as a precaution all the troops were to be armed and ready. As we descended soldiers drifted out to join us, yawning and hitching up their greaves.

At the main City gate I clattered up the stairs to the battlements. Days ago Silverhand had chosen Sisters who were deadly archers to man the walls. Their arrows were triple-barbed with bronze, for the weapons forged of their special metal must never leave the Order's hands. The tough, compact women saluted me, raising their tall bows, as I panted up into view. The weight of my lamellar coat made long flights of stairs a trial. Caydish arrows were already rebounding from the tile facade.

Silverhand led me to a crenel. "Don't stick your head too far out," she cautioned. "There—you see?

They're dashing from the warehouses into the shops at the base of the wall."

"So they are." From this perspective the Cayds, skittering across the gloomy marketplace in their brown leather armor, could have been a plague of cockroaches. Though they held bucklers and pieces of wood above their heads, our arrows did a good deal of damage. As I watched, a bold Sister leaned right out of her nook to drive a barbed arrow down at the correct angle. It caught a running Cayd in the thigh, where the leather legging left it bare. He screamed and tumbled over. From so high the blood on the cobbles looked unconvincing, like paint.

"We ought not to have let those shops be built," I said with agitation. "No one could even approach the walls then."

"They could always have crept up at night with scaling equipment," Silverhand reminded me. "Lucky for us the Cayds don't think that way."

But she was wrong. From the edge of the nearest roof below a head stuck up. No, two—and without helmets. Someone was climbing the shop wall. Before I could open my mouth to cry warning grayfletched arrows pierced them through. Astonishingly, they continued to rise. "A ladder! They've built ladders, Ennelith's blight on them!" Silverhand cried, and dashed off shouting for the Master Magus.

I clung to the embrasure and watched with awe as our stubborn foes climbed up. There was no cover on the flat roofs below. As each Cayd scrambled over the edge, arrows hissed down. At this close range the impact pinned their limbs to the dirt roofs, or tumbled them right back over the edge again. Yet no one below seemed to notice the dreadful slaughter. With undiminished enthusiasm the tall fair warriors shoved their dead aside and pressed on. After many attempts a second crude ladder was hoisted up to the roof. I saw it was long enough to reach from the roof to the top of the wall, and glanced wildly around for a spear or pole. Our only chance would be to push the ladders away.

The Sun should have risen long ago, but the sky was now muffled in an overcast thick as quilts. Only a groggy parody of morning crept through; we seemed to be endlessly caught in a dreary time neither day nor night. Now, very quickly, the clouds rolled closer, frowning right over our heads. With only one preliminary rumble of thunder the heavens opened. A driving rain scoured down, spattered on the tiles facing the wall and utterly obliterated all sight of our foes. But only a few fat drops hit me. Abandoning my nook I leaned out laughing with astonished delight, holding my hands out into the rain-wall not a foot away.

"I've always wanted to see a herognomical storm so close," I told Silverhand as she hurried up.

"Get ready to duck again," she replied, peering out. "The Magus said this storm would be brief."

"I'm sure the wet will annoy them," I said, "but it won't do us much good. Those ladders can take a little rain."

She smiled at me, the expression incongruously sweet in so tough a countenance. "Anyone could tell Your Majesty's of leisured status," she said. "If you'd ever been in one of these shanties after a rainstorm you'd know earthen roofs leak terribly."

Still I did not see her point. "They're not planning to take up residence down there," I said foolishly. "They're just passing through."

With the suddenness of a slamming door the rain stopped. I was still leaning over the parapet, and Caydish arrows instantly flew. But they faltered and fell back harmlessly. The Caydish bowstrings were now wet, and consequently powerless. So I leaned even farther out, exclaiming, "Look!"

Perhaps a dozen Cayds had taken advantage of the storm and mounted to the roof just below us. With a flourish and a shout they hoisted the second ladder above their heads and raced through the Sisters' arrow-fire to throw it against the gleaming-wet wall. As they swarmed up we hurried to a nearer crenel. The top of the ladder was barely within reach of my sword. With its tip I pushed the ladder as hard as I could. The topmost Cayd's sword was out but Silverhand leaned over me and shot him in the chest. As he fell I saw the arrow sticking out red a full foot beyond his back.

The ladder wobbled and then toppled sideways, spilling warriors over the roofs. It was too much to hope, that they would break their necks, for the drop was barely two stories. I kept my eye on the nearest Cayd's fall anyway. One never knew. But to my amazement when he hit the roof one thick leg *sank* into the softened surface. Fatally, he tried to wrest it free. The whole structure sagged, crumbling wetly into the room below. Another Cayd leaped to help him and fell straight through with a plop, like a stone into the sea. Through the disintegrating roof I could see the light timbers and reeds that support the dirt.

"And is this happening everywhere along the wall?" I asked.

"That's my sincere hope," Silverhand said jauntily. The shouting from either side along the wall seemed to confirm her wish. "This will put paid to ladders for a while." And indeed without an intermediate stop the ladders would fall quite short; the Cayds would have to build new ones.

With great loss of life our foes extracted themselves from the muddy ruins and fell back "to think it over," I suggested. "I suppose this concludes today's assault?"

"They do appear to have lost interest," Silverhand agreed. "Let's go down and find some breakfast."

I assented with enthusiasm, having been too anxious to hunger until now. As we descended the stairwell's sudden quiet rang in my ears, and I realized how noisy the assault still was. No doubt the Caydish yelled to keep up their nerve.

We emerged into wan sunlight and chaos. The gatekeepers' courtyard was crammed with wounded soldiery in a froth of excitement and fear. It was impossible to learn what had happened, impossible to even make a shouted question heard over the din. "We must get through this," Silverhand bellowed into my ear. "Look, there's Pardia on that crossing-block, she must know." With that she began to worm through the press. I hastened after, treading close so that her aggressive elbows and bronze-clad knees would clear my passage too.

The crossing-blocks allow the pedestrian to cross from curb to curb without stepping into the street. From that vantage point Pardia could have seen us over the heads of the crowd. But she was looking the other way down a side street, standing on tiptoe to shriek inaudible advice to someone invisible. When Silverhand battled near enough to tug on the loose leg of her trouser, Pardia whirled to attack, her face distorted with emotion.

"Oh, Commander!" I was near enough to hear her exclaim. All of a sudden she seemed about to weep.

"We can't talk here," I said, panting, and pointed. On the south corner of the intersection was a tavern, strategically placed to attract thirsty travelers.

The proprietor was putting up his shutters, preparatory to closing up. When the three of us shouldered in anyway he snapped, "I'm not open for service, messir and Sisters, so you can step right out again."

Pardia seemed disposed to make a violent reply. But I took off my helmet and mopped my brow, remarking, "You have a mort of potential customers outside."

So much of the tavern front was shut up the big common-room was in dimness. The clay-brick walls were plastered, and decorated with humorous frescoes of drunkards weaving their way home. I could see our host shaking his head vigorously. "It's a forlorn hope, but if I board up maybe the barbarians won't recognize the place for a tavern."

"The barbarians?" I asked. "You expect the Cayds?"

Unable to contain herself, Pardia interrupted. "They've forced the river-gate!"

She buried her face in her hands. To the taverner I said, "Since we'll have to hold a brief council of war here, messir, perhaps you would favor us with a jug of wine."

"Let's see the color of your metal," he retorted.

I sighed. Ordinarily the Shan King is too quickly recognized; the man must be quite upset. But time was too short to argue about it. Silverhand slapped a few coppers on the trestle table and when the wine came made Pardia sit and drink. "Now," she ordered, "let us have an account."

Pardia took a deep breath through her nose. "You know the underwater chain that blocks the river-gate. They strung leather hawsers around the base of the river tower to it, and then from there around to the docks."

"And then laid planking over," I finished for her. I remembered the Caydish style in bridge-building.

Pardia nodded. "They took us in the flank. The river-tower's holding, but the streets are a slaughter-house. The common folk are caught between the soldiers, everywhere. The army can't charge them." And the first impulse of the townspeople, as with the taverner, would be to escape. Never would it occur to them to join together and drag the enemy down.

Though I couldn't recall tasting the wine, looking down I found I had drained my cup. It was of ordinary cheap earthenware, such as one would find in any drinking place—red and smoothly cool under my thumbs, with a neat design of coiling vines impressed round the outside. In the storm of this great disaster only trivialities anchored me. Across the table Silverhand was drawing on the scarred age-darkened oak tabletop with a wet fingertip, noting the extent of the Caydish incursions on an imaginary map as Pardia recounted them. "That fat idiot!" she seethed when Pardia was done. "Horfal-yu should be rendered down for axle grease!"

"That won't help now," I said wearily. "Besides, I dare say he has. What instead should we do?"

Both pairs of eyes glinted sharply at me in the comfortable dimness. "This time," Silverhand said, "you're going to keep yourself safely inside the gate—of the Upper City."

I quite forgot I was Shan King, and banged my cup on the table. "It's not fair," I protested. "I've worked so hard to become a warrior, and no one will let me fight!"

"Easy on my crockery, messir, if you please," the taverner growled from his corner.

"I never liked your learning," Silverhand admitted. "It's never been custom, and now you see why."

"And it won't be the only unfairness today, either," Pardia said.

"They were glad enough of me last month," I grumbled. But Silverhand was deaf to all my complaints, and I soon found myself trudging alone up the main road I had descended this morning. The streets seethed with anxious townfolk demanding news or fleeing from where they imagined battle was. I had been strictly enjoined not to begin organizing the resistance, and so plodded by, unseen and unspoken to, my helmet under my arm. With a distinct feeling of being stuck in a plaiv—and a repetitive one at that—I instructed the keepers of the Upper gate to prepare to close up, upon my signal.

CHAPTER 6:
Over the Divide

Now that the magian influence was dissipated the day had become heartlessly clear. A bright Sun graced a merry blue sky and a cool wind rumpled my hair. The Upper walls were old as time, but neither as high nor complete as the lower ones. They did not need to be, for the Upper City perches high on a shoulder of rock. On the Palace side the cliff falls sheer for nearly three hundred feet, invulnerable to all except perhaps dragon-fire. Every inch of the zigzag road up the shallower side of the rock was commanded by the walls, and the cunning dog-leg in the walls blunted any assault on the gate.

When I looked down from the wall's wide top the gigantic stone blocks still gleamed with a smooth finish. Everything Shan Xao-lan the first and mightiest Magus laid hand to was built to last. Even the gates were utterly trustworthy, being closed and opened daily.

My lonely vigil lasted all day and into the night. Everybody seemed to get the idea of taking refuge in the Upper City at the same time, and once more the wagons and refugees poured through the gate. Neither soldiers nor Sisters were among them; somewhere in the Lower City a bitter battle hung in the balance. More than once it occurred to me that if it came to a second siege this torrent of oldsters, care-laden mothers, and timid shopkeepers would be worse than helpless. A practical ruler would deny sanctuary to the useless mouths; the survival of the Shan might depend on it. I was absolute monarch. No one would dare say me nay.

But I could not bring myself to do it. My very kingship had taught me too well to feel the pain of others. Mother had always complained I was more than any of us a helpless prey to emotions of *chunhei*. But this was the first time I knew she was right. The sudden realization of my own power terrified me. There was nothing the Shan King could not do, no cruelty beyond his command, no pain beyond his order, no life out of his grasp. That they would perforce be necessary cruelties and pains and deaths was irrelevant. I was Shan King, and could not bear my own sovereignty.

All of a sudden I yearned for human contact. Alone, high on the wall, I might as well be a god. I wanted to smell my own sweat, feel someone else's hand in mine, hear another voice. Had this not been wartime I would have gone up to my gardens—transplanted a stubborn young tree. or pruned thorny klimflowers. Instead I sent a guardsman with a note to Zofal. An elder brother can always be relied upon to keep one down to earth.

As night fell I ordered torches set up along the road below, so that we might distinguish friend from foe. In the City below, night thickened swiftly, though up here on the hill it was still day. The guardsmen set up torches as far as the first bend in the road. squeezing themselves against the flow of traffic and then thankfully hurrying uphill with the press as soon as a torch was fixed in place.

"Hallo, Liras-ven, enjoying the show?"

I nearly jumped out of my skin. "Siril-ven, what are you doing here?"

"I read your note," she said, shaking out the hems of her trailing sleeves. "You ought to make them dust that stairway. How pretty the view is from here. Is that silver line the ocean, on the eastern horizon?"

"Of course it is, the harbor opens out there. I sent the note to Zofal. Where is he?"

She glanced at me in mild surprise. "Oh, didn't you know he went down to join the battle?"

I clutched at the stone parapet. "I didn't bring him down with me!"

"He heard the alarm-gong and decided it was his duty." She spoke with calmness, as if Zofal had merely announced a wish to go swimming. "Where are you going to put all these folk, Liras? Thre isn't room!"

"There's plenty of room in the Palace." Of course Siril was not pleased to hear this, since she enjoyed having an exclusive privilege. But refusing to be distracted from the main issue, I demanded, "Where did he go? Did he say?"

But Siril had spent the morning in her bath and so could not say. I leaned out, peering through the flickering torchlight for any gleam of bronze, and prayed desperately for my brother's safety. "What are all these oil jars, Liras?" Siril wanted to know. "Surely the gatekeepers don't cook up here."

"There's cloth scrap as well as oil in there," I said crossly. "A variation of the General's idea. They'll be set afire before we drop them on the Cayds."

It was full night now, and getting cold despite the brazier. An oily smoke from the torches below stung in our throats and noses. "Would you like some tea?" Siril offered. "I'll go down and get some."

She vanished down the narrow stair before I could order her back to the Palace. This was no place for noncombatants. Nepotism is our besetting sin; grimly I resolved to preserve Siril at least. She was gone a long time. I fidgeted from cold and nerves, and battled the temptation to dash up to the Palace and look in on Yibor-soo. For once she had been right. There were too few of us now.

When Siril reappeared, struggling under the weight of a large basket, I said, "You had better go home, Siril, before it gets too late."

"The least you could do," she panted, "is let me eat something."

"You could dine properly, with Dasan and Yibor,"

I argued, but she ignored me and began unpacking the basket.

Tension fluttered in my stomach so that I turned from the food with loathing. But I was thirsty. Just as I swallowed my first sip of tea the low murmur from the road below changed. Shrieks and yells rose up. Those still trudging up the road began to run in terror for the gate. A picked dozen of Palace guardsmen, warned by the noise, clattered up the stairs. "Get those jars ready," I told them. "Siril, you mustn't leave now, just keep out from under foot." With scared obedience she tucked the stoneware tea-bottle, fruit, and the palm-leaf twists of barley groats back into the basket.

Red heads, bright as coals, bobbed round the bend in the road. Was no one left alive to oppose them? Desperately I told myself the Army must be outflanked, that our forces still lived and fought somewhere in the Lower City.

There was nothing to be done as the Cayds began swinging their axes like scythes. Our fire missiles were intended only for the ultimate necessity of guarding the gate. And even the best archer would be hard put to hit the correct targets in the milling, torchlit roadway.

The townspeople screamed shrill as gulls and ran to clog the gate. Some bolder folk tried to dodge past the axemen and escape downhill. For a while this seemed successful. Then another group of Cayds arrived to completely block the roadway, and they began to advance in earnest. Red stained the cobbles, and flowed down the central gutter. The roadway looked like a slaughterhouse. A grip of bronze seemed to be choking off my breath.

"They can't be doing this," Siril wailed. "Those are people they're killing!"

"I'll shout up the stairs," I told the guardsmen, "when I want the missiles lit. Remember, drop them directly in front of the gate, never mind who's below."

Siril followed me as I ran down the spiral stair.

"How can you give an order like that?" she cried to me in the darkness. "Zofal is out there trying to get in, suppose he's at the gate when they drop?"

With weary pain I replied, "Then he must die for Averidan, as so many have."

These gates were shut by wheels and gears, not oxen. The great spoked wheels of bronze were manned by terrified gatekeepers; between them the tunnel-like gateway overflowed with a torrent of horror-stricken refugees. Though I tried to convince her the stairway was an excellent hidey-hole, Siril insisted on clinging to me as I fought against the tide of people. I was tall enough to see a little over the press; what I dreaded now was not slaughter but a Caydish rush for the open gate.

At last I reached the nearer gatekeeper, clapping him on the shoulder so that he started violently. "Close the gate," I shouted in his ear. "Can you shut just this side?"

He nodded. His assistant helped him to drag the wheel around, slowly at first and then a little faster as the great bronze gate began to swing around. "You can't close it yet!" Siril cried in unfortunately loud tones.

Those in hearing took up the cry. "Not yet!" "Uncle is just behind, wait for him!" "Not so fast!" "Don't dare to shut it!"

Angry hands plucked at the gatekeepers. I defended them with outspread arms, shouting, "I'm the Shan King, and I order it!"

Oddly enough no one doubted my claim. For the first time my people cried out against me. "Cruel!" "It's not fair!" "Drag them away!" But no one dared actually do so, and with a hollow boom the gate swung home. The gatekeepers ran to shoot the bolts that secured that side, top and bottom.

Through the remaining open half pressed a dreadful mill of hysterical, bleeding refugees. I fought my way across to the other gate's keepers, fearing the crowd would rend them to pieces when their side began to shut. "I have to do this," I found myself explaining as I went. "If the gate isn't shut the Cayds will come through. The war will be lost. We'll all die." Through the din I doubt anyone caught, or was in a temper to heed, my excuses. I made them to myself only.

Oil-dipped torches do not burn long. When I stood on tiptoe to glimpse the dog-leg beyond the gate it was much dimmer. Without the slightest warning those actually on the threshold fell forward, spilling red down the backs of those in front. A Caydish axeman loomed above them.

"Close it!" I snapped to the gatekeepers, and dashed forward. Too late I realized the guardsmen could have helped me better here below. Yet I was the last surviving remnant of the Army of the Shan. Siril screamed as I drew my sword. "Go and tell them to drop the jars," I called to her, but dared not linger to see if she obeyed me.

There are probably worse places for a forlorn fight then the dark gate-tunnel. The axeman was too busy chopping up the helpless; in the gloom I was able to edge quite close. I saw him start as he noticed the glitter of torchlight on my lamellar, and swung quickly before he should be ready.

The wide slicing blade took him at the side of the waist where the leather armor is thin. He tottered sideways and then leaped within the circle of my return stroke, dropping buckler and axe to throw me down. Battle etiquette in Cayd is to die killing one's killer. I fell back with a stunning bronzen crash onto the cobbles.

Hands big as cargo hooks tore at my throat, and a roaring din filled my ears. Through glazing eyes I saw the sheen of torchlight on moving bronze above me as the door swung around. If I did not strangle I surely would be cut in half like a slug, when the massive door banged shut on me.

I saw the jar suspended above, and in confusion wondered how the guardsmen had managed to throw them inside the gate. It hit my assailant square on the head. Someone else looped a string tied in a running knot over the Cayd's head. "Tug! One, two, three!" And the cruel hands flew apart as he was dragged away. I rolled to my stomach and crawled clear of the door. Outside fire-jars were shattering, spattering Cayd and Shan alike with burning oil. The gate's sudden closure made the tunnel utterly black, but willing hands helped me toward the light at the farther end.

"Oh, Liras!" Siril wept aloud over me. "Look at your neck, are you hurt?"

As I sucked in the sweet cold air my eyes cleared. I lay propped on a bulging satchel as its owner, a shopkeeper, applied a wet cloth to my throat. Anxious people stood close around, one timidly holding my sword out at arm's length so it should not drip on his shoes. Beyond, the more robust were messily battering the Cayd to death.

I coughed. "A good sign," a gatekeeper comforted Siril. "Means his voicebox isn't cracked. And he can walk, so his neck isn't broke."

"Make a great plaiv, this will," someone else offered.

"I'm never going to listen to plaiv again," Siril sobbed. "I'd always see him holding the gate all alone." There was a murmur of approval at this dramatic vow.

"I shall live," I croaked. Both talking and breathing were painful. Blood mixed with water puddled around me, an impressive sight that did not soothe me at all. The Cayd had worn gloves sewn with copper plaques, which bruised and cut, but I had no serious wound. Still, Siril hovered ready to support me when I staggered to my feet again.

With a respectful bow the sword-holder returned my blade. I jammed it gory back into its sheath, for cleaning later. "What shall we do with the Cayd, Your Majesty?" someone asked.

At least I did not have to waste precious breath to ask if he was dead. Foggily I searched my mind for a suitably colorful disposal. "Haul him up and drop him off the wall," I suggested in a hoarse whisper. The words were repeated and greeted with enthusiasm. A minor noble offered me his sedan chair, and I gratefully collapsed into it.

Before I lost my senses again I realized what had really saved me. No one had pitched in until I had offered a chance to participate in a real-life legend. I was its hero, stepping out alone against a terrible foe. Then they had followed me willingly, over the divide between reality and myth. Somehow problems dragged to that plane lost power. One needed no Crystal Crown, no special link to the god. That was what poor General Horfal-yu had done with the linen wagon. That was what the Sisters of Mir-hel were: living legends. "We've got to do more of this," I mumbled aloud. "It's the solution to everything."

Siril was walking beside the chair, and for some reason understood my words. "Do this again," she sniffed, "and I'll—I'll tell Yibor-soo."

I woke next morning in my own bed, aching all over. A peep in the mirror showed my neck swollen and black with bruises. My head seemed to run directly into my shoulders. It hurt so much to get about—I was unable to move my head and had to turn my entire body when I wanted to look around—that I was glad to spend a recuperative day in my chambers, with a towel spread with pungent liniment round my throat, and leave the Upper City's defense to the guardsmen for a while.

Yibor, Siril, and Dasan called and were so solicitous and respectful that in irritation I sent Dasan out to count the new additions to the Upper City. "The Sun Temple is housing most of the new refugees," I told him. "But we'll need an exact count to allocate supplies. And perhaps someone saw Zofal yesterday. I'm sure Yibor and Siril will be a great help to you on this." I also summoned the store-keepers and demanded complete tallies of all our foodstuffs.

After they had gone Melayne accused, "You said you were going to rest."

"I am," I defended. "But that's no reason why anyone else should. Is anything of interest to be seen outside?"

"They're keeping watch from the walls," she assured me. "But there's no sign of the Army or the Sisters or the magi."

"Of course they realized the gate was shut," I argued more to myself than my wife. "They probably scattered, to hide somewhere in town. And it's notoriously hard to kill magi." Neither of us voiced the more likely possibility, that they had all valiantly perished. So that Melayne should not worry, I took a bath, and closed my eyes to soak in the herb-sweetened water and think it over.

The Upper City had never fallen by storm. In the time of Tsantelekor a small stubborn garrison had held it for years, until everyone grew bored and both besiegers and besieged relaxed into token conflict. Tsantelekor had had to win the Crystal Crown by wedding its wearer, the Shan Queen. Then the garrison surrendered, for a wedding present. We had water from a deep hidden spring on the fortified southern slope—I made a note to go inspect it—and somewhere thereabouts there was a secret postern, a door that let one beyond the walls. I had never seen it but like most City residents knew where it must be.

From the contributions this past autumn I knew we had great store of food, admittedly of a tedious and humble sort—dried beans, dried fish, potted fruits, and above all barley, jar upon gigantic jar of barley. The memory of those jars, rank upon rank stored safe in the cellar, was as comforting as a quilt on a cold night. The lack of fresh meat or seafood would be a trial, but if put to it we could raise vegetables in the gardens come spring.

But we had neither weapons nor the warriors to bear them. No doubt a motley fist could be scratched up from assorted peasant lads, guardsmen, and servants. But the armory had been cleaned out. "We can't use our fingernails," I said aloud.

"We can throw rocks," Melayne said firmly.

Very softly I said, "Do you realize, Melayne, I've never had to fight alone before? I could always ask the General or Silverhand for military advice."

"And their counsel wasn't notably successful," she replied with spirit. She poured liniment from a bottle onto my towel, and asked, "Are you hungry?"

"Oh, yes." I had of course breakfasted, but not very heartily. Five meals a day is the standard in Averidan. I climbed up the three steps out of the square sunken bath and sat wrapped in a robe on a couch on the tile verge. The servers brought in a bath-side table and approached with a generous repast—a heaping platter of little roast quail, potted eggs, barley groats, preserved cabbage, and four sauces. I stared at the parade and exclaimed, "Take it away!"

With smooth and graceful obedience the servers circled away again. "Wait!" Melayne objected indignantly. "You said you were hungry!"

"Quite right, no, bring it back," I told the servers. "Melayne, you must join me. Chamberlain, let all the Palace cooks be informed: Henceforward there must be only three meals a day served. Small ones. We don't know how long our stores must last. Where did you get these quail?"

The servers looked at one another, and at last one said, "At market, Your Majesty, yesterday."

I sighed. The last quail the entire Upper City would likely see for weeks, and here they all were on my plate. Zofal had loved quail. I pointed at the two plumpest little birds and commanded, "Remove those to another dish, and bring them with my compliments to my half-sister-in-law."

A chair had been brought up for Melayne, and she eased her growing bulk into it. She said, "*I'm* not hungry, why do I have to eat?"

"You're eating for two," I said severely. "I'd rather

starve myself than have you hunger, now of all times."

The quail were tender, deliciously greasy and spicy, and Melayne watched with sardonic amusement as I tore the first one apart with my fingers. "You don't even know hunger, let alone starvation," she declared.

"I may well find out, soon. We can't possibly eat all of these birds, shall I send some to Siril too?"

"Or what about us?" A ragged red sleeve shot over my shoulder, and a grimy hand snatched up a piece of quail from my plate.

"Xalan!" A stab of agony in my neck rewarded me when I tried to turn. Instead I leaped up to embrace him, nearly upsetting the food into the bath. "Thank the One you survived!"

"You're greasy," he said happily when he broke free, "and I'm both dirty and ravenous." Behind him the Master Magus drooped, evidently at the last extreme of exhaustion. We sat him down on the couch and poured him wine. While he recovered I demanded of Xalan, "However did you escape? How many magi are with you?"

"We lifted from roof to roof, and so up here," he replied briefly. "Nearly all of us are back; magi are elusive. We spent all night snatching our men, here and there as we found them, away from the Cayds. One can't just flutter about in broad daylight any more, so our return took awhile." He sat on the free end of the couch and stuffed a crisp quail leg into his mouth.

The Master Magus took off his peaked red hat, revealing straggly white locks. "Despite our best efforts, Your Majesty, I'm sorry to report the slaughter was terrible. Their ferocity and sheer numbers overwhelmed us."

"I knew that must be the case," I said in a low voice. All of a sudden I wasn't hungry anymore. "Did you happen to see Zofal-ven?"

"Your brother was down there?" Xalan stared in dismay.

"When we've rested a little I'll set the scryers to look for him," the Magus promised. "But Your Majesty ought not to hope too highly of our efforts. The invaders have set the populace to clearing the streets. The slain are being thrown into the harbor."

"That will spoil the fishing," I said, aghast. Viridese funerals are ordinarily conducted well out to sea, the dead being burned in small boats.

"No ship will put out to sea now," Xalan predicted. "They fear Ennelith's anger."

"You can't expect Cayds to know that," Melayne pointed out. "This is the first time many of them have even seen the ocean."

We found this difficult to imagine, but realized it must be true. Melayne herself was the proof; even river-barging made her edgy, and she had never set foot on a seagoing vessel. The hungry magi had made short work of our meal. "You will want to bathe and sleep," I told them. "We'll discuss the situation later." It was clean against custom, but I embraced them both as equals, cheek to left cheek. "I'm glad you're back. I thought I'd have to cope alone."

"Our powers in Your Majesty's service," the Magus replied formally, flushing with embarrassment.

Xalan sniffed pointedly and demanded, "What's that? Did you fall down another flight of steps?"

"Liniment," I said. "A Cayd thought I was a chicken and tried to wring my neck."

So much had happened that the Magus did not even raise his eyebrows. "I trust Your Majesty taught him proper respect," he said mildly.

CHAPTER 7:

Of Posterns and Provisions

The next day found me up and about again. I went to the Temple and after a thank-sacrifice discussed our situation with the High Priestess. She was newly elected, bony and very conscious of her rank. She glanced disapprovingly at my plain, unregal tunic. "We're housing the mothers with babes in the colonnades and halls," she reported as if it were a personal injury. "Everyone else is camped in the courtyards and streets; the Upper City is as full as a beehive in summer. Something must be done before everyone catches cold. Living in each other's laps like this opens us to plague."

That had never occurred to me. "I'll open up the Palace," I promised quickly.

"And there's a great deal of worry about food; Your Majesty knows the Temple maintains no great store."

"I will see to the feeding of all," I assured her, "if the Temple will do its part also." She stared at me, lips compressed, and I plunged hastily on. "No sacrifices of food must be made, for the duration of the siege."

As I feared, she was outraged. "How dare you meddle with such high traditions? No flowers bloom in winter, and what else shall we give, but what is dear and beautiful to us? Will you dare to stint the Lord of Life?"

"It's my belief the god would prefer live worshippers to dead ones," I said firmly. "We must allow for all contingencies. I propose we offer scrip instead, a

105

written note of what will be sacrificed after all this is over."

"This will surely bring down a curse," she warned me in portentous tones. But I refused to believe it, remembering that uncanny affection in the heart of the central fire. The god would understand.

After this disagreeable conversation I felt I owed myself a treat, and sent my attendants back up to the Palace. Xalan, two stonemasons, and a hydromant named Xadok waited for me near the gate. When I came up they were leaning on staffs or mattocks, listening to an itinerant rhetor recount yesterday's doings to a rapt audience.

"Round and round they went, as both armies paused in wonder," the fellow declaimed energetically. "Lamellar scales flew off the King's armor like dust from a carpet, so mighty were the barbarian's blows. Only the golden charm hung round the King's neck by Princess Melayne of Cayd saved him—"

So long as Melyane held such a positive role in the popular imagination, she was safe enough. I tugged at Xalan's sleeve. "Is everyone ready? Then let's start."

As our little party moved off down the narrow lane I was uncomfortably conscious of the stonemasons' round eyes, and thanked Viris I had had the sense to dress simply. Even Xalan was impressed. "Did you really leap off the wall to confront the foe?" he asked.

"Of course not," I said with irritation. "It must be a forty-foot drop; I'd have broken both legs." I wondered whether my great-grandfather had ever had to put up with such nonsense. Then it came to me: that was why the gear from his pirate-campaign had been so carefully stored—so that anyone who seriously looked into the episode could learn the facts. A sense of kinship with my long-ago ancestor warmed me, and I grinned to myself.

We walked almost due south, with the wall looming over our left shoulders. It diminished rapidly in height, as the slope on its other side became steeper, and ended at a little round tower. Beyond, the sheer cliff fell down to the main City walls, and the Mhesan river flowed on the farther side. To our right the tiny white houses were heaped like children's blocks up the narrow strip of slope. Behind and above them a Palace wall topped with green and blue ornamental tile gleamed bright against the hill. On its other side were my fruit orchards.

The tower was one of the odder erections in the Upper City. Some ancient Shan King had ordered a high egg-shaped dome to be added, so that an exotic point of interest would finish one of his favorite views from the Palace. So the squatty lower walls were of prosaic gray stone, while the ornate white fretted marble dome gave the entire structure the look of a snowball balanced on a dirty finger.

Xadok had a key to the wide wooden doors. The tower's exterior glories did not extend into the high stone chamber within. A narrow stone stair descended along one wall from the floor above, and on the other side of the room another stair wound down. In the middle, taking up all the space, was a great treadmill. A plump brown ox drove it creaking around, and a Palace official tended it. "Would Your Majesty care to see the works?" Xadok invited.

From a locker he took oil and lamps. When these were lit and distributed we descended. The center of the tower was hollow, and as we went down the hempen hawsers ran ceaselessly up and down beside us. The lower story showed low and dark in the faint light of our lamps. A tangle of bronze gears, copper pipes, and wooden pulleys were anchored to the stone-flagged floor.

There were no more stairs. Instead we took the sole passage, which I judged ran north and east, parallel to the road we had come by. Only one copper pipe, thick as a horse's body, followed along beside us. Xadok stroked it lovingly with one hand as we went along.

The stonemasons' regard on the other hand was

given to the tunnel, which was very low, made post-and-lintel style out of blocks the size of a bed. The massive roof just cleared my head. "You realize, Your Majesty," said one, "that the tunnel runs underneath the wall itself." And they pointed to the floor beneath our feet, which I saw was indeed virgin bedrock.

The tunnel was not long. Quite suddenly we arrived at our destination—a square hole in the floor, lined with masonry. The copper pipe curved to dive down into the darkness. I held my clay lamp low and saw the dark gleam of water far below. "Here we are," Xadok said with fond pride, "the spring. What did Your Majesty wish to see about it?"

"Besides inspecting the pipes and tunnels and pumps?" I smiled at them in the wan lamplight. "What do you think? Now that the Upper City is besieged I want to visit the secret postern."

Xadok seemed surprised—magi are dreamers, and he had probably not noticed the war—but the elder stonemason nodded. "It's improper for anyone to accompany Your Majesty, except by your command, so we'll wait back in the pump room for your return."

"I shall bring only Xalan," I said, for I knew I would need at least one geomant.

We waited until their retreating lights vanished around a bend in the tunnel. The silence curdled coldly around us. Xalan's dark eyes gleamed in his narrow face as he smiled at me. "Who'll go first?"

"I will." Carefully I edged around the well-shaft and went on. The tunnel ran for perhaps twenty more paces, and then ended without ceremony, as if its builders had lost interest. A single enormous block closed the tunnel, so we stood in a massive box of stone. No sound from the lands of the living could ever penetrate into this chamber in the deep heart of the fortification. Our ears rang with the uncanny quiet. "Melayne says the Cayds *bury* their kings," I said in a low, mysterious tone, "deep in stone mounds. I wonder if this is what it would be like."

Xalan shuddered. "Gruesome. It reminds me more

of being lapidated." He touched the huge cold block above our heads; it was just about as long as a man and probably no less thick, a titanic cube. "That would squeeze the juice out of you fast enough."

I smiled at him, and he smiled back. "Let's give up trying to scare each other," I said, and turned my attention to the right-hand wall. To the casual eye it seemed one solid stone, but when we moved our lamps this way and that we could see it was in three pieces—two mighty side chunks, and a door-sized one in the middle. A faint door-wide trench was cut at right angles across the entire width of the tunnel. "How many people know of this?" I asked.

Xalan shrugged. "I suppose everyone knows there's a door somewhere," he said. "The acute could even place it near the well. But to spot the correct stone from the outside?" He shook his head, and handed me his lamp. "Shan Xao-lan himself built this door, so it's well disguised. Allow me to open it for you."

Willingly I stepped back as he unslung the stone wand from his back. No single geomant had the power to shake the Upper City with an earthquake, but a trained magus could call the stone out of its place. Now Xalan held the wand up, and beckoned gently to the stone while muttering beneath his breath. With a grating, grumbly sound the center block quivered back perhaps a finger-width. "This is harder than it looks," Xalan panted. "It must be terribly thick."

It was, as a matter of fact, only a little less thick than the tunnel was wide, and took Xalan nearly an hour's hard geomancy. When at last a sliver of daylight appeared, I said, "You'd better rest, while I stick my nose out. Remember, you'll have to push the stone back, too. Xadok is only a hydromant."

Strictly speaking it was unnecessary to go out. All I had needed to determine was whether the door still existed. But now I could not resist a look. Xalan was too drained to argue. He sat down on the remaining sliver of floor and fanned himself with his hat. "Just don't let anyone see you," he gasped. "Right now I couldn't rescue a mouse."

I edged into the opening, which barely allowed for a single man to pass. Naturally the wall on either hand was as thick as the block was long—it would never do to leave a betraying dent on the outer side—but it was made up of several slightly smaller stones. Framed at the end of the tunnel-like passage was a chunk of afternoon sky, and a flat white-washed roof with a clothesline on it. The slope below was very steep.

Stepping warily I moved forward, listening intently. I was sure no one would tell the Cayds of the existence of this postern. Nor could anyone move the stone without magery. But a casual watcher on the roofs below seeing me emerge might exclaim or shout with surprise at the sight of me. A commotion would be disastrous. As a final concession to caution I got down on my stomach and slithered, snake-like, along the last few feet.

The Lower City looked quite as usual. On the gate-tower, however, the royal green banner of the Shan King had been cast down. In its place was the Caydish emblem, a ram's skull with gilded horns, lonely and absurdly out of place. I slid my chin over the edge and peered down. My heart jerked crazily in my chest. A white, strained face hung not an inch below, staring up at me. With an involuntary yelp of surprise I dodged back. A sinewy hand flashed up after me. It grabbed the slack of my tunic, and several other hands helped haul me forward and down. "Xalan!" I gasped for help almost inaudibly. Grips like pincers restrained my wrists, and the toes of my boots found no purchase on the smooth granite.

For a moment I hung, bug-eyed, over the void. Below, a half-dozen cloaked and hooded figures clung like monkeys to the stony slope. "Viris and Mir be praised!" the closest one exclaimed. "It's the King!"

Rapidly I was manhandled back up into the gap again. My assailants followed swift and silent as leopards, shoving me back into the shadows. I scrambled to my feet just as they pushed back their hoods. The dim slanting light made their faces look like wax sculptures, but I recognized one. "Pardia!"

"I hope we didn't startle you too much," she said harshly. "She was right," she said to the other Sisters. "How could she have known what the King would do?"

I rubbed my aching neck. "Who?" I asked.

For answer the Sisters flipped open what I had taken to be a bundle of armor. A battered and grubby head lolled within, and I had to kneel and look closely in the shadows. "Silverhand," I whispered. "What happened to her?"

"She was captured and tortured," Pardia said tensely. "We rescued her. We must move, before someone sees us."

"I can carry her," I offered, for the Sisters were plainly tottering with exhaustion. Their eyes flicked me over sharp as needles as Pardia hoisted her into my arms, tucking the cloak well in. Through the fine cloth I could feel naked flesh. Of course there would be no finer torture and amusement combined, to rape a woman vowed to virginity. In my daze of horror I almost forgot to whisper a warning to Xalan. But Pardia poked me forward, and I called, "I found some friends, Xalan, and we're coming through. Prepare to close the door."

We edged inside. I was careful not to scrape my burden against the rock. As soon as I appeared Xalan hissed, "What do you mean, you found friends?" Then he blinked as he recognized the Sisters.

"Silverhand's been hurt," I told him. "Can you manage the door alone?"

"Just leave me a lamp," he said. Pardia took charge of mine, and went first to light the way. The other Sisters hung on in a long line from my belt, and in this way we passed the well-shaft.

Xadok and the stonemasons were astonished to see me so accompanied, but I brushed aside their questions. We hurried to the Palace, and when I laid Silverhand down in Melayne's pink-tapestried quarters I sent for herbals and the Crystal Crown. "I'll have her healed up in no time," I told Pardia.

She looked up from her washbasin—the Sisters had gone straight for water—and said flatly, "Her first act will be to leap from those windows."

This was difficult to understand, and I said so. But Melayne, who had brought me the Crown, agreed. "The horror of her experience will be too close," she told me. "Let her body heal slowly, at its own pace, so that her mind may heal with it."

So I laid the Crown by. But then a new idea struck me. "Will she still command the Sisters?"

"I don't know," Pardia said sadly. "This has never happened before, that I know of." With a sense of shock I saw tears were running down her tanned cheeks. "And suppose," she gulped, "after all, we ought not to have saved her? She begged us to kill her, you know, and we defied her."

All of a sudden I was weeping too: for my friend's pain, for the agony of all my people. I was Shan King. Somehow, I should have managed better. All the tears I had not been able to shed for Rosil, and Mother, and Zofal, rose up in my chest, and I sobbed as I had not done since childhood.

I counted on the Cayds to manage the second siege as they had the first. If they dispersed to spend a fortnight or so reveling and looting we could dislodge them from the harbor at least. Through the mirrors the Master Magus had spread word of our plight. Any day now a relieving force from Mishbil and Ennelith-Ral might arrive by sea.

But Musenor was unfortunately too wise a Warlord to let his forces off the leash like that. Our one attempt at a formal sortie nearly ended in disaster when the Cayds rushed the gate again. We fell back on time and chance, contenting ourselves with archery contests from the walls and occasional secret excursions. The Sisters especially became adept at rappelling from Melayne's old windows down the cliff-side of the rock in the dark. They would gather news, knife any Cayds they came across, and return to climb their ropes again before the tardy winter dawn.

One vital mystery to be resolved was the main Caydish effort. Buildings just south of the Upper City, between the main road and the wall, were systematically dismantled by work gangs under Caydish duress. We watched roofs removed, walls thrown down, and the rubble flattened with stone rollers, all without comprehension.

On their night forays the Sisters questioned the crews without result. Though Caydish is an easy language hardly any native of insular Averidan speaks it. The invaders had to make their wishes plain with mime or a few cobbled phrases of pidgin-Viridese. But they quite naturally discussed all their own plans in their own tongue. The casual eavesdropping so popular in Averidan was thus rendered worthless. Public rumor had King Mor asearch for some vast treasure; his deity had indicated the general area of search. But Melayne scoffed at this idea.

Though we did not know it Xalan found part of the answer in his magic mirror, when he descried Bochas the rhetor. "He's in the Caydish headquarters," he reported. "So he did get your message through."

"I had wondered if they killed him," I said with relief. "Is he a prisoner?"

"No, he seems quite free of their camp."

I instructed the Sisters to try and contact him—a spy would be very useful, and Bochas had a smattering of Caydish—but they were unsuccessful. The whole business would have been more worrying were it not for the news that a relieving army was assembling in Mishbil. A more irregular opposition was also coalescing, in the Cliffhole district across the strait from Ennelith-Ral.

For several weeks a determined cheerfulness pervaded the Upper City. Refugees were housed in Palace attics, offices, and anterooms—the Shan King's business had drastically shrunk anyway. I allowed the bureaucrats and officials to maintain a pretense of regular work for the sake of morale, and set tasks for the newcomers as well. Wood had to be cooked into charcoal for braziers; stones carried atop the walls to hurl at the Cayds; food and oil distributed daily.

In an attempt to harness the powers I had stumbled on once already, I devised a minor gesture of defiance and *chun-hei*. I organized a scratch crew of gardeners one fine day to transplant eighteen trees. Their winter dormancy meant it was possible to shift small shrubberies and sycamores around the grounds to form more pleasing plantings. Somehow this greatly delighted everyone, since it indicated my utter confidence in our future, and I was well content. The only folk it failed to impress were those who had to lever frigid balls of tree root out of the earth and replant them to my exacting specifications.

The first portent of the end was at the close of Ekrep, nearly a month after the second siege began. I woke up one morning fevered and sick. "It feels like I'm going to lose my breakfast, even though I haven't eaten any yet," I complained to Melayne.

"I'm the one who's supposed to be sick of a morning," she said. She leaned her head on my thigh—I was sitting on the platform of the bed—and commanded, "Let me feel." I winced as small competent fingers probed my belly. "You're surely not pregnant," she teased, and then added, "We had better call a herbal." The herbal smelled my breath, looked at the color of my urine, and prescribed a vile-tasting tea. By lunchtime I was well again, and thought no more about it.

The next day my chamberlain had the same illness, and more severely. In spite of the herbal's treatments he was ill for a week, with nausea, flux, and fever. By then a dozen others in the Upper City had fallen ill. Slowly, my folk began to die. The ailment struck without warning or reason, reaping both the strong and weak, the wounded and the well, the elderly and the babes. Yibor and Siril, in terror of infection, kept their noses perpetually covered in handkerchiefs scented with brandy.

My chief fear then was that it would fasten on Melayne, for she was nearly in her seventh month. The herbals ceased all other work to search for a cure, and the magi devised ways to track down possible sources of contagion. It did not take them long.

"The barley," the Magus intoned, deep as a funeral gong.

"The barley? What's wrong with the barley? We have enough of it to last years."

He held up a pale hand to stop my frantic questions. "We noticed that those who ate barley frequently fell ill. Then we narrowed it down, to those who ate the barley in store for more than a year. Such ailments are not unheard of, if the weather was damp when the grain was threshed. And even they are not serious if there are plenty of other, untainted foods."

"Can you prove that's the cause?" I scrabbled on my work table for the grain tallies. "Two-thirds of our supply is more than a year old!"

"We could devise a test," the Magus said thoughtfully. "Someone could eat of the questionable grain. Would Your Majesty have anyone in mind?"

"For a trip to the Deadlands?" I was incredulous. "There isn't anyone I want lapidated, and who would volunteer?"

"It's not a sure thing," the Magus pointed out. "Think of it as a gamble. If no one will offer to try, you must nominate someone."

Unhappily I began a list of possibles. The one tested must be in health, not of one of the necessary categories of residents—no magi, Sisters, herbals, priestesses, bonesetters, or anyone able to wield a

weapon of any sort. I found that even having got so
far, there were still plenty of candidates. We had all
too many useless mouths.

In a turmoil of indecision I poured out my difficulties to Melayne. She, who never suffered from
wooliness of mind, suggested, "Ask for a volunteer
first, before you start winding yourself up in lists."

At the time we had just finished a family supper.
Dasan-hel shook his head. "No one holds life so light
as that," he affirmed. "Suicide is only allowable to
those who have been utterly disgraced."

"You see," I told Melayne.

"You would find no difficulty in Cayd," she retorted with spirit. "There, it's considered an honor
to die in saving one's fellows."

For a moment we stared at her, across the seemingly unbridgeable gap between the races. Melayne's
nation was of such different stuff, it was a wonder
she and I were so happy together. Then I thought of
our child, unborn yet already uniting our dissimilar-
ities. It was exciting, yet perturbing to consider.

Yibor-soo put down her teacup. "I will try, if you
like," she said.

I goggled. "*You* will? I mean—"

Siril cut in before I could untangle myself. "Grief
has disordered your brain, Yibor. Liras, don't listen
to her."

"Liras certainly didn't refer to any of *us*," Dasan
assured Yibor. "Why, we're all essential to the war
effort!"

"Certainly not I," Yibor said firmly. Her sagging
plumpness seemed to take on a new dignity as she
spoke. "You, Dasan, can help Liras govern what is
left of his realm. Siril, if put to it, could carry stones
up the walls to hurl down. But what of me? I'm an
old woman." She looked at me. "Let me be of what
use I can."

A storm of dissent erupted from Siril and Dasan,
while Melayne sided vociferously with Yibor. But I
said nothing, as the Shan King struggled quietly with

Liras Tsormelezok. For Yibor was right, she was an ideal subject. That she was my half-sister-in-law ought to have made no difference. I had sacrificed Rosil, and Mother, and Zofal. What was one more? Furthermore, I recognized now a dramatic gesture when I saw it. If Yibor found herself able to step into that realm, I ought not oppose her. On the other hand, though we had had our quarrels Yibor was family. She was the last who had seen us born and given Mother unwelcome advice on our upbringing. With her would perish the last remnant of our childhoods.

"The only one who can decide is Liras," Melayne was retorting hotly to Siril. "What do you say, dear?"

I shivered, silently cursing my destiny. No other Shan King had been riven like this. Why had disaster befallen my reign? I felt I was plucking the heart from my own body but the judgment emerged: "If you wish to take the gamble, dear half-sister-in-law, I will honor your decision."

Inevitably the experiment gathered to itself an aura of ghastly ceremony. The suspect grain was steamed, ground and baked, or pounded and fried, and served up with all the appropriate condiments. The cooks, weary of austerity, vied in the glory of their preparations. The magi sat around a table with a single place-set, watching with clinical interest as Yibor put away a repast such as no one had eaten for weeks. I had forbidden Siril and Melayne to attend—my sister would surely weep, and the business was too morbid for an expectant mother. But Dasanhel insisted on attending, and my presence was the least honor I could offer Yibor. It was far worse than attending a lapidation. If she died it would be suicide. I sat hunched in misery at the far end of the room, listening to the clink of eating utensils on porcelain and Dasan cracking his knuckles.

At last Yibor rose and called for tea. "Thank you, Liras," she said. "What a lovely banquet, your cooks are marvelous."

Very impolitely I demanded, "How do you feel?"

"Full," Yibor said happily, patting her podgy middle.

"I'll wager they were mistaken after all," Norver said with a sidewise glance at the magi.

"Let us give it time," the Magus retorted with dignity. "No one would be more delighted, I assure you, to be mistaken."

We loitered about for a while in a truly morbid manner, waiting for some dramatic collapse. But when it became plain Yibor had no such intention we had to adjourn for the night. As I went to bed I confided to Melayne, "Perhaps we'll get off after all."

But it was unlikely. It was the time of the Mid Year holiday, when the Sun is farthest away, and no project begun goes well. When I rose in the morning Xalan was waiting for me. "She fell ill in the night," he reported grimly. "There's no doubt about it."

I covered my face. "How is she?" When Xalan did not reply I knew it was serious.

That afternoon we burned the tainted grain, stoking up a bonfire in the main Palace courtyard and scattering the contents of jar after jar. All day and throughout the night a toothsome smell of roasted grain filled the cold air, and the smoke of its burning rose up straight and black against the winter sky. "They'll know we're burning something," I said, "but not what."

"How long can we fool them?" Manfully, Xalan tightened his sash. "What will it be, two meals a day?"

"One," said I, and he winced. A terrible sense of disaster oppressed me. The holiday is the time to render up taxes and tithes, so our harsh necessity seemed even more cruel. Every jar of grain thrown on the blaze was like a kick in the belly. Yet for the sake of my watching people I could not show it. Only to Xalan could I say, "This is our hope of victory here, going up in ash."

CHAPTER 8:
The Door Closed

Though the winter solstice had passed the days were colder than ever. It was the worst possible weather for fasting. With so little grain left our other supplies had to take up the slack. For years everyone had been accustomed to the generosity of the Shan King, and now the cutback was resented.

I set up a dole system, to apportion the remaining foodstuffs fairly and foil hoarders. As yet no one actually starved, but no one had enough either. We are not a patient or enduring folk, and stomachs are our weak spot. I was badgered by one and all for special favors. Clemmed servants dropped me hints, mothers egged their children on to cry at me in the halls, and Siril took to calling at mealtimes, hoping to cadge an extra meal. Dried fruit instantly became a second currency. Even Pardia remarked, "A horsemeat steak would go down nicely now."

It struck me as particularly unfair because I was as hungry as anyone. Melayne had been right. The sensation was novel, and unpleasant. The thought of food obsessed me. I mused for hours on the gorgeous dishes I had only picked at in the past, vainly taking oath never again to take the gods' bounty for granted.

Worst of all was stinting Melayne. I had planned to ordain her the sole exception to the new frugal regime, but to my dismay she refused to cooperate.

"If you do, your subjects will rise up, Liras, and slay you," she warned.

119

"No one would dare," I maintained. "I am Shan King, my word is absolute."

"This is the one area where you must be scrupulously fair," she insisted. "You think all this naggery is bad? If you make any exception, for anyone whatever, it will quintuple. You'll be lost. Those left out will unite against you. We're in bad enough straits as it is, don't split your folk now. That's how traitors are made."

That was a shrewd blow, in view of the news coming in from the Lower City. "But you're pregnant," I pleaded. "What about the child? Your health, your delivery?"

"You people are addled about food," she said, "and see the price! I'm not—the baby and I will be fine."

With enormous dignity she waddled away, putting an end to the debate. She was so short, her pregnancy seemed especially pronounced. I tore at my hair, but had to accede. She would not even permit me to give her some of my share. My only consolation was the frustrated gleam in Siril's eye, when she dropped by and saw our meager meals—beans, a dried fish, a cup of thinned wine.

The Lower City was a hotbed of rumor now, of which the Sisters could glean a sampling. The Shan King had died. The Shan King's wife had died giving birth prematurely (to twins), and the Cayds were going to behead him, in revenge. The viceroy of Mishbil, a spinster of at least fifty, was arriving next week in full battle armor at the head of ten thousand troops, which she had acquired by marrying some barbaric island baron. Everyone in the Upper City was dead of plague—the black smoke had been the burning of the bodies—and the walls were now held by three children under the direction of Silverhand herself, who proposed to raise them to adulthood to save the Shan.

But most consistent were the rumors concerning the rhetor Bochas. He moved freely, from Caydish camp to city and back again, and soon the story coalesced so solidly, we increasingly suspected it was true: Bochas had turned tail.

"The taverner I bespoke said he boasted of it openly," Pardia reported to me. "The Cayds promised him enough gold to sail a dinghy on, and safety for his kin."

I glanced at Xalan. "You realize what he—what someone—must have done?"

Xalan nodded. "That's what all that earthmoving must be for, on the south side. They've learned of the well, and the tunnel, and the door."

"Not even Silverhand knew exactly where the door was," Pardia objected.

"Not even I did." I shook my head. "But I'll tell you what the magi descried, outside the City. They're working on a battering ram, a log reinforced with bronze and suspended on a framework. They raise it to the level of the wall, on the earthen ramp. They batter at every stone. Sooner or later, they'll hit *the* stone. It weighs tons, but it only needs to shift an inch to show its position. And then it's a matter of time, only."

"If I ever see Bochas in town," Pardia vowed, "I'll gut him!"

"You mustn't," I said wearily, "until we learn if he's to blame. Will we have time to seal the door?"

Xalan grinned wolfishly; never plump, in the past weeks he had become downright gaunt. "We can make time," he said with a humorless chuckle. "Let's see what a flood will do for those earthworks."

Earthquake could be even more destructive, but we dared not endanger our own walls. Very slowly, over a week or so, the weather-wizards prepared their stroke. They called down snow, day after day of steady cold and driving white flakes. Ordinarily snow in this clime lingers briefly, and then melts. But under the magian influence deep drifts began to accumulate in the streets. The gardens vanished under white, and the golden dome of the Temple wore

a high white cap. Everyone shivered around braziers, and bundled up in layers of clothing. I tired
myself out floundering through the grounds, brushing snow away from treasured bushes and covering
sensitive plants with old hay. But almost all the purple klims froze anyway, for such a cold snap is unknown in our temperate land. The devastation of my
gardens was almost harder to bear than hunger.

News of the treachery spread faster than the snow.
One of the rhetors in the Upper City—there were
only two—was mobbed by a gang of old ladies, who
walloped him with brooms and pelted him with snow-
balls before rolling him over and over in the drifts.
His fellow, one Calis-yu, rescued him, dragging him
into the Hall of Justice and pleading for protection.
"We're faithful subjects, Your Majesty," Calis complained. "I'm sure all the members of our guild
deplore Bochas' dreadful acts."

The white light from ground and afternoon sky
made the Hall look foreign. The wide windows, so
pleasant in summer, now made the room intolerably
drafty, and the chill from the tile floor soaked so
painfully through my shoes that I sat cross-legged in
my throne. I released the scroll I had been reading,
letting it coil back up, and stared down at the two
miserable rhetors. They had tracked in a consider-
able amount of snow, and the younger, who had
been beaten, had a black eye. "No one truly blames
your guild," I said. "It could have been anyone. I
fault myself, for choosing an emissary so casually."

We had found that unless the single meal was
eaten at nightfall hunger could vanquish sleep. More
and more, the days seemed to be nothing but long
cold sunless afternoons. Some of them I burnt up in
a sort of frenzy, torturing myself with recollection of
past feasts until I prowled the chambers and halls
like a ravenous tiger. This afternoon, however, I had
been too tired to warm myself with imagination.
Instead I doggedly read reports, trying to distract my
mind. My domain had shrunk so, judgments were

not often needed. Impulsively now I said, "Tell me a story, messirs."

The rhetors glanced at each other; then Calis dusted snow from his trousers with his battered hat, and asked, "What plaiv would Your Majesty care to hear?"

"About my great-grandfather," I promptly replied. "One that I haven't heard before."

I knew it was a difficult request, for I always made the same one and by now all the well-known tales had been told. But after some thought Calis asked, "Have you ever heard the plaiv of his meeting with the Ennelith?"

"Is it a version of my own adventures?" I demanded a little suspiciously. For I had once, through misadventure, actually met the White Queen, and the story had got out. Plaiv about myself gave me the nervous feeling that I was no more than a character in a lurid series of fantasies.

"No, not at all," Calis assured me. "You know, of course, that Shan Norlen King is now surnamed 'the Merciful.' But he never let the epithet gain currency during his reign, and the way of it was this." Bit by bit the rhetor's voice shifted from the speaking tone to the rhythmic half-chant of recital.

"On a day, the Shan King said, 'Let us go down, and assail the pirates in their stronghold at Cliffhole.' So the captain of his fleet, Rumil of Ennelith-Ral, called out the ships. They sailed east and waged a terrible sea battle, which dyed the very rocks and shoals scarlet. And the spilled gore drew a mighty sea-drake up from the ocean depths. It was slick and green as the scum on a still pond, with long glittering red eyes, and all fled before its hunger. So huge was the drake, however, that its mighty tail writhed for half a league through the waves, and the scaley tip smashed the nearest pirate-ship in two.

"Seizing a swimming pirate the drake choked him down whole, as snakes do. But the other pirates clung to the wreckage of their craft, and cried out for rescue.

"Rumil commanded the sails to be furled, so that a rescue might be made. But the Shan King said, 'These are pirates. It would be better to sail on.'

"Yet Rumil prepared to lower anchor. 'Pirates or no,' she declared, 'they are your subjects and we must rescue them. Only pirates abandon the ship-wrecked.'

"'I forbid it,' King Norlen said. 'We shall make war on them, and every pirate eaten by the drake is a pirate less.'

"But too long had the Captain paused to dispute the King. The treacherous current pulled the pin-nace onto the shoals. Captain Rumil was thrown across the deck and over the side. Only the Shan King was close enough to catch her by the wrist as she fell, and so both fell into the sea.

"Yet still the King did not release his hold. The foamy sea was cloven by a long green snout, and the sharp white needles of the drake's teeth circled them round. Then he was swallowed, and the cold wetness of the reptile's throat enrobed him tightly from fore-head to toenails, like a skin around a sausage. He found breath only by turning his head toward his upraised arm—like this," Calis broke off demonstrate by standing on tiptoe with his arms raised.

"I don't believe it," I said uncertainly, but since that had no relevance to plaiv, Calis was not in the least deterred.

"The squeezing muscles of the drake's huge throat soon forced the King to release Rumil's wrist. But then the snug passageway opened out into the utter darkness of the beast's belly. The King found him-self on a slimy yet resilient ledge of flesh. Immedi-ately he slashed at it with his dagger, and through the living walls he could feel the drake's hoot of distress. Cold worm-blood poured down around his feet. He raised the knife again, and a voice cried, 'Hold!'

"'Who are you, who calls me to spare my foe?' he shouted into the dank, echoing darkness.

"Then a tiny spark of light began to glow, so far away he doubted his eyes, for there ought not to have been so much space in the innards of any beast. Rapidly it grew and came nearer, and he saw it was the greenish glow of phosphorescent sea-slugs, which had draped themselves like bracelets over the limbs of octopi, for transport. They lit the way for a most royal lady, her long green hair dressed with pearls and her silken robes trimmed with sea-grass knotted into lace. By her finery the King recognized her, and bowed his face down to the slimy pools at his feet. For this was Ennelith, ruler of the Sea and all that is in it.

" 'You recognize me,' the goddess said coldly. Though she was no goddess of words, yet the power of her displeasure was sharper than the most caustic tongue. 'I do not as yet intend you any harm. But you may not slay my sea-drake. He has prayed to me for help, you understand, which you did not, and so he has priority.'

"Very timidly the Shan King said, 'I apologize for the omission. And does the Sea-Queen recognize me?'

"The goddess looked him over closely, and then nodded. 'You are the King of the Shan,' she said.

" 'My folk are your loyal worshippers, as am I,' The King said. 'I came here by accident only, trying to rescue my friend Rumil. As soon as I find her, we will be more than happy to leave your sea-drake in peace.'

"Ennelith frowned. 'The ship-captain Rumil is passed to the Deadlands,' she declared. 'Is it your wish to follow her even there? For though it is not yet your time I can easily send you.'

" 'I think not today,' the King said hastily.

" 'Then I will leave you,' the Sea-Queen said, and the light began to diminish.

" 'But wait!' the King cried. 'If I am not to perish here. and yet may not cut my way out of this belly, what shall I do?'

" 'Wait,' the goddess commanded, and the King dared not disobey. For a period of five days he waited in the drake's snaky innards, and on the fifth day he emerged."

"Vomited up," I suggested.

"I'm sorry to say not," Calis said. "Rather, he was passed out the other end."

"It shat him out?" I demanded, and when Calis nodded I began to laugh.

"That was precisely the Shan's reaction," Calis said with a grin, "when their King was rescued at sea afterwards." Then, shifting back into recital, he continued, "But after he had recovered from the experience the King found time to mourn his friend. Said he, 'Rumil spoke rightly. To abandon my subjects was a cruel judgment, and justly were we served by being wrecked ourselves.' And he abjured cruelty forever, and resolved to embrace mercy even when it was foolish. But never did he allow anyone to name him merciful. For the sake of the royal dignity it was held that his one harsh judgment had forever lost him that epithet, but the truth of the matter was also remembered."

I laughed until my sides hurt, then sobered to think it over. This obscure offering was not one of the simple and happy plaiv told to children, but a puzzler, like those ivory carvings that show different aspects as you turn them between your fingers. "There is a moral, of course?" I asked.

"What would you suggest?" Calis said to his associate.

The younger rhetor, with a sycophantic glance at me, suggested, "That it's always unlucky to defy the Shan King."

Ignoring this I rubbed my upper lip thoughtfully and said, "The King must have done rightly; doesn't the Crystal Crown enjoin justice?"

"I've often wondered," the rhetor said, "whether it would force the monarch against his own will." I tensed; this cut too close to my own doubts. But he did not seem to expect a reply. "I expect it both does and doesn't," he continued reflectively. "Everything has two sides. Being a King must be yet more subtle and complicated."

The worst rhetors are flatterers, but if heroes were birds in flight the best rhetors were painters of birds, capturing what would otherwise be lost. They knew as well as any the ways of the domain beneath the commonplace, and I realized there was much I could learn from them. But I was too hungry to consider it further, and the last gray light had faded from the grim winter sky. "You have diverted my leisure," I said, to thank them. "We will talk of this again. In the meantime, keep within doors, and away from crowds for a while."

It was about this time that Yibor-soo died. The cold was too much for her sickness-weakened state. So many had preceded her to the Deadlands that only the family mourned her. The ground was frozen too hard for a burial. We did the best we could, chopping out frozen earth with hatchets and picks, and I promised her departing spirit to amend it at the first opportunity.

At last the magi were ready. In the space of an hour one morning summer seemingly arrived. The Sun blazed down hot as in Arhem. We hastily stripped off our extra garments as the heat kneaded our winter-weary bodies. Icicles arrowed off eaves, endangering passersby, and bowed branches of the trees lifted themselves up again. And the snow melted, cold floods rushing madly down the streets of both the Upper and Lower City. From their vantage-point on the walls the hydromants, led by the Master Magus himself, raised thick glass wands. And the torrents moved, slowly shifting their courses to run sideways and even uphill. They ran, rills into runnels and runnels into creeks, and the many creeks into mighty street rivers, to converge round the earthen mound below the south walls. The dirt and bricks and rubble began to wash away, the foundation of the structure undermined nibble by nibble.

The Caydish realized our intent and dashed up with sandbags; stinging arrows and slingshot drove them back. Then they herded up the Shan townsfolk to the work, counting on us to spare our own kinsmen. "Fire on," I commanded in a loud, even voice. "We, also, fight for our lives." The Sisters shot at their feet, and with yelps of dismay the Viridese cringed, dropped their loads, and ran.

"And a little rain," the Magus directed, "to erode things further." With unnatural speed a storm-cloud gathered—not the thick wintry pall that had dimmed the sky yesterday, but a summer thunderhead, mountain-high and black as pitch. Lightning crackled right over our heads, and a ferocious downpour swept friend and foe away below. We could see nothing for at least an hour. When it was over, odorous mud clogged the byways of that whole sector of the Lower City. Roofs were collapsed, trees uprooted, rats and donkeys drowned. But the earthworks were no more.

Still the Cayds did not give up. A new ramp was begun, of logs and great stones pried out of the lower walls. What appeared to be the entire population of the Lower City was mobilized to haul logs and rock. To divert our attention a second ram was deployed at the gate. It made no impression on those mighty portals, but we had to split our forces.

Meanwhile, the stonemasons sealed the secret door. Shan Xao-lan's great stone fitted so snugly no mortar could be forced into the joints. But the masons began a stout brick wall to seal off that entire end of the tunnel. The cubical room thus formed was packed tightly with rubble, a little more with each course of brick.

Yet all this time we were slowly starving. The dole was cut, to stretch provisions. I ordered the donkeys slain and roasted. Their hides were fed to the draft dogs, which we ate the next week. That evening everyone got indigestion from a satiety of dog stew. After that I was driven to the final resort, and ordered Sorrel butchered. He was skin and bone, having been maintained for so long on nothing but straw. I was too hungry to turn down that evening's meal—horse soup—but that night dreamed that the hapless beast's skeleton was trotting up and down the terrace below my window, the moonlight shining through his well-gnawed ribs. "If he's alive, Zofal will never forgive me," I said to Melayne.

On the last of Olhem exciting tidings arrived by mirror. After more than two months of siege the relieving force was on its way from Mishbil. Five merchanters had been commandeered by the viceroy. They would arrive, crammed with fighting men, in two days.

Plans for a sortie were instantly set in motion. The unfortunate stonemasons had to pry apart their wall and haul the rubble out again. We would maintain a flashy defense at the gate, and sneak out the postern. Timing would be crucial; once the Caydish were occupied at the docks we could assault them from behind. Trapped between two forces, their defeat was quite possible.

Our one amateur fist was set to drill in the Palace courtyard. In a fury of anticipation I raided the kitchens for knives. Xalan helped to bind them to poles, forming crude pikes. "I think," he said, "the first thing I'll do after we win is go down to the harbor. There's a tavern that does redfish with four herbs in the gravy."

My mortified stomach growled audibly. I pretended not to notice. "Can I come too?"

Smiling, Xalan looked me over. "Wear your plainer clothes, and we'll creep out without telling anyone," he said, agreeably.

The relieving force planned to arrive under cover of darkness. That evening we began a noisy and energetic defense at our gate, rattling the door-wheels and shouting as if we planned to emerge. The deftest Sister lowered a noose, and snagged the head of the ram. With her mighty tug the ram jerked up like a startled horse, and tumbled sideways off its four-legged framework. The hide screens that shielded its masters also fell away, exposing the half-dozen Cayds behind. We had run out of arrows, but a hail of stones crippled one and killed two.

By then it was full night. The bray of Caydish horns showed the ships had been seen. I clattered down the battlement stairs. Since only the Sisters and I still had armor the army had formed up below. "All right, men!" I ordered. "Around, to the water-tower!" I was proud of them, this little army I had schooled myself. With brisk speed yet no jostling they marched down along the wall to the water-tower and filed down the stairs. The Sisters stayed behind at the gate, to keep the Cayds busy.

Deep in the tunnel the magi were ready to move the stone; this time five geomants made the work swift. But before they began I had several hydromants descry the battle. No one must see us emerge. "Like viewing the inside of a bag," one complained. The night was deliberately cloudy, to cloak the moon, which was just nearing its full. We waited, fidgeting, for as long as possible. At last I had to decide, "Our foes must be gone. We'll risk it."

Everyone knew their part. The door slid grating back and we hurried through the gap into the velvet night. The air was cold and almost dizzyingly sweet after our long stuffy wait underground. It was too dark to see anything, and the rocky slope was almost gone, hidden under the second Caydish earthwork, so we had to go carefully. All the Viridese forced labor had fled the moment the Cayds answered the battle-horns. As quietly as we could we began to climb down.

Something hit my middle with a hissing thump. Absently I brushed at my lamellar coat, half-expecting to find an early beetle or dragonfly. Then the man beside me lurched heavily against me and fell. I bent to help him up, and in the darkness felt the arrow sticking out of his chest.

Something flew up, glowing, and fell down among us—a bale of straw, burning merrily. Its light glittered off the bronzen heads of a dozen arrows in their flight up from the roofs below, and then down. They were collapsing all around me, my unarmored army with their kitchen-knife pikes. Only I was proof against the deadly rain pelting down. "Back!" I shouted. "Everyone get back, into the door!"

We ran. The word was passed swiftly back uphill; those still safe within did not emerge. The arrows rebounded from my armor. I darted back and forth, last in the line, to shield the unarmored backs before me. It was hopeless. Even in this light the Caydish were crack archers, and to get into the door we had to bunch close together. They fired into the mass of us with terrible effect. I found I was sobbing as I stumbled up the steep slope, tripping over bodies and broken rock.

As the last survivors crowded inside I sheltered them with outstretched arms. A final arrow drove through my left hand, pinning it to the back of the lad before me. I scarcely felt the pain, even when his collapse tore the arrow free.

We squeezed past the great stone into a tunnel stinking of fear. "Close the door!" I commanded harshly. As the magi obeyed the deadly slice of night narrowed and vanished.

Someone lit a lamp. The little flame showed me my own bloody handprint on the wall. I stumbled out past the well into the lower room and gasped, "Call the stonemasons. The wall, the rubble—seal that door, the Cayds know it now!"

My own panting breath filled my ears. I could not tell if anyone heard me. But Xalan was here, quietly squeezing my left wrist to stanch the flow of blood. The wounded member had swollen remarkably in so short a time. "Don't worry, everything shall be done," he said. I leaned against the cold stone wall and bit back a moan of pain. Hot blood ran down my arm, and my little finger stuck out at a strange angle. Xalan pressed gently on my shoulder. "Sit down and rest, the bonesetter's on his way."

"Don't *do* that!" I snarled. "Help me up, I can walk to the Palace. Then you can get to your mirror. Don't you see, only Mishbil can save us now. We must learn how the battle's going!"

"No more battle for you," Xalan said, but obediently hoisted me up. The floor seemed to rock alarmingly under my feet. When I ignored it, however, my surroundings steadied. In awkward tandem we climbed up the stairs. At the top Xalan abruptly let go my wrist. The blood spurted anew, and the world spun around me. "See, the bonesetter's right here," Xalan persuaded. "It won't take a moment, to stick you back together again, and then you'll feel ever so much better."

No longer able to resist, I sat on some sacks of cattle feed. The bonesetter spread out his tools and bandages on a piece of cloth. "Watch the ox, Your Majesty," he suggested kindly, but I closed my eyes and listened instead, to the steady hollow clump of hooves and the creak of the gears.

When I opened my eyes my left hand was a neat tight roll of white bandage, from which four discolored fingers and a thumb protruded. "Your Majesty may with luck regain the use of as many as four fingers," the bonesetter said as he knotted a sling round my neck.

I hardly heard him. The respite had allowed me to recover a little; as soon as the sling was done Xalan and I hurried away. A few wintry stars glimmered through the clouds, and our cloaks snapped in the apparent wind of our speed uphill. The narrow street was empty, though when we came to the corner war cries and conflict resounded from the gate to our right. We could offer little aid to the Sisters there, and instead turned left. "Where is everybody?" I asked.

Under his red robe Xalan's flexing and straightening knees kept time with my own as we strode up the stepped way. "There," he pointed. Above and to our right the Temple glowed white and gold. Dozens of torches and lamps made it shine in the night. "Light our darkness," Xalan invoked the god.

I was shivering from shock and cold. "Do you really think he hears?" I asked. "How can this be happening if he does?"

"We're not done yet," Xalan insisted stoutly. "What fun would the plaiv be, if there weren't a cliff-hanging, suspenseful climax?"

At the Palace Melayne met me in the courtyard. Word of our setback had spread; when she threw her arms around my neck I could feel her heart's frantic beat. "You're hurt!" she exclaimed, not in dismay but in anger. "How dare they!"

"Actually I came out of it quite well," I said bravely. Then I hid my eyes again in her braids. "So many died," I said in a low voice, "I ought to have too."

Melayne had no patience with this. "You're cold and hungry," she scolded. "Come in and rest. It's the middle of the night."

"No," I said. "Let me get out of this armor. We're going to the court of the magi."

The round scrying pool at the far end of the magian courtyard was scummed with ice. Apprentices skimmed it off with rags and sticks, while servers brought jars of hot water to fill it brim-full. Lamps and braziers warmed the air around the pool and the mightiest scryers of Averidan knelt on its verge.

The Master Magus greeted us with a reproachful glance. "I don't know what Your Majesty hopes to discover," he said. "The night makes it difficult to both scry and see. There's little in any case we can do at this distance to influence the outcome of the battle." Then he looked more closely at me, and blinked. "You've been wounded!"

I brushed his agitation aside. "It's the turning point of the siege," I said. "We *must* know."

We took seats on the stone benches around the pond. Even with the braziers it was chilly, and the magi's chamberlain brought us thick warm cloaks and cups of hot mulled wine. Now that I could sit and rest, my hand began to throb in earnest. It hurt far worse than when I had actually been shot. I nudged Xalan and whispered, "What did the bonesetter mean, 'with luck'?"

He made a face, half sympathetic and half horrified. "You didn't look at the wound closely," he said. "The arrow didn't hit plumb center, otherwise they'd have amputated. As it was, there were tendons and bones and what not torn right through the edge of your palm. The bone will mend, but not the sinew. But you can get by, with three fingers and a thumb."

I stared down at the stricken limb in its sling. "I'll never play the flute again," I said dolefully.

Xalan raised his eyebrows. "I didn't know you were musical."

I grinned. "I'm not. Nor will I ever have to be, now."

The brimming water in the pool was now clear and still. Only the reflected light of lamp and brazier made it look like a pool; in daylight the water would be nearly invisible. With a gesture from the glass wands these reflections melted into nothingness. The magi bent over the water.

"A ship is on fire," we were told.

"One of ours, or a troop-ship from Mishbil?" I demanded.

"I can't descry a banner," one hydromant said after a pause, "but it's just inside the harbor, listing to port. The Cayd are using fire-arrows and slinging burning missiles."

"As they did to us," I remembered.

"If there are no armed men fleeing from it," Melayne suggested, "then it must be an ordinary merchanter."

"What of the battle?" the Magus asked. "By the light of the fires you should be able to make out something."

"A terrible fray on the north dock," another magus reported. "Yes, I see men in Viridese armor. The Cayds hold the landward portion, while our folk try to push them back."

"That is where we ought to attack," I moaned in regret.

The water still looked invisible, but deep in the center of the pool vague lights and shadows writhed and swayed. The magi stooped lower, carefully holding their trailing sleeves back out of the wet. Then all at once they leaned back, defeated. "The fire is out, the ship must have sunk," one said. "Nothing can be seen now."

I could have screamed with frustration. The Magus stroked his mustaches back. "We'll scry again at dawn," he promised. "Why doesn't Your Majesty get a few hours' rest?"

I was certain I could not sleep, but Melayne needed rest. So we went home. She seemed disposed to wait up with me. With what I flattered myself was real cunning I lay down beside her fully clothed, resolving to get up again after she dropped off. I closed my eyes, and when I opened them again the Sun was blazing in through the tall windows. Melayne was gone, and a quilt had been tucked over me. I threw it off, jarring my left hand horribly, and cried, "What happened?"

The silence and orderly luxury of my silk-hung chambers mocked me. For the first time no one answered my call. I tugged at my sleep-rumpled clothes and dashed out to the antechamber. At the table in the far end of the room a silent crowd had gathered around Xalan. His round mirror lay uncovered on the table, and he propped his head above it, elbows on either side of the glass. I pushed past the unheeding Palace workers to tap him on the shoulder. He looked up, focusing bleared eyes with difficulty. I did not have to ask what had happened.

"Mishbil is no more," Xalan said in a hoarse voice. He had talked himself dry. "The Cayds never let them land. Two of the ships are sunk, and one captured, with all hands."

I could not speak, but there was nothing to say. Melayne tucked a cold hand under my good arm. My folk huddled around like lost children, silently begging me to save them. The pain of my own helplessness tore at my insides, stung in my throat. I wanted to run, find a refuge myself, but there was not help anywhere. Or was there?

The Crystal Crown was beside my bed. I fetched it, gently disentangling myself from my people, and told them, "I'm going to the Sun Temple, if any would care to come." Everyone did; I felt like the fisherman in plaiv who acquired a charm, and found shoals of obedient fish trailing behind his dinghy. By the time I arrived at the Temple courtyard nearly everyone in the Palace was following me.

In ordinary times the courtyard is empty and peaceful. The colonnade leads the eye around to the door and in, while the long walk across the pavement fosters calm and introspection. These days the colonnade was partitioned off with canvas and lath. Each wedge was crammed with refugees. Bundles and baskets of possessions were piled in every nook, and breakfast cakes fried on pungent braziers. Children wailed, women scolded, men gossiped, their voices joining in an eerie parody of the song that linked us to all creation. The noise and misery struck all the senses like a hammer-blow.

All at once I was angry. We had trusted the deity utterly. How had he come to fail in his trust? If I, a mortal, felt such pain on behalf of my subjects, how could a god feel less? The unfairness of the entire disaster cried out for an answer. I brushed past the anxious priestess on door duty and went in to the sanctuary.

Here also was change. Worshippers huddled around the polished walls, hoping by sheer persistence to win the god's mercy. The ashes of a thousand offerings were heaped high on one side of the central altar. A priestess swept some off into a dustpan, and trotted off to dispose of them somewhere in the back precincts. Then she returned for another load. All the time I was there she bustled back and forth, tireless and patient, removing the detritus of a thousand incinerated wishes.

My hand shook with fury as I put on the Crystal Crown. The High Priestess appeared at my elbow to ask, "What offering does Your Majesty bring?"

I stared at her as from a great distance. "I came not to offer," I said, "but to demand. The god has a great deal to answer for."

If she expostulated I did not hear her, for my entire attention was given to the flames. They were low and yellow-clear, full-fed from the night's sacrifices. I was close enough to feel the heat strike on my brow, close enough to whisper my plaint.

As it had before the Crystal Crown seemed aquiver with leashed power. The heightened sensitivity fueled my rage. I avoided pain when wearing the Crown. It hurt too much. Only the healing hand made it at all endurable, the knowledge that I could drive pain out. Now the agonies of my people rent me, and I could do nothing except suffer it with them. "You're in charge of this situation," I said aloud. "Help us, why don't you help? Is it that you can't?"

There was no reply, no sensation of a watching gaze from the flame before me. The silence was total. I could have been addressing a statue. Had the immobile stone ever moved with life and emotion? Could I have been mistaken? My power was still there, coursing in my pulse, warm with my blood. "You know the truth cannot be hid from me," I said softly, and reached out in power.

For a moment I groped mentally in the fire, seeking out the door. I soon found it, for I knew the way. But to my utter consternation I could not pass through. The door was shut. The face was no immobile statue, but someone sitting with eyes tight shut and lips pressed together, pretending not to hear.

A horror fell on me. Though the sanctuary was as busy, the fire as bright as ever, I was alone in the dark with an appalling idea drumming in my head. This was what the god was really like. Our pain did not touch him; though he could interfere to spare us he would not. In fact, since the deity was all-powerful, he quite possibly had authored our downfall. For such a one, to allow an evil is to participate in it.

For a moment despair beat dark wings around me, and my realm, the entire world, closed in like a vicious trap. Then with a choked exclamation I wrenched myself free. The golden pillars whirled around me. I ran, my demons howling at my heels, out of the Temple and into the courtyard. The people there surged around me, plucking at my consciousness, touching me, calling questions. Impossible to explain, impossible even to know if I had seen truly. I had lost a lot of blood, had not breakfasted, had not even eaten properly for months. So long as there was hope I was wrong, I could not destroy their trust. If the god proves faithless, yet I could not.

CHAPTER 9:

The Counsel of the Magus

The Cayds spent the remainder of that day licking their wounds. At first light of the next, the ram was hoisted up to the south wall. Blanket-draped screens shielded them from our nooses and stones. This ram was of the same make as the other, but mightier: a massive section of tree trunk fitted at the business-end with a bronze sheath shaped like the head of a curly-horned Caydish sheep. They positioned it at the secret door, and began.

The noise was terrifying, an inexorable rhythmic smash of metal on stone that could be heard all over town. I watched not from the wall above, where the Sisters were managing the defense, but in the tunnel below, where the din throbbed through stone and flesh like a gigantic toothache. The stonemasons had sweated to rebuild the wall and pack the end of the tunnel again with rubble, but the work was less than half-complete when the ram began. As a temporary measure beams were wedged tightly from one side of the tunnel to the other, to hold the moving block in place. As I watched, these timbers seemed to tremble with the strain. I told myself the flicker of lamp-light deceived the eye.

By that evening it was plain we were too late. The block had slid in about a handspan, squeezing rubble and timber before it. And now the door was known our foes could attack the blocks to either side with chisel and lever. Certain of their success the Cayds kept at it in shifts all night. I went up to the Palace for my scanty meal, but could not swallow a bite. "If

139

you're not hungry, can I have your roll?" Siril asked me.

Melayne was furious. "Is your dainty belly all you can think of?" she demanded. "Liras needs to keep up his strength."

Absently I pushed my plate not over to my sister, but to Melayne, who scowled at it. "Siril, would you consider masquerading as a ladies' maid?"

She gaped at me. "Certainly not! I'm well-born!"

"Before you commit yourself, hear me out," I said quietly. "When they force the secret door, our water supply will be cut off. The end will be ugly. But Melayne can get out. She can go to her brother; he may roar and knock her about but he won't kill her."

"I will do no such thing!" Melayne cried.

I pretended not to hear. "You could go too, dressed as her maid," I told Siril. "You could even carry Sahai, in a basket." I looked across the table at Dasan. "I'm sorry, brother-in-law, but I can't think of any way to smuggle you out with them."

Dasan smiled a ghastly smile. "Wouldn't think of it," he declared weakly. "Rather go down with the ship."

"*Chun-hei*," I nodded. Then I turned to Melayne. "Be sensible, dearest. Think of the baby."

"I am," she flared at me. "How long do you think he'll live, under Caydish custom? Mor means to be king of Averidan. Could he really afford to spare the only son of the previous monarch?"

"It might be a girl," I asserted.

"It's a boy." Melayne patted her arching belly and glared at me. "If you want me out you'll have to *put* me out, like an unwanted cat. And I'll sit right there in the road and cry, just like Sahai would."

I shifted uneasily in my chair. "Don't be stubborn, Melayne," I begged. "Please, just this once, accommodate me."

"If they're not going to kill me, they can just as well not kill me here," she said flatly.

By morning the main stone had shifted a little

more, snapping one of the timbers, and several of the side blocks had been prised out. The inside wall was nearly done, and I had the stonemasons begin another just past the spring, with slits for spears and arrows. Meanwhile, the Sisters on the battlements above had twice set the Cayds' blanket-screening afire, and on one of those occasions halted the battering completely by sluicing boiled bran down on the warriors thus revealed. The magi called up another storm, hoping to erode or soften the ram's footing, but this time the ramp's stone-and-log construction foiled them. Their final resort was lightning; the ram at least ought to burn well. Thunderheads boiled around the Upper City all day. But no pirolurge remained in Averidan to guide the bolts down, and they persisted in hitting the wall or taller buildings beyond instead of our foes.

That day was pervaded with despair. The chamberlain was weeping when he opened my shutters; the servers crept about like mice and the Palace guardsmen put off the army tunics to resume their green-and-black uniforms—"so the Cayds will understand when we won't surrender," their captain informed me.

"We'll go down with all the flags flying," I approved, "drag as many to the Deadlands with us as we can."

The captain's eyes sparkled. "Will Your Majesty slay Prince Musenor?"

I smiled grimly. "If I do I'll die happy," I said.

But that evening the Master Magus paid a call. I had been recounting the tale of Melayne's intransigence to Xalan, and we both stared at the Magus's full formal red silks.

"There can't be a party tonight," I said tentatively.

The Magus shook his head. "I have two things to say to Your Majesty," he said. "First, I must ask you to release Xalan from your service."

Xalan and I looked at each other, puzzled. "I had planned to perish in that service," he suggested.

"Tomorrow, you mean?" The Magus looked down at us; he was tall and since we were seated on brocaded floor cushions in my sumptuous private salon he loomed above us like a flagpole. "I'm sorry, grandnephew, but if you die tomorrow you won't even perish a magus."

Xalan's cheeks turned white. "I won't?"

"Sit, Magister, and explain yourself," I urged.

We had been pretending to divert ourselves with Thumbprint, and the Magus now carefully stepped around the scattered playing pieces to take a chair. But for us the wide chamber, paneled in green and white, was empty. But the Magus spoke in low tones anyway. "Your Majesty knows I intended Xalan to succeed me as Master Magus?" Xalan shook his head, but I nodded. Very few secrets of that sort can be hidden from the Shan King. "Magery makes these barbarians nervous. It is quite possible the Cayds will try to eradicate it—kill every wearer of the red robe they can find."

"Oh, surely not," Xalan protested. "They're frightened of our power."

"We can't risk that," the Magus said in somber tones. "Your Majesty, I foresee a great persecution. I can accept my own end, for I am old, but not that of the magian arts. They date back to the founding of Averidan. I want you, Xalan, to don a server's garments—the chamberlain can find you some—and hide yourself in the rear halls. You are young. Someday, if you live, you can bring magery back to Averidan. Our scrolls and records are being walled up in the basement of your tower tonight."

"You can't die!" Xalan clutched frantically at his grand-uncle's trailing sleeve. "It's too soon—I've never mastered any of the arts, really—I won't be able to teach them to anybody, not by myself. Don't make me do this, find someone else!"

The Magus glanced at me. "As always, the final decision, Your Majesty, must be yours."

I weighed it, drawing on my knowledge of both

peoples, and had to admit, "I forebode your assessment is right." Xalan had hidden his face in his hands, and I waited until he looked up before saying, "All those excuses sound familiar."

Then he grinned, though with a remnant of his usual cheer. "I shouldn't have laughed at you. Serve me right. When do I have to start? Now?"

"We don't know how long we have," I said. "Although I must say I hope the stone holds out until day. Candlelight is bad for swordplay."

"Stay a little longer," the Magus instructed him, "and go to bed tonight in the servants' quarters. If you are to be Magus, someday you may need to repeat what I have to say to His Majesty."

"There's more?" I quavered. Once I had wanted to learn courage. I had, and had need of it. One of these days I feared I would run out.

"Your Majesty has heard the plaiv of Tsantelekor Sea-Reaver?"

I nodded. "He married the Shan Queen, and so became King."

"Almost certainly that is incorrect," said the Magus. "We magi have a different story."

"I'm not surprised," I said with relief. "It's always pleasant to hear old plaiv. What is it?"

"He almost certainly killed her," the Magus said quietly. "The Crystal Crown has only one living wearer."

I felt my hands grow cold as the implications of this sank in. Pitilessly the Magus continued, "The Crown is the foundation, the soul of the realm. So long as the Shan King wields it we will always be the same, always be the nation Shan Vir-yan founded us to be. My dear Liras, there is only one action your country now asks of you—to die, and let the Crown pass on."

My tongue was stuck to the roof of my mouth. Xalan announced, "I'm never going to tell this to a Shan King. It's cruel."

The Magus glanced at him with irritation. "It's

necessary that Liras know. He's a fighter. Suppose in the struggle he kills both Mor and Musenor? If the Cayds start fighting among themselves for rule there could be disorder."

"There's already disorder," Xalan argued. "And from what I've seen of him Mor could be a terror as king."

"Not if he wears the Crystal Crown," the Magus insisted. "The Crown itself will force him to rule justly. Unfortunately Caydish justice may demand the end of magery. That's where you come in. Sooner or later, these barbarians will be assimilated. The Tsorish were. Sooner or later, the Cayds will become Shan. When they are, you'll be ready."

"You have it all figured out," Xalan said with admiration. Then he crumpled a little. "I'm never going to be able to do it."

"Neither am I," I said huskily. "Magister, I'm not brave by nature. It's only courage, a learned skill. I tell you, I won't be able to stand there and let Musenor cut me down. And what if he doesn't, after all?" I shivered, remembering Mor's promise. "They favor torture, in Cayd."

"There's no help for it," the Magus said. "If you fight you must somehow contrive to lose."

"They say he's a fell warrior," Xalan offered. "And you're one-handed. Perhaps you'll fight your very best, and be killed anyway. A pretty pass we've come to," he added dismally, "if that's the only consolation to offer."

The Magus rose. "No one knows what tomorrow will bring. I may not see Your Majesty again."

I scrambled to my feet and clasped his offered hands. "I remember," I said awkwardly, "when you came to tell me I was Shan King. Xalan winked, but you whispered to me what to say. It was clean against custom, and I never thanked you for it."

The Magus blinked back tears. "We'll meet in the Deadlands," he prophesied, "and laugh."

"I can't imagine it, but I daresay you're right."
Then I turned to Xalan.

"I almost wish I were coming with you," he said.
"I'm sure Mor won't be as much fun to serve."

"What's so bad is being alone," I agreed, past the
lump in my throat. "I wish *I* were coming with *you*."

He made a rueful face. "You can't, but if you like
I'll come by tomorrow, and wash your windows or
something."

"You'd be safer washing dishes," I said. "Let's say
farewell now." We embraced, not bothering to hide
our tears. Then they were gone. It seemed a pity to
sleep away the last night of my life, but between
hunger and emotion I was exhausted, and crept
gratefully under the covers beside Melayne's sleeping warmth.

The next day I rose and called for the Wardrobe
Master. "Armor, of course?" he suggested eagerly.
"Your Majesty's lamellar has been newly burnished."

"No," I said. "Find me the grandest, most sumptuous robes. Royal green silk. Only, not too confining,
please."

Melayne stared suspiciously from under the bed-
covers as I was dressed: A loose, pale emerald silk
shirt. Matching pants loose in the thigh and snugger
below, long enough to leave generous gathers when
pushed up around my ankles. A gorgeous satin robe,
supple as oil and heavy as gold, of a green so rich it
was nearly black, with wide triple sleeves that trailed
from my wrists to the tile floor. The inner sleeves
were in tints of peach, and the hems and orange sash
were stitched with gold, crystal beads, and starry
emeralds. My hurt hand was set in a white silk sling.

Sahai wound in and out around my ankles, purring. She detested fuss and change, and therefore
abhorred the armor that I wore of late. Also, it was
hard to claw. This superficial return of the old life
delighted her.

It seemed only kind to live up to our prosperous

reputation and give the Cayds generous spoil from my corpse. So I slipped into my sash all the proper accouterments of a Viridese noble—embroidered purse, silk handkerchief, gemmed knife. Nor, when the Master's chief assistant produced the jewel chest, did I disdain a kingly necklace of adamant and jacinthe.

When I was done Melayne pushed the green silk bedhangings aside and hoisted herself out of bed. "That's no outfit for a battle," said she. A sharp, foxy expression glittered in her gray-green eyes. "What are you planning?"

I dreaded the explanation to come. Without replying I flicked a finger at the chamberlain. "What word, from the water-tower?" I asked.

"I believe they've nearly forced the stone through, Your Majesty."

"Keep me informed." When he was gone I sat beside Melayne on the bed's carven stone ledge. Her red-brown hair, not yet put up for the day, hung in two long thick plaits past her waist. Her face glowered between them, and I kissed the frown on her forehead. "You are beautiful, like a ripe peach, have I told you?"

"Liras! Answer me!" she exclaimed crossly. "Are you planning to surrender? Is that why you're all dressed up?" It won't impress my brothers, you know, they'll—"

She stopped. I finished for her, "They'll kill me anyway?" I knew my smile must look false as a wooden pearl. "I have a rather busy day scheduled, and I'll need these rooms. Call your maids, and have them move you back to the Lady's chambers. You can easily share with the Sisters."

"If you're going to surrender I want to be here," she said.

"I'm not going to surrender."

She smiled her approval; submission is quite foreign to the Caydish nature. "If you're going to fight I can help." She rummaged under her pillow and brought out her knives, which masqueraded as hair ornaments.

"You're eight months gone and more," I pointed out patiently. Her courage and stubborness were both exasperating and heart-rending. "It would relieve my mind, if you were where Musenor would expect to find you. The sack will be confusing enough; someone might chop you in half by accident."

"And what are you going to do?" She pressed for the answer, sensing the core of my reluctance. "You've only the one hand, are you going to make a final stand, with the guardsmen, here?"

"No, the guardsmen plan to hold the courtyard," I admitted. "I don't want anyone here, not even you. You see, Melayne, I am Shan King until I die. King Mor must have me killed, and take the Crystal Crown, before he can succeed me."

"You're not going to fight?" She looked closely at me to be sure my brain was not disordered. "You're just going to stand there, all dressed up, and let them cut off your head?" When I nodded she exclaimed, "I won't let them!"

My control snapped. "Curse it, Melayne, do you understand, I don't want you to see me die! Is that too much to ask?" It was a mistake. Black, salt horror washed over me. I flung myself away from the bed, huddling on the floor to hide my face in my sleeve. The dread was too deep even for tears. I pressed my cheek down hard enough to feel the tiles through the layers of heavy satin, and shook. My astonishing superficial bravery had to be husbanded only a little longer.

Warm arms hugged my shoulders, drawing my head up onto a rather knobbly knee—Melayne's lap was occupied by her stomach. A tear trickled down onto my hair. "I don't understand it," she whispered, "but if it will help you feel braver I will obey."

"It will help." When I leaned my ear against her belly I could almost fancy I heard a heartbeat not my own, or Melayne's either. "I wish I could have seen the child."

"I will tell him all about you."

Her hands stroked the hair from my temples. The tears were falling faster now, spotting the front of my robe. I sat up and embraced her. "Come, don't cry, it's bad for the baby. I love you."

"And I you," she sobbed. "You are the spouse I would have chosen above all others." Of course our union had been fixed by treaty. "I'll never find anyone like you again."

"I hope not." Her collapse had stiffened my spine a little; one of us had to be strong. I helped her to her feet. "Go now, and send your maids back for your jewels and clothes."

"I don't care about them."

"You may not have them long," I said, "so take them while you may. At least if they're with you they won't be looted outright. Musenor won't let his men strip you of everything." I had been gently walking with her toward the door, and now I opened it. On the threshold we kissed until we were breathless, and then stood in each other's embrace for so long the chamberlain became uneasy. His duty is to remain one room away, within call yet out of eavesdropping range. Finally I told him, "Have the Lady escorted to her chambers." At the last moment I scooped up Sahai and put her in Melayne's arms. And with a final stricken glance back they went.

Back in my bedroom I opened one triple-arched window. It was nearly noon. Cool moist air rolled in, and a distant sound of men shouting. I judged the door had been forced. The tunnel could not be held long now.

Leaving the casement ajar I crossed to a cupboard. Inside on a wooden stand hung my armor. The worn sword-belt had its own peg. I took it down. Though I thought I could die bravely, I had decided enduring torture was beyond me. No doubt Musenor still hoped to strangle me, as is traditional for witches in Cayd. But if I rushed at him with my sword, his warrior instincts should take over. One-handed and unarmored, I should die fast.

The only other item to keep at hand was the Crystal Crown. I did not trust the Cayds to recognize its casket, and would wear it when the end came. I lifted the lid and looked at it, recalling the plaiv of its origin and purpose—"so that the true king might be known." Shan Vir-yan had ordered its creation.

But Shan Vir-yan had been fathered by the Sun himself. The Crown itself bore light, in memory of the corona of his sire. If the god had cast us off, how was it I still held this symbol and focus of our kin-ship to him? Perhaps its power too was gone.

I was tempted to put it on and see. But I was no longer alone. The servants were creeping about on tiptoe, trying to set the sleeping chamber to rights without disturbing my meditation. Though they tried to keep their countenance, I could see their fear. No one knew what the Cayds would do.

"Wait," I commanded abruptly. "Don't go away." I hurried into the adjoining wardrobe room and jerked open drawers and cubbyholes in the jewel chest on its stand. Many of the gems were heirlooms, the royal jewels of Averidan. But there were plenty of less important items, rings and brooches and arm-bands, probably minor presents to Kings of old. I gathered up a double handful, and swept back out.

"Here," I said, and pressed a carbuncle-set brace-let into a sweeper's work-worn hand. He gasped and dropped his broom. "In thanks for faithful service. Pry the stones out of the sets; have the metal melted down separately. Hide the stones around your per-sons. The Cayds probably won't search you all." Quickly I distributed jewelry. Everyone got some-thing. They gathered around with vociferous thanks. The noise drew the chamberlain, and I gave him a gold ring set with a great beryl.

"All of you, heed me," I said. "For today you are released from the Shan King's service. Go down to the Upper City and busy yourselves with tasks at home. No doubt in a few days' time things will be as they were." I was proud that my voice did not waver. As they left I called the chamberlain back. "I forgot," I said. "Take these—" I poured the last of the jewelry into his hands. "Go and find my sister Siril. Give her these and conduct her to the chambers of the Lady." Melayne would understand, and keep Siril safe. The gems should give the last of my kin a start, wherever Siril ended up.

CHAPTER 10:
The True Stalwart

When they were gone I was completely alone. Nothing stirred within this entire wing of the Palace. From the open window came the sound of yells and metal on metal. I shut the casement, for the room was growing chilly, and shook the coals in their copper brazier. I had forgotten to ask for more, and now did not know where charcoal was kept.

I had never had occasion to explore the servers' pantry in the antechamber. Now, instead of charcoal I found there a loaf of barley bread, obviously intended for my meal later in the day. There was no point in hoarding it further. With it and a jar of sour-cherry preserve filched from the shelves I made a pleasant meal.

Barely a season ago I should have turned up my nose at such simple fare. Barely two years ago fear would have destroyed my appetite completely. Now as I wiped out the jar with bread crusts I realized my wish had come true. I was afraid, but fear no longer disabled me. I had become almost completely the Shan King. Liras Tsormelezok lived but had as little to do or say as the child Melayne carried.

It was a very peaceful thought. The Shan King could manage everything; that Liras would at the end have to do the actual dying was unimportant.

So I finished my meal in good spirits, and washed my sticky mouth in the basin. The noise from outside had steadily grown greater even through the closed window. Dispassionately I listened, and decided the Sisters were making a stand somewhere in

the Upper City. I peered from the window, but saw
no one, not even the gardeners who ought to be at
work. The afternoon Sun slanted golden through
the ornamental plantings, shifting and dancing as a
boisterous winter wind tugged at the boughs.

A splintering crash sounded quite close by. They
must be assaulting this wing at last. I took up the
Crystal Crown and put it on, taking a seat in a tall
carven chair near the window. The sheathed sword I
kept across my knee. The worn leather belt looked
rough and strange against the rich silks.

For a long moment time hung, breathlessly, in
midair. At last heavy footfalls echoed down the hall.
With a mental gesture I lit up the Crown, bleaching
the bright colors of wall and floor with my own white
light. The hall door was kicked open. Then the inner door flew in, rebounding so hard a piece of
green-tinted plaster cracked off the wall behind. The
Cayd outside gaped as the light poured past him.

"Come in," I invited, smiling, but with a scrabble
of boots on tile he was away, running like a hare.
Musenor would soon hear.

I felt calm and happy, completely at home in this
legendary realm though I had not entered of my
own choice. Here in the myth I had found the only
solution. And through Melayne's tales to my child,
and through Xalan's testimony if he lived to revive
magery, I should not be forgotten.

A tiny noise came from the outer room, and then
a sleek gray form appeared in the doorway, preen-
ing herself against the carven doorpost as if she had
been very clever. "Sahai, go away!" I cried. My cat
must have escaped from Melayne and run straight
back here. Ignoring my exclamation she leaped onto
my lap and draped herself over the sword, purring
like a hive of bees and sticking needle-claws into the
silk to make herself a nest. In my one hand I grabbed
her with the strength of terror. I had a tryst with
death; everything I loved must be safe away.

I leaped up, tripping over my sleeves and drop-

ping the sword. One-handed I tried to both restrain
her and unlatch the window again. A cat could easily
survive the one-story drop. But already many booted
feet were tramping into the antechamber. And as I
turned there was Musenor, towering in the doorway.
The uncanny light of the Crown glittered off his
leather and bronze armor, made his yellow hair shine
like beaten gold. Behind him crowded in others, his
friends and nobles. For a moment I forgot my pet.
We looked into each other's eyes as if across a great
divide, and yet with understanding. So long had I
striven to encompass Musenor's battle plans and way
of thought, that my heart leaped at his appearance
as if he were a friend. He was only Warlord; his
brother Mor would be King. But after all I was glad
it was Musenor who would kill me.

"Your Hell gapes for you, Witch-King," Musenor
said in formal Caydish.

"It is death, to defy the Shan King," I replied in
Viridese, not bothering to mention whose.

Then Sahai heaved her head out of the pinch in
the crook of my elbow, and spat. She loathed strang-
ers, especially odd-smelling ones. With sudden energy she twisted free of my grasp, and fell to the
floor. She landed on all four feet and scampered for
the door. "His familiar!" someone shouted. A tall
noble caught her by the hind leg. She yowled and
lashed out, drawing red gashes across his wrist, and
he swung her around with dreadful force. A splotch
of cat-blood was left on the wall. The furry body slid
across the tile to Musenor, who kicked it away in
disgust.

"You vermin!" A bubble of hot anger almost choked
me, and I scooped up the sword. Musenor laughed
aloud at the sight; I would wipe the smile from his
face. I reached out with the power of the Crown,
stopping Musenor in his tracks. This close, his mind
was as open as a fishpond to the sky. I saw Pardia's
body, bristling with arrows, pushed to one side in the
tunnel; heard the gatekeepers yell as they were taken

from behind; flung myself on my belly to thirstily scoop water from the courtyard pool while my men guarded my back. Plans: a meal, wine, a victory feast, a woman. Gold and wine, jewels and land, all to be acquired, safeguarded, then doled out to the good fighters. The best for Mor, of course, then myself. The Crystal Crown, that perilous talisman of witchery, should be smashed, and a proper crown made. Perhaps set with pearls. Pearls were so common here—

Then something utterly strange happened to me. I was shunted aside in my own head, as another intelligence snatched the reins away. The white fountain of light vanished. My hand opened, letting the sword clang to the floor. My legs sped me round my chair. With a resounding crash my body dove straight through the glass window as if it weren't there, into space.

My wide sleeves saved my face from glass-cuts. Razor-sharp shards and scraps of wood mullion fountained out with me. One story down was the marble terrace. The impact would likely have broken my every bone. But by the mercy of Viris a Cayd was there, kicking in the terrace doors. My sudden descent knocked him flat; while he lay stunned I bounced to my feet and began to run. From the window above Musenor roared, "After him! Chase the coward down!"

Branches and evergreen needles slashed past my face as I plunged through the shrubbery. My lungs labored to draw in the cool air. Though all that I, myself, felt was bewilderment, my body was panicking.

I grappled with this unseen rider for control at least of my legs. The struggle disoriented us both, and my foot trod on my own wide sleeve. I tumbled head over heels down a retaining wall. When things stopped spinning, I found myself lying breathless in a narrow asparagus bed. The crackling-dry fronds cushioned and hid me, and while my heartbeat thundered in my ears I mentally shouted, "What on earth is going on?"

The Crown's beautiful voice had never sounded more shaken. "They mean to destroy me."

"Well, that's nothing new," I said callously. "They're out to kill me, too. And where have you been, all this time? The entire realm's been falling apart; I could have used a little sage advice!"

"Though your use of my powers is constrained, I do not usurp your mind and will," the Crown meekly offered. "You had learned well, and had no more need for guidance."

I stared blankly up at the afternoon sky, astounded. I was so accustomed to the thought of being carried, Liras the passenger, while the Shan King strode along. But all this time I had been doing the walking myself, alone. The Magus had been wrong, I had been wrong, and the rhetors had been right. No one forced the Shan King to rule rightly. The realization was terrifying, and I shut it away for consideration later. "So you don't want to abuse your power?" I demanded in a nasty tone. "Then why shove me out of the saddle? This is *my* body. *I* get to steer it."

"I apologize," the Crown said. "The sudden threat of dissolution—"

Oddly enough, I could sympathize. It had taken me a long time to conquer the urge to break and run. "Running from trouble never solves anything," I said, a little mollified. "And I can understand your viewpoint. An immortal must fear death greatly."

"It's not that," the Crown said, unconvincingly. "The continuity and stability of Averidan are rooted in me. Without the Crystal Crown the realm will literally be no more."

"But Musenor will have none of you. I should have seen he wouldn't. I don't suppose Mor will think different."

"Someday he will," the Crown predicted. "I must be kept safe against that day."

Shouts and the sound of snapping branches came

from farther up the hill. The Cayds were beating the bushes, hoping to flush me. As quietly as I could I rose and slunk further into the kitchen gardens. My sleeves, already in rags from my headlong flight, caught on every stick and thorn. My sword was gone, but I had a knife. With it I sawed at the trailing silk, knotting up the ends as best I could.

"Going about with you will be like wearing a flag that says, 'Here I am, chase me,' " I grumbled as I worked. "How about burying you here in the garden. I'll get word of the location to Xalan before Mor has me killed."

"It's cold in the ground," the Crown complained. "I need warmth."

"Viris above! Nicety's not a luxury you can afford right now!" Then I thought of the Navel Room, the cup-shaped chamber at the top of the Temple dome. If I could find a way to seal off the door and stair it would be a perfect hiding place, being designed to house the Crystal Crown between reigns.

"I approve," the Crown told me.

"I hadn't even suggested the idea yet," I said sourly, and lifted the Crown off my head. Not until then did the reaction hit me. The nightmare had come true— the thing had taken over my body! My own casual bravery just now, in the face of this horror, took my breath away. For it was bravery, the innate grace of the hero. I had never aspired to more than courage, its learnable substitute. Apparently all this time, while I had admired the Shan King's mettle, it had been me myself. So long as I was in charge I had been a true stalwart. Only when the Crown seized control had I—or we—run. "If I had known learning courage would lead to this, I never would have begun," I said aloud. Then I could not help smiling at the picture—the stern hero-king, blundering out the window and skittering away to hide under the leaves like a mouse. Rhetors to come would have their work cut out for them, to make that look good. With unsteady hands I rolled the Crown in the severed tatters of silk, and hung it for safekeeping over my shoulder. Then I made my way further down the slope, among the fruit trees.

The apples and pears were long since harvested, and the gnarled gray boughs sifted the westering sunshine. At the bottom of the orchard was the wall. Even one-handed it was easy to climb an apple tree and step from a bough to the wall. From the Palace above a horn-call echoed. Someone had seen me. On the wall's other side was an alley and the orange-washed back door to one of the cramped white houses. No one seemed to be home, so I hurriedly dangled from the wall and dropped off.

The Upper City could have been designed to foil pursuit. Alley ran into lane, which turned down three crooked steps, arched over a courtyard, and led me to another narrow porch, scarcely two feet wide and painted with whitewash and yellow checks. From there I took a winding route that was half lane and half staircase, threading past thick-walled houses, around terraces, between gutter-pipes and over earthen roofs. Though no one uses maps of the Upper City I knew enough to maintain a more or less steady course east and north, around the Palace grounds and toward the Temple. The few Shan I saw were too busy with their own troubles to pay me any mind. Several times I was spotted by Cayds—my tattered finery marked me—but by hiding behind doors and darting softly down stairs I was able to elude them. I was greatly helped by the shadows here on the eastern side of the hill. On the other side the Sun was setting, and it was getting cold.

I was sneaking around a corner when someone ran slap into me. We both tottered back gasping, ready to run for it. Then I exclaimed, "Xorlev?"

The magus pushed his red hat back onto his head, a dazed look in his eyes. "Your Majesty? The Master Magus said you were dead."

All of a sudden I was buoyant. "Not yet I'm not," I almost laughed aloud. "Now I've found you, I lack

for nothing." For Xorlev had the missing skill I
needed. I hauled him to his feet. "Can you trans-
mogrify a door to look like its parent wall?"

"Surely, but—"

"How long does the glamor last?"

"Uh, I don't know, at least a year or so—as long as
I'm alive."

"Perfect!" I grabbed his thin arm and began to
hustle him down the twisting alleyway. "We're going
to the Temple; I have need of your talents."

"But the Caydish are there, the Master Magus told
us to run and hide!"

"I am still the Shan King," I said sternly, lifting the
Crystal Crown. Then, realizing it looked like a beg-
gar's bundle, I pushed the silk rags aside to show
him the Crown's distinctive white substance. Xorlev
gaped at it.

"You were supposed to give that to the Cayds," he
said suspiciously.

"Musenor decided it was witchery, and plans its
destruction. You're going to help me hide it, until
the Cayds learn better."

I urged him along, closing my ears to his feeble
protests, until we were just below the Temple. Columns flanked the main entrance into its outer court.
We crouched in the shadow behind the first one, and
listened.

We heard nothing. But I did not like the look of
the thick red stream that choked the central gutter.
Everyone in the Upper City had crowded into the
Temple, for either help from the god or sanctuary
from the Cayds. Surely when they burst in the Cayds
would have seen their helplessness and fear. A slaughter would profit nobody; the Cayds needed servants
and cooks and farmers as much as anyone.

I had forgotten to reckon with the Caydish battle-
lust. As we crept through the entryway a butchery
odor of spilled gore assailed our noses, an almost
visible stink of fear and death. Nothing moved in the
courtyard which had once been so sunny and peace-

ful. The bodies lay hacked and split, thick as driftwood on a beach after a storm, sprawling in every direction away from the Temple. They must have run, and the Cayds had chased them down.

"I'm going to be sick," Xorlev announced wanly.

"Not now," I said between gritted teeth. My own stomach clenched tightly on itself; I wanted to close my eyes but feared to step on someone. The red-splashed pavement was sticky under our shoes as we made our way across.

We tiptoed into the antechamber without meeting anyone. I held on tightly to Xorlev, for comfort and also because he seemed inclined to turn and run. The sanctuary itself seemed curiously different. "The fire," Xorlev gasped. "Look!"

The central altar had been defiled. The fire which never goes out was scattered—the embers doused with the blood of its priestess. As I approached my legs quivered with shock and rage. The god might or might not have cast us off, but now we would never know. The door was shut.

Xorlev plucked frantically at me. "Listen!" he whispered through chattering teeth. I did so, and heard deep voices from the precincts to our right.

"That's why the sanctuary's empty," I whispered back. "They're looting the treasure. Now's our chance."

Xorlev did not seem to feel this, but I dragged him the other way, around the dreadful altar to a further opening. The brass-bound door that had sealed it had been broken in. A few steps down the corridor, on the right, was another door. "This is the one," I whispered.

"But you realize all I can change is appearance." Xorlev faltered. "If they feel, it will feel like a wooden door, not a stone wall."

"They won't feel," I said. Thrusting my fingers into my purse I brought out my keys. "And if any of the Sun Priestesses notice the change they won't be inclined to babble to Mor about it. The illusion only has to hold for a few years. I place my faith in the Shan."

My confidence seemed to infect him a little. "What do you have in mind?" he asked.

The lock snapped open and the door swung in. Beyond, the stairs rose away into darkness. "Start laying your magery," I told Xorlev. "It won't take me long to run up and put the Crown into the pool."

"I can't work unless the door's shut," he said as he followed me through. "If I wait inside here for you to—"

He choked. Instinctively I caught him as he fell forward. Hot blood gushed from his mouth onto my hands and robe. Stunned, I stared over Xorlev's dying body at his Caydish killer.

"Hoy! Brothers! He's here!" the Cayd shouted, and dragged his axe out of Xorlev's back.

With the strength of desperation I thrust the corpse at him, blocking his path. Then I ran. Only I knew where the stairs went, the Cayds would have to run blind, watch every moment for ambush. I tore up the three short flights, slowing down a little only when I reached the endless curving stair to the dome. I dared not collapse on the long ascent. My side ached from the climb, and my hand in its sling throbbed in time with my galloping heart.

The steps curved ever so slightly to the right as they ascended inside the dome to the keystone. There were no landings, no doors, and only one low window halfway around. But the Cayds could not know that; they would fetch lights, proceed carefully. I might yet have time to deposit the Crown, and run back down to die somewhere on the stair. In the excitement of killing the Witch-King the Cayds might, just possibly, forget to explore the stair's destination.

As I trotted up I undid my bundle and freed the Crown. I needed it to open the door into the Navel Room. Once it was on my head I began to run again, for the sounds of pursuit were waxing from below.

The temptation to keep looking over my shoulder

was constant, but I smothered it. One glance back showed me the glow of torchlight from around the curve. Though the stair was high-ceilinged and drafty sweat dripped down my forehead and into my panting mouth. My legs grew heavier and heavier, and my throat was dry as a lime-kiln.

At last the stair began to level off. My pursuers were catching up, hallooing in a most terrifying manner whenever they caught sight of my torn flapping robe. Dredging up the last of my strength I put on a final spurt of speed, and leaped down the final passage to the handleless door. After an instant the charm unlocked it, and it swung towards me.

I sped in. Too late now to try anything; even a Cayd could see the stair was ending. The Navel Room is open to the sky; under the spur of desperation I could claw my way up its wall, dropping the Crown into the water as I passed and then—after drawing my pursuers up after me—leap. It is the highest point in the City. I would fall more than four stories, onto stone. But it was my final hope; at least my end would be certain and quick.

But I had forgotten the Navel Room has no floor to speak of. Blind with my own haste I slipped. I tumbled headlong into the cup of shallow water. The Crown jarred off my head, making a faint musical tinkle as it rolled along the narrow paving beyond. As I lunged for it a rough grasp on my ankle jerked me back. My chin hit the stone verge with a vicious crack, and my strength seeped away. Big legs stepped over me, muscular hands scooped up the Crown. My last sight was a booted foot swinging toward my head.

PART II

CHAPTER 11:
The Break

Consciousness announced its return with pain and thirst. Hammers beat a fierce rhythm in my brain, and my body seemed to be one huge, angry bruise. My tongue felt like old, cracking leather. A hardened mat of blood and hair clung stiffly to one side of my head, and one eye was swollen shut. Peering through the other I saw, not, as I had hoped, the Deadlands and the White Queen waiting, but two threads of light suspended above darkness. I lay stripped and shivering on clammy rock.

Waves of hot and cold made everything nightmarish, but I recognized the place. I was just about to be lapidated. The slabs of wood above me would be heaped with stones. The weight would press me slowly to death. In the darkness I screamed, but my mouth was so dry it came out a croak, barely audible.

When I clawed my way back to awareness again, some time had passed. The pain and thirst were worse, but my head was a little clearer. This could not be Execution Rock. For one thing, my stony cell was too deep. The thick wooden planks above were at least ten feet away.

As I watched, a shadow crossed a thread of light, and the planks creaked. Someone above began to snore, a deep regular noise like a saw in hard wood. I must be in an old dungeon, deep in the Palace cellars, and my Caydish guards were above. One put a prisoner in—the cells were no more than deep holes scooped in the living rock—and set planks across to keep him there. So long as the guards stayed in the room, weighting them down, escape was impossible.

The realization was even more fearful than imminent lapidation. They were keeping me prisoner, for what? Nausea rose sour in my throat as I recalled the stories of torture I had heard during the Tiyalor war. I remembered Silverhand's fate, and Mor's promise. The shuddering pains twisting through my frame were only a foretaste of worse agony to come.

With a convulsive effort I sat up, breath rasping hoarsely through my bruised lips. Though the stone was icy my body burned with fever. Joint by reluctant joint I dragged myself upright, breaking the fingernails of my hand on the cold rough-hewn rock, forcing my quivering legs to bear me. Black water seemed to slosh perilously in my skull. A hero in plaiv would have been able to claw his way in the darkness up the wall, push a plank aside against the weight of the Cayds above, and then, one-handed, fight his way free. But I could not do it. Like a fly in glue, I was stuck in reality. The saving power of legend's country had never been more remote. My knees unstrung themselves, and I sagged onto all fours, retching.

Only bile came up—my stomach had been empty for what felt like years. When the spasms passed I lay prone on the indifferent rock. Though it could not be of the least use, my mind weakly revolved on its treadmill of thought, like an ox that has forgotten rest.

I had lost everything, throne and kindred, freedom and country, even my cat. There was not even "the Shan King" to rely on anymore; had he ever existed? So long as I believed the Crystal Crown was running me, I could hope it was in control of events. Now I was alone. I had thought I was safe asleep and dreaming, when all the time I had been awake. No one was responsible for Averidan's wreck, but I. The thought made the sweat stand cold on my body.

This line of deliberation was too painful to sustain

for long, and like a light-crazed moth my mind fluttered around, to a new angle of the central agony. Once, when I had been younger, more innocent, I might have turned to the god. Despite everything I had nursed a secret hope it was all a mistake, that somehow everything would yet be set right. But now I was shut out indeed. If it was my life's last act I would return the favor. Though I did not know if it was day or night I rolled painfully over, to face where the sky should be.

"I abjure you," I whispered aloud. "If this is the sort of deity you are, we are quits." It was not worthwhile, to tense myself in anticipation. No weapon was left for the god to strike back at me with except death, and I welcomed death. But there was no change in the dank darkness or the two threads of light above. Listening to my own heartbeat, waiting for it to stop, I slipped into a cobweb-fragile slumber. Through the thin skin of sleep I still knew the clammy gloom of my cell. But as the eye can take in only the net, and not the fish distending it within, I dreamed over and tautly around physical distractions.

In the dream snow sifted thickly down from a leaden evening sky. As I slogged through the drifts the snow crept under my leather leggings and into the high tops of my boots, where it melted to soak the fur lining. By my woolen and leather clothes I recognized the place—this was Cayd, and I was on the road with my army to Ieor, to defeat the renegade magus Xerlanthor.

But where was the army? I halted to look around, and saw virgin drifts, marred by only my one set of prints. The tall pines all around seemed to turn away from my glance, pretending I was not there. "I must have wandered off the main way," I said aloud. "If I follow my tracks back, they'll join on and I can catch up with the others."

I did so, fighting an irrational surge of fear and loneliness. No beast in these forests would attack me, except perhaps a wolf. "And I'm armed," I rebuked myself, feeling at my belt. But my fingers found not a Viridese sword but a Caydish battle axe hanging there. No Shan uses them.

Somehow this was far more frightening than the prospect of wolves. I fled, floundering and stumbling over roots and logs hidden by the snow, lurching from one tree to the next like a drunkard reeling his way home. As I fell against the trunks great heaps of frigid powder were shaken off the boughs above, so that I ran practically blind. At last, my heart pounding fit to burst, I almost collapsed against a tree, leaning my forehead on my arms while I gulped down the cold air.

My eyes, open yet unseeing, were directed toward the foot of the tree. Suddenly I realized I was not seeing gnarly tree roots. There were toes in the snow, the toes of leather boots. My spine crept as I timidly raised my head. I leaned against the sash of a tall man. He was Shan, dressed suitably for the weather. An old-fashioned split-reed hat lined with quilting covered his head, and a tall spear was in his hand.

"Xerlanthor!" I gasped. Though this one did not in the least resemble the evil magus as I had last seen him, I did not doubt it was he. Xerlanthor had been a master of disguise. Then I must be the unfortunate Cayd who would be compelled, under a magical geas, to betray our cause. Choking with terror I flung myself away. But a bramble caught my heel, and I fell backward, helpless, into the deep snow.

But the magus, if he was a magus, did not stir. To my fevered eye he looked unnaturally tall, taller than the Master Magus or even the Cayds. His hat brushed the tops of the trees, and under the plaited brim the dark eyes were deep and warm, like the depths of a cup of mulled wine. The snow drove steadily down, sticking to my hair and eyelashes, but the flakes melted instantly as they touched this other's shoulders.

"I never use geas," the magus said in so quiet a

tone I had to keep still to hear. "Your will is free. What good should I find in slaves? Run, then, and when you have run yourself a little wiser seek me again."

So glad was I to be dismissed I hardly took in these words, which were quite uncharacteristic of my own turbulent dealings with the evil magus. I thrashed in the snow and underbrush to haul myself upright, and jerked myself right out of sleep.

I came back with a painful start. Something was going on above, bottles rolling about and metal thumping on wood. My guards were waking up. "Gods, what a hellhole," a deep voice moaned in Caydish. "Might as well sleep in a tomb."

"Light up that silly tray of coals. if you're cold," someone else growled. "I'm hung over, as bad as you."

Booted feet began to move about above me. The door creaked open, and then shut. From the talk, it had been a fine sack. They compared loot, shared food brought out from a pack, reminisced about the slaughter, and speculated on honors and land grants to come. I could tell these must be Musenor's most trusted men. No mere incompetents would be posted here. I listened for mention of me or my fate, in vain. Any discussion must have already taken place.

For what must have been a full day I slipped in and out of oblivion, listening muzzily as one set of guards was replaced by another, and those by yet more. In the fevered spells I could doze, but my own uncontrollable shivering often woke me. No wonder I had dreamed of snow. The room above was never empty. No one lifted the thick planks to inspect me; whether I lived or died of cold and thirst seemed to be a matter of indifference.

At last it was plainly time for sleep again. The talk above was of the day's doings—Musenor had set a squad to clearing out corpses and drunks, and sealed off the treasure rooms again. "But we got some nice stuff out first," I heard one guard confide. "Look at this thing, it's made of solid gold."

"Hist! 'Ware visitors!" his companion hissed, for the door was creaking open.

"Hallo, soldiers!" A familiar voice greeted them cheerily in Caydish. "Why, it's cousin Galj! I haven't seen you in years!"

"Little Melayne! Limaot's mercy, but you're very pregnant!"

Stunned, I recognized my wife's voice. For an instant a crazy hope stirred in me. But as I strained my ears it withered. Melayne seemed in the best of spirits. "A temporary condition," she laughed. "Here, I've brought you a greeting-gift—plum brandy."

"Ugh, I had some," another guard said. "Give me ale any day."

"Ah, but this is the Shan King's private stock," Melayne purred. "Smooth as milk, but virile as a ram in a new herd of ewes."

A clink of bottle on metal, as she set the tray down. A prolonged gurgle of fluid into cups. After one taste the Cayds brayed their approval. "Delicious!" Galj coughed and sputtered. "Let's have one more cupful, there. Who are these two, your women? Oh, midwives! Well, I can see you're near your time. Sit down, little cousin, and tell us who you fancy for your next!"

"Me, I volunteer!" one guard crowed.

"Oh, definitely a Cayd," Melayne said.

"Was it very bad, wedding a barbarian?" the other guard asked. The pity in his tone, and his casual 'barbarian,' made me blink.

"Well, there's no denying they're not like us," Melayne said with the coyly confidential air of one revealing a marital secret. Though I knew the Cayds talked far more lasciviously than they lived, still I was startled to hear her.

"Ah, and you want a real man this time!" the lewd one chortled.

"They're certainly a very small folk," said Galj.

"In every sense," Melayne agreed.

A shout of ribald laughter greeted this remark. The lewd guard made several suggestions so sexually technical they escaped my grasp of the tongue completely. The sympathetic one refilled his cup and drunkenly intoned, "I always say, good marriages are made in bed. Virgins have to be initiated correctly, or they're spoilt."

"That's right," said Galj, as earnestly as if some fundamental truth had been propounded. "Pass the bottle, there."

"These wimbly Shan, now," the other continued. "Though their women seem so loose, that doesn't mean what it might in Cayd."

The lewd one laughed. "Do you remember that forest girl—"

But his reminiscences were interrupted by Galj, who had been working steadily away at the brandy. "This stuff is stronger than it tastes," he announced in thick wavering tones. "I think—"

A heavy thump made the planks quiver, and Galj was extravagantly sick. Vomit dripped through into my cell. The others thought this very funny. Melayne, especially, hooted that the only cure for such a delicate digestion was yet more brandy.

I tried to close my ears to the noise. Vainly I told myself Melayne was lying for her life—I had made her happy, I was sure of it. But hardly any male is absolutely secure sexually, and after all it was true, the two peoples did have sharply differing ideas about it. Before Melayne had learned to speak Viridese she had been so compliant and tame, I had nearly forgot she was a person, and not a sexual toy. Now my wounded pride overwhelmed common sense. Melayne had never loved me. My downfall made her, if anything, glad. When I died she would shrug, and happily choose another spouse.

From this stupor of self-pity I was roused by the sudden quiet. The laughter and voices were gone. A small, metallic noise scraped at the farther side of the planks, while low women's voices conferred. Then with a sudden creak one thread of light grew fatter, and a plank rose away. A block of yellow lamp-light slanted down to illuminate the rock wall at my feet.

Two heads appeared, black against the light. "Liras!" Melayne called softly. "Liras, are you there?"

Treacherous bitch, I wanted to reply, but my tongue was so dry it stuck to my split and cracking lips. The heads went away, and a long narrow shadow snaked down—a rope. Then a female figure, skirted and bloused in the Caydish style, clambered nimbly down—not Melayne, for this one's waist was belted in slim. With fastidious care she lifted her wide woolen skirts over the pool of vomit, and crouched beside me.

"Is it he? Is he dead?" Melayne called down, in such a pathetic tone that I instantly forgave her.

"They beat him," my visitor said, "and he's cold as the inside of a melon. But his pulse still beats." She reached to explore my bruised temple, and I caught sight of the face under the headscarf. It was Silverhand. I must have made some noise, a groan or mumble of surprise, for she smiled down at me and said, "Don't fret, we'll take care of everything."

Carefully she hauled me up to a sitting position against the wall, and then to my feet. The room whirled sickeningly around. She knelt and caught my sinking body round the waist. I collapsed over her shoulder and with a grunt of effort she rose, carrying me. Through blouse and vest I could feel the sinewy warm strength of her frame. With the aid of the rope she slowly climbed part-way up the wall. Then Melayne and the other woman—a genuine herbal, I thought, middle-aged and stout—dragged me to the planking. After so many hours in darkness the glare of the single lamp hurt my eyes. But I saw all three were dressed in the bulky Caydish style, presumably to distinguish them from the rapable Shan women.

"They hurt him," Melayne whispered. Her warm tears dropped onto my bare leg.

"No time to mend that now," Silverhand said, climbing briskly up from below. "Mistress Rodis's herbs won't last all night. Where's that bundle?"

They dressed me with painful speed in Caydish clothes—my own, I recognized, the one outfit I had obtained in Cayd. The warmth of leather and wool was infinitely comforting, as was the water Rodis gave me from a stoneware bottle.

"Now the cloak and hood," Silverhand directed. "Which of these topknots do you fancy, Melayne?"

"The longest," she replied, and to my foggy surprise Silverhand began to chop off a Cayd's long blond braid. The severed tail was unbraided, and Rodis swiftly pinned it to the inside of my hood. When the hood was drawn up dirty yellow hair obscured my face.

Silverhand looked me over critically. "Too clean," she said. "Where's that brandy? Now keep your mouth shut, Liras, this stuff is drugged." She splashed the liquor generously down my woolen tunic-bosom. "I know—we'll roll him in your cousin's puke."

"Yeargh!" Melayne wrinkled her nose. "He'll stink."

"Yes, and no one will care to examine him closely," Silverhand predicted. I dared not object as they dragged me through the filth.

Rodis coiled up the rope while Silverhand and Melayne fitted the plank back into place. Everything was stowed away in Silverhand's bogus midwifery bag. Then Silverhand took me under the arms while Rodis took my ankles. They lifted me, and Melayne fluttered around to tuck my wounded hand up out of harm's way. "Relax," she told me softly. Then she opened the creaking door.

"Lock it behind us," Silverhand said. Melayne did so, sliding the key back under the door again, and then led us down the corridor. Since my last visit lamps had been set up at intervals for the convenience of the guards, making the cellar passage look very different.

"He's terribly heavy," Rodis whispered.

"We can rest any time after we get up the stairs," Silverhand said in a low voice. "Just don't look scared. Look annoyed, if you can."

We met nobody as we moved down the corridor. The only sound was the stealthy shuffle of their thick-soled Caydish boots. The climb up the narrow twisting stairs was slow, Melayne carrying the child and the others carrying me. But they had chosen their time well. It was after midnight, the deadest hour of the night. The solitude that oppressed me before was now my friend. Once at the top they paused to rest, laying me down inside a darkened office. Melayne gave me another drink and a kiss, cradling my head on her bosom. My confidence in her was so great I felt no fear whatever, and actually nodded off when we began moving again down the endless marble hallways.

A shout woke me. "Hey, who's that there?" A minor Caydish prince bustled up, only a little tipsy and bristling with suspicion.

"Hallo, Rin," Melayne greeted him in Caydish. "Put him down, girls, for a moment."

"Princess, you ought not to be wandering about at this hour," Rin scolded her. "The men are still wild, you could get hurt."

"Oh, but I was so anxious to see my cousin Galj again," Melayne explained. "We had a little party, to celebrate. And then when we came back the stairway was just completely blocked by this fellow! Look, he's drunk himself sick!"

Rin nudged my ribs with one foot, hard. With an effort I relaxed, not allowing myself to stiffen with pain. Neither Melayne nor Silverhand objected, though through my eyelids I saw Rodis twitch. "He must have worked through gallons of the stuff," Rin said enviously.

"I thought I'd have him thrown in the fountain," Melayne said, "as a penalty for stopping up staircases."

"You do that," Rin agreed. "There's a good one, a little farther on." With that he moved off. Silverhand sighed faintly at the narrow escape, and hoisted me up again.

"Not far now," Melayne encouraged. The Lady's rooms at the far end of the Palace were well-guarded. But Musenor, not knowing the Palace, had posted his sentries only on the main corridor. The women took me through several side chambers, a narrow pantry, and a closet stacked high with linens, unlocking and then locking the doors as they went. We emerged from the closet into Melayne's quiet bathing-room. They set me down on the tile with gasps of relief.

"Viris is truly merciful," Rodis said, flexing her cramped hands. "Fill up this bath, and we'll clean him."

Melayne tipped the waiting hot-water jars while Rodis laid out her herbs and preparations. Were I not so ill I would have perished of embarrassment, as the women stripped and scrubbed me like a babe. But the water was hot, and the soft soap scoured away the humiliating filth of imprisonment. I relaxed gratefully into their care. "Hot tea and proper food may keep the damp from settling in his chest," Rodis told Melayne as she poulticed my hurts. "We must cool his fever and draw away the bruising as fast as possible. Marked like this, he's too noticeable."

"We can keep him here a few days," Melayne said. "I'm going into labor."

I pushed the wet compress away from my face. "You are?" I croaked.

"No, no! I mean, I'll tell Mor I am," she explained. "Don't do that, darling, you'll hurt yourself. It'll be a long, hard labor, a lot of coming and going and commotion. But no men, of course."

"You, for your part, must rest and heal," Rodis said.

They laid me on a pallet beside Melayne's bed. Her pillows and mattress were rearranged on the marble platform so that she could lie nearer the door, and higher. Anyone in the doorway would see only the bulk of a very pregnant woman. Hot, bitter tea was spooned into my mouth for the fever, and then some broth to nourish me. Beside me, Melayne held my good hand until I fell asleep.

I lay hid in the women's rooms for three days. For a goodly portion of the first, no one noticed my escape. Cousin Galj and his companions, racked by severe hangovers, suspected nothing, and no doubt put the forgotten haircut down to drunken revelry. Melayne had visited all her relatives, and made merry with all. When my absence was discovered that evening, no one could say how long I had been gone. A noisy search was made, and a destructive one, for the Cayds had never had such luxurious dwellings, and suspected the thick Palace walls were riddled with secret passageways. But Rodis met them at the outer door, saying, "The Princess's pangs have begun. Must you disturb her? After all, the sentries keep the door of the suite." Melayne lay on the bed and made loud pathetic noises. So the soldiers went muttering away.

I slept, waking only to take medicine and food, and slept again. My skull had not been actually cracked, and the innumerable scrapes and cuts were ugly and painful but not dangerous. Though the next morning I woke still aching, the concussion had abated and my head was clear.

The window over the cliff was ajar, letting in cool air, but a copper brazier at the foot of the bed warded off chills. The rose-hung chamber was far less neat than it had been when Melayne was its sole tenant, for no one had been allowed in to tidy it. The white pierced-porcelain lamps were askew on their stands, and dirty crockery and medicine spoons stood on the broad window sills. Silverhand sat on the tile floor beside me, splicing two thick ropes together. She looked very unlike herself, with the wide Caydish skirts tucked around her. New grim lines were etched around her mouth and eyes. Only her hands were the same, the wiry tendons sliding under the tanned skin as her clever fingers worked the strands and the awl.

"What's that for?" I asked sleepily.

"You're awake! How do you feel?"

"Infinitely better," I said. I eased myself up, cautiously peering over the heaped covers and pillows to my right.

"Don't worry, the inner door's locked," Silverhand said, smiling. "Everyone not in on the secret we keep in the outer rooms."

"You women are insane!" I sat up too suddenly, and set my head to pounding again. "I'm not ungrateful for your efforts, but you do realize I ought to be dead—I'm no longer the Shan King!"

Her eyes grew hard as onyx, and about the same color. "Don't you dare give up now!" she said in a furious whisper. "After all our work! You asked what this rope's for. Well, we plan to lower you down the cliff-face, and smuggle you to Cliffhole. There's a group of Shan partisans there."

I hardly heard this last part. "The cliff? It's a three-hundred-foot drop! I don't know how!"

She waved a dismissive hand. "We'll deal with it. Don't worry."

I lay back on my pallet. "Don't worry!" I echoed in disbelief. "What about Melayne?"

"She will come too. The new Shan King and his Warlord won't appreciate her efforts in this."

There was no arguing with that. But mention of King Mor brought other tidings to mind. "He may be King," I said, "but he won't be Shan King. The Cayds decided the Crystal Crown is witchery. They plan to destroy it."

Silverhand stared at me. "Destroy it! You're sure? They can't, they'll destroy Averidan!"

"I know." It was hopeless. My incredible rescue had been for naught. Desolate tears burned in my throat, and I covered my aching brow with my good hand, lest Silverhand should see.

"Then we must steal it back again," she said firmly. "I'll question the servants, try to learn where it is."

"It's impossible."

"Rescuing you was impossible," she retorted. "Yet here you are."

The door to the bath opened and Melayne came through, her wet hair wrapped in a towel. "Don't talk to him too much, Silverhand," she ordered. "Let him rest. Are you better, dearest?"

"Somewhat," I said. I looked her over carefully. Under the blue silk bathrobe she bulked larger than I would have believed possible. Nor could I grasp the idea that she had risked all, at this awkward time, to save me. More snappishly than I meant I scolded, "In your condition, you oughtn't be running around at night, drugging soldiers and stealing prisoners! Gravid women need a full night's sleep!"

She scowled at me. "You're an ungrateful one—" Then the frown melted into a smile, and she pushed me back onto my pillows. "Now you're here I'll sleep better, and leave the worrying to you again."

Now the siege was lifted, there was food in plenty. Large meals arrived at frequent intervals to feed the "midwives," and Silverhead and Rodis took it in turns to slip out and forage for more. Late that second evening Silverhand filched a whole basket of oysters. We lounged about as she shucked them, slurping the delicate flesh raw and then tossing the shells off the cliff. "Women in labor aren't supposed to eat like that," I teased Melayne.

"Women in labor aren't supposed to eat at all," she replied calmly. "When I genuinely go into labor, I'll stop. I've been so hungry for fresh foods."

"These are undeniably fresh," Silverhand said, skimming an oyster-shell far out into the cold air. "Your cooks, Liras, are miserable. The Cayds wouldn't even try anything so raw."

"Not yet, anyway." Melayne noisily sucked the excess salty juice off the shell, and then pried the oyster up with her knife.

Just as she was tipping it into my mouth the door flew open. Rodis darted in and slammed it, leaning her back on it as if to keep it shut. "King Mor is here! He wants to search the rooms!"

Like lightning Silverhand threw the basket of oysters out the window and swung the casement to. My eyes popped as Melayne shook out her braids and began to tear off every stitch of clothing. Rodis leaped onto the bed and hauled the head of the soft mattress up. "Quick, Liras, lie down here!"

My muscles were frozen with shock, but Silverhand jerked me to my feet. I tottered to the platform and lay down flat across the head of it, next to the wall. Rodis dropped the mattress over me and then shoveled all the pillows over the betraying hump. Stark naked, Melayne clambered swiftly onto the bed and leaned against me. Rodis threw a sheet over her, while I sweated and wriggled, trying to get some air. Two dozen fat pillows overflowed over this end of the marble platform. I wormed forward under the suffocating mattress and poked my head out among them.

From behind the sheet, Melayne's raised knees, and the pillows, I could glimpse Silverhand dashing to scoop up stray oyster shells and discarded clothing. Rodis dumped a fistful of powder onto the brazier, which instantly began to smoke and give the room a mysterious air. Then she sprinkled Melayne's face and hair with water. Silverhand pulled her scarf well down over her forehead, and took up an attitude of concern beside the bed.

They were just in time. The door swung open, and there stood King Mor. Some fair men are hot as fire—Musenor was one. But Mor was red, yet cold. The first time we had met, shortly after I had be-

come King, I had thought him shy. Now I realized
he was hard, hard as ice. Perhaps his rule had changed
him as much as mine changed me.

Even taller behind him was Musenor's blond head.
As they strode in he growled, "It's like an oven in
here! And what's that smell?"

It was oysters, and smoke. I thanked Viris Musenor
didn't eat them, otherwise he could hardly fail to
recognize the aroma. "Oh, brothers, go away,"
Melayne moaned in Caydish. "I don't want you to
see me like this."

Musenor shuffled his feet unhappily. "I'm sorry
you're having such a hard labor, Melayne," he said.
"But we've scoured the Palace, and can't find the
Witch-King."

Mor spoke coldly. "Be grateful, little sister, that I
keep it in the family, and don't call a squad of soldiers to ransack your suite. Musenor is confident he
can deal with the fugitive alone now that he's been
deprived of his necromantic Crown—if he's here."

"You think I'm entertaining men *now?*" Melayne
panted in a most convincing manner. "Then be swift
about it, Musenor, it's unlucky for you to see wom-
en's mysteries."

Embarrassed, the Warlord drew his short sword
and vanished into the bathing room. To my dismay,
however, King Mor took up a position beside the
brazier at the foot of the bed and watched his sister
with a disapproving interest in his eye. Rodis and
Silverhand hovered on either side, adjusting the sheet
over Melayne's 'pangs' and pretending to wipe her
damp forehead. I could just see the red-gold hair
furring one huge forearm, left bare by Mor's Caydish
vest. In the warm flickering light of brazier and
candle the uncouth metal ornaments in Mor's pierced
ears glittered like a second-rate jeweler's display. I
hardly dared breathe, lest he notice the movement.

"When will the birth be?" he rapped out.

"They don't speak Caydish, Mor," Melayne lied.
In Viridese she repeated the question, and then trans-

lated Rodis's deferential reply. "At least a day. I don't think I can bear it."

"Have you told the midwife about the babe?"

Melayne shifted her bulk restlessly. "I told you that's not the custom here. Anyone can be Shan King. Why, Liras himself was only a minor noble, the youngest of his family. His son will have a title, but be completely harmless."

"Nevertheless, Melayne, we do things differently." Mor moved a little, and I glimpsed his hard gray stare. "If this were Cayd, his seed would rule even after I killed him. Just accept my decision—the babe will die."

"He's not even birthed yet!" Melayne shouted in protest.

"I told you before—if he has the sense to be still-born, he can save me the trouble of drowning him," Mor retorted. "Dead or alive, the midwife must bring him to me as soon as he's born."

Musenor had finished searching the bath, and now came in and remarked, "You can't feel reasonable about it now, sister, but later on you'll understand. You'll have other children, and forget this half-breed pup."

"If I can find anyone to wed you," Mor said. Under the sheet I saw Melayne's small fist clench the hem of the sheet at this old taunt. She was not thought a bargain in her homeland; the royal Caydish line prides itself on height.

The copper amulets strung round his wrists jin-gled as Musenor threw open cupboards and ward-robes, and poked his sword under the couches and behind the pink hangings. He even opened the win-dow and leaned out into the night, whistling softly at the sight of the drop. I gulped as he stopped right before me to kick the marble platform of the bed, but what with Melayne's uneasy tossings and the solicitous fuss Rodis made with the sheet, he saw nothing. "Solid," he reported. "I told you this was futile. He's not here. Why would Melayne try to hide him?"

Mor scowled down at his sister; for a moment the family likeness was startling. "The rhetor said you two were like turtledoves, always dewy-eyed. Women can always be won over in bed."

"You think I was going to be frank to a witch?" Melayne snapped. "He'd soon take it out on me." She let her head fall back onto the damp pillows, and writhed. "Those story-mongers are liars anyway, everyone knows it."

"So he's a liar, and you were a liar," Mor said with a tight smile. "You're acquiring far too many Shan perversions, Melayne. I must make sure to tell your next spouse to beat it out of you. He and Musenor here can confer on effective methods."

With that he whirled and strode out. Musenor, to my astonishment, bent to pat Melayne's hand. I could see the jagged half-healed scar on his muscular arm where Zofal had speared him, and a green silk Viridese cloak, no doubt looted from my wardrobe, tightly strained over his massive shoulders. "Don't lose sleep about your next husband," he said kindly. "Mor will be busy for a long time, he'll probably forget all about it if you keep out of his way."

He left, shutting the door behind him. Rodis sagged with relief, while Silverhand crept over and shot the bolt. Melayne sat up, holding the sheet around her nakedness, and I pushed the pillows aside and crept out from under. My crumpled garments were soaked with sweat, and I was very thirsty. When I poured out some water I noticed my hands were shaking. We all were.

"That was too close," Rodis quavered. "You warriors may be used to it, but I'm not."

"And the way Mor talked about the babe was blood-curdling," Silverhand said.

"I can understand that," I said, drawing outraged glances from the others. "But what did he mean, about Musenor's methods?"

Melayne glanced at Silverhand, who reluctantly said, "You've been too sick, Liras, to ask about your sister, and we didn't want to upset you."

"Siril-ven?" I looked around, half expecting my sister to step out of one of the open cupboards. "Isn't she here? I told them to bring her."

"She was," Melayne said, "and in the sack Mor kept the army out of these rooms. But when he and Musenor came by, to look over the women, she wouldn't pretend to be a servant."

"She wouldn't even climb into these Caydish clothes, and blend in with Melayne's ladies," Silverhand snorted. "She put up her hair, wrapped up in a purple silk robe, and announced to Mor she was your sister."

Obviously our entire family was insane. I sat down on the bed and held my aching head. "And what did Mor say to that?"

"It could have been worse," Silverhand comforted. "Mor already had a wife. So he called Musenor forward, and gave her to him. I hear there'll be a big wedding, when things settle down."

"I tried to tell Mor that your relatives don't hold any rank," Melayne said, "but he can't believe me. It's not like that with us."

"Just as well; that probably saved her life," Silverhand said.

"I suppose Dasan-hel is dead then," I groaned; Silverhand confirmed this. Poor Dasan, he had been so transparently snobbish that once, in a cruel moment, Zofal and I had dubbed him Old Piecrust—all pastry in search of a filling. "Siril will kill herself."

"It could have been worse," Melayne repeated. "Of course he can be unpleasant in battle, but Musenor is the nicest of my brothers and half-brothers. Much nicer than Mor—Mor is a snake."

But I refused to be comforted. I remembered that idiotic plaiv I had had Bochas recite for the Cayds nearly three years ago. In it the sea-reavers had married "the fairest ladies of Averidan." That had probably put the idea in Mor's head, though even a barbarian could hardly call Siril a beauty. If she had not had the misfortune to be my sib Siril would be free now—a widow, to be sure, but not a captive wife.

There was no point even to discuss her rescue. The Crystal Crown must take priority. When I had been about to die these responsibilities had fallen into abeyance. Now they leaped up from their premature pyres, all clamoring for solution. So, limp with exhaustion and misery, I returned to bed.

CHAPTER 12:
North and East

The next day, the third since my rescue, I again woke very late. I felt almost myself again. The swelling had gone down so that I could see out of both eyes. Assiduous nursing had saved me from the chest cold I should have caught in the chilly dungeons. My head no longer hurt at every motion, my bruises were fading into purple, and my cuts scabbed over. "We leave tonight," Silverhand said. "I'll start scrounging supplies."

Not until then did the folly of our plans strike me. "Melayne's well-nigh at the child-bed," I protested. "She can't swing down ropes and hike miles to safety."

"I will if I have to," Melayne stoutly maintained. "And Rodis will be meeting us with a wagon."

"Yes, I told the guards I needed some childbirth potions from the Sodality." Rodis had changed from Caydish dress to her Viridese herbalist-white again. She pinned a brown shawl over her gray hair.

"A boat would be safer," I grumbled.

But Melayne scowled, "No."

"I will wait at the grain-store you marked, Silverhand." Rodis glanced at me. "The birth isn't due for at least two days, I can assure you of that."

She left by the main door, and we locked it behind her, while Silverhand slipped out the back way. For the first time in days we were completely alone. I lost no time in taking my wife to my arms. She was too big now to hold comfortably on my knee. Instead we curled up very close together on a couch. "You are so brave," I murmured into her hair. "It appalls me."

"If you persist in becoming snared in confoundments, I have to fight for you," she said in the reasonable tone of one stating the obvious. "The gods alone know where you picked up this idea that womenfolk must be kept safe at all costs. This isn't Cayd. You have the excellent example of all your female relatives."

"Averidan was a matriarchy once," I admitted. My good arm fitted neatly around her, in the warm crease between bosom and baby, and I held her close. "But I can't help it. It's instinctive, to want you and the babe to be safe. Did Mor really mean what he said? What if the babe's a girl?"

"He might let a female live," Melayne said, "and wed her to his heir. But I'm sure it's a boy, and I told him so."

"And you call Siril a goose! If you had assured Mor it was female, you could stay safe here."

"There, you're doing it *again!*" She scowled sideways at me, laying a possessive hand over the mound of her skirt. "I know I'm right, so I must escape. And as for you—there's to be no more of this hustling me away to safety. I'm your *wife*. You need me."

There was no denying that. In the teeth of our plight an absurd happiness sang between us. To need and be needed, love and be loved, was sufficient. I buried my face in the red-brown coils of her hair. Through the thin skin over the temple I could feel her pulse under my lips. "I'll never willingly be parted from you again, Melayne," I said. "That is, if you won't mind sharing in the exile of a fugitive Shan King."

She pretended to think it over. "Is that a promise?"

"If you wish it, of course."

"Good." She leaned against me, her arm tight around my neck in that same gesture of possessiveness.

Silverhand ordered a large, early dinner for herself. It was supplemented by a Caydish cheese, two cold preserved pigs' feet, and day-old barley bread, all these being items purloined from a pantry. "Eat well," she warned. "Our next meal will be far less easy to steal."

I gnawed hungrily at a salty-spicy chunk of pigs' feet and said, "It's not stealing. This is genuinely my provender."

"Think of it that way if it improves the flavor," said Silverhand.

Our packing was soon done. For lack of other garments I put on my green Caydish clothes. Silverhand had stolen for me a straw hat and a wide robe of coarse gray linen—the sort of outer garment worn by peasants on feast days. With these I could pass for either a Shan or, at a distance, a Cayd. Melayne, on the other hand, donned loose trousers, boots, and a loose tan tunic quilted with green. She had to tie the trousers up over her shoulders to keep them on, since Silverhand had had to purloin big ones. "You look like an overweight innkeeper," I teased.

"Trews are far warmer wear for climbing," Silverhand reproved. "The draft that blows up these skirts is amazing." She herself also wore male peasant garb. Melayne and I did not comment. The tacit acknowledgment was that the brown outfits of the Sisterhood would be imprudent wear.

The Cayds kept weaponry far closer than their food. Even table knives were scarce. The best Silverhand had been able to steal was a pointed Caydish stabber. I did not know how to use it; our swords are slicers. So she slung it at her belt.

My pack held the spare clothes and Melayne's jewelry—she had no money. Silverhand carried a little food, water bottles, and blankets in hers. But when Melayne set her bag down beside ours at the foot of the bed we saw it was huge. With a glance at Silverhand I pushed the flap back. Inside was lime-green silk, embroidered with golden turtles. "Melayne, what is this?" I scolded. "You will not be needing a party dress."

"You haven't the forethought of a sheep," she retorted. "Party dress indeed. Here!" She grabbed the bag and shook it out. Tiny silken robes, fine linen shirts and diapers, and even a pair of soft leather shoes no longer than my thumb cascaded out onto the bed. "The baby will need something to wear."

Awed, I fingered a wee jacket, green silk quilted with merry blue gryphons chasing a dove. In the lamplight, the pea-sized buttons twinkled with dozens of tiny sapphires. They were all boy's garments: the clothes of a prince. "He can't wear these anyway, Melayne," I pointed out. "They're too grand."

"Yes, in our humbler array we'd be haled up for kidnapping a scion of nobility," Silverhand said.

Melayne stowed the clothes neatly back into the bag, and refused to budge. "My baby's not going naked," she said. "Find him some plainer clothing, and I'll discard these." And with that we had to be content.

It was night by then, but we had to wait for people to go to sleep. "What do you hear about the Crystal Crown?" I asked.

Silverhand frowned. "Not a thing, no word of anyone either wearing it or destroying it. Mor has it, but he's not telling anyone where. They're concentrating on finding you."

"I must have put fear in them," I said, pleased.

"According to the servants, the Cayds will believe anything," Silverhand said with a grin. "Some wit told them you can walk through walls. So Mor keeps a guard of ten with him, day and night. They have to sit up in the dark around the bed as Mor sleeps, and aren't allowed to so much as sigh."

Melayne snickered at her brother's folly, but I said, "I wish I could, and get the Crown back."

"There are plenty of tales about you, too," Silverhand said to Melayne.

"About the birth?"

She nodded. "The story is twins. The lower halls are seething with it."

I eyed Melayne nervously. She seemed enormous, almost circular. Rumor has its own life in Averidan. "You think so?"

"You'll just have to wait and see," Melayne replied serenely.

At last the Palace was quiet. Silverhand doused all the lamps. Fresh chilly air nipped at our noses as Melayne opened the window. Outside, frosty stars hung in a deep midnight sky. Silverhand took the great coil of rope from its hiding place on top of a wardrobe, and ran one end through the ceiling-pulley that ordinarily holds the lamp-cluster before tying it to the marble window-bench. "The way we'll work it is this," she said. "I've made a sort of rope sling at the free end. You, Liras, will get into it and climb out the window. I'll lower you down. You can fend yourself off from the cliff-face with your feet."

I leaned out the deep sill and looked down. The white marble wall went down for a few fathoms, and then the rock overhung darkness. It might have been my unhappy imagination, but a few thin clouds seemed to be drifting across the chasm below. "It's a fearful way down," I said, aping a calm I did not feel. "Are you certain there's rope enough?"

"Of course," Silverhand said "Now, the more you think about it the harder it will be—"

We froze. From the darkened bathing room had come the click of a door's lock. Soundlessly Silverhand drew her sword and sank to her knees, fading right into the shadows. Melayne and I shrank back against the walls to keep out of her way. Whoever it was had to be silenced.

For a long tense moment we heard nothing. Then a shuffle, the squeak of furniture on tile, and a muttered curse. The entering intruder had walked into a bench. I stared into the shadows, straining my eyes to recognize him, but saw only a dim figure.

But at this sort of game Silverhand was unequalled. As the intruder passed she rose out of a pool of darkness and caught him round the neck. With a complicated jerk and twist she threw him in a sideways somersault. As he hit the floor I heard the "whouf!" of out-driven breath. The pointed sword glittered at his throat before he could recover.

"Who is it?" I asked, leaning forward.

"Shush!" Silverhand glared reprovingly at me, and I stepped back into the shadow again. The fewer who knew of me the better. Melayne helped Silverhand slide the intruder toward the window, where the faint starlight shone in.

"Twins, huh," he wheezed, staring up at Melayne's bulk against the light. He wore the humble outfit of a junior kitchen-worker, the kind who perpetually washes dishes and pots.

"A snoopy servant!" Silverhand growled as she put her sword up.

"No—" Melayne leaned awkwardly closer to peer at his face. "It's Xalan!"

"You've about broken in my ribs," Xalan complained. He sat up to rub them. "And I didn't know women could turn their labor-pangs on and off like that—" His eyes widened as I came forward.

"Xalan, you idiot," I said happily.

"You aren't supposed to be alive," he said in wounded tones. "Grand-uncle had your demise all worked out, what a disappointment."

With a catlike pounce Silverhand bowled him over again, her fingers poised to break his neck. "You weak-spined, lousy man!" she cried. "If you intend to sell us out I'll send you to the Deadlands now!"

"No, no!" I pulled at her wrist, but it was like tugging the arm of a statue. "He's joking. Besides, we haven't told anyone yet that the Cayds mean to smash the Crystal Crown."

"Do they really?" Xalan rolled his eyes at Silverhand as she let him up. "The barbarians. That changes everything."

"We're going to try to get it back," I said. "You've just interrupted our escape—you wouldn't by any chance care to join us?"

He grinned. "I was waiting for you to ask. Just let me fetch my wand and mirror."

"And you can lift," Silverhand remembered, "which could be very useful. If you untie the rope after we descend, and shut the window, the Cayds won't pick up our trail."

So when I stepped into the sling and then climbed over the sill Xalan already stood on thin air beside me. His presence was not nearly as comforting as I had hoped. "Let go the ledge, Liras," Melayne urged above me, but it took a distinct effort of will for me to relax my fingers and trust all my weight to the rope.

When I stared down between my toes no ground was visible. I told myself the darkness hid everything, and not the height. The wind tugged unpleasantly at me as I dangled, and I clutched at the rope as it swayed in its descent. But Xalan's hand at my back kept me from whirling like a chestnut on a string. "Don't look down," he instructed, his breath a white plume on the air. "And don't look so distraught, Silverhand won't let you fall. I thought you were dead, until the Cayds started their search for you. However did you do it?"

Fixing my eyes on the rope before me I gave my mind to recounting the tale. It was not a short one, but when I concluded, saying, "And they hid me there until today, when I was well enough to escape," we were still fairly high up. Silverhand was lowering slowly, taking no chances on losing control.

"The people are right, it would make a delightful plaiv," was Xalan's admiring comment. "What's the plan now?"

"We wait for Melayne and Silverhand, and then make our way north and east to Cliffhole, where some supporters are banding together." Since the rock leaned outward at the top I could no longer touch the cliff-face. I dangled in empty space, like a spider on its silk. But now when I looked down I could make out a sloping moraine at the cliff's foot. It was dark with scrub and thorn. Broken pottery, rotting fruit-rinds, and oyster shells showed the Palace was casual about trash-disposal. Guiltily, I looked for Silverhand's oyster-basket, but did not see it.

I reached with my toes for the landfall, and Xalan guided me clear of a thornbush. The loose rock slid under my feet while I clambered out of the sling and tugged it, twice. The rope paused, and then retreated upward again. "Keep out of sight," Xalan warned, and rose up with it.

Unslinging my pack I went uphill a little, and sat with my back to a rock. It was well after midnight, and a late moon shimmered down from behind me across the valley. The shadow of the Upper City stretched out and away before me like an inky carpet. At the bottom of the moraine a low wall of timber kept the rocky gravel out of the pasture. The oxen that usually lived there were gone. I wondered if the Cayds had roasted them.

Against the starry sky Melayne's plump descending figure looked like a fat grub baited on a fish-line. I hurried forward to help her alight. Xalan lifted back up again, but the rope dangled limply on the rocks. "Isn't she going to pull it back?" I asked.

"You don't believe the Commander needs to be lowered," said Melayne. And as we watched the dangling rope began to jerk and sway, and in due time Silverhand slid gracefully to earth. She tugged the rope twice, and after a pause it fell in coiling loops all around us.

"You should have had Xalan wind it up," I grumbled, as I helped untangle it from branches and thorns.

"Trust a magus to coil my rope?" Silverhand exclaimed. "I do it better."

Fortunately Xalan did not hear this. He bounded lightly down the three-hundred-foot drop, and I gave him Melayne's bag. Silverhand led us leftward down the slope. The rocks crunched and rolled underfoot, and we trod as cautiously as we could in the dark. I held Melayne's elbow, and kept on her downhill side in case she slipped.

The moon had risen high enough to pour its blue light past the scarp. So after we climbed down the retaining wall its light guided us across the fields. The ploughed earth was frosty and firm underfoot, the ridges glittering in the cold light like the white-caps of a frozen sea. Not a candle or lamp showed in the distant farmhouses, for it was very late. No Cayds were to be seen. In its silent sleep Averidan was mine again.

At the edge of the field was a hut, used to store straw and grain. We waited while Silverhand crept up and looked inside. Then, at her signal, we came forward and went in. The low doorway was half-blocked, so that we had to climb to enter. Inside the sacks of grain had been arranged for our comfort, solidly paving the earthen floor. The straw was heaped neatly on top. The smell of barley and chaff was dusty-sweet, an appetizing assurance of food to come. On this warm and comfortable couch we spread out our cloaks. Silverhand went to fetch Rodis and the wagon.

"How do you feel, dearest? Tired?" I asked Melayne.

"A little," she sighed, leaning back. "What an awkward time to be pregnant."

"You don't feel any more pangs, do you?" Xalan asked in an anxious voice. "Magi don't know anything about birthing, and I'm sure Kings and Sisters are no better."

She smiled pityingly on him and said, "Count on my son to choose a convenient time for his birth."

"I didn't know they could divine the child's sex as well," Xalan whispered to me, impressed. I too wondered a little. Cayds, male and female, regard sex with both distrustful restraint yet unwilling fascination, as I might approach a poisonous yet beautiful plant. So perhaps their intentness lent them an insight we Shan, with our plain common sense, did not possess.

The low door creaked as Silverhand pushed it open. "Come around," she called softly. "Rodis and the wagon are in the lane."

The wagon was the usual sort, two high wheels supporting a box and a hay-rack. It was almost full of hay, and Rodis sat on the plank seat in front. Carefully, I helped Melayne into the back, while Xalan lifted up our packs. "This is Hoob," Silverhand introduced, "the owner of the wagon and these lands."

"We've met," I said, smiling.

The moonlight lit the old man's gap-toothed grin. It seemed incredible, after war and siege and sack, that Hoob was unchanged, lean and cheerily generous. "Dear, dear, how terribly brave of you, young sir, to escape the Cayds!" he congratulated me in a reedy whisper.

This living reminder of all we had lost brought a lump to my throat. "It is you who are brave, Hoob," I said with difficulty. "How you dare to defy them, loaning us an ox and wagon, after all they've done—"

"They're donkeys, two of them, young sir," he corrected. "The Cayds stole my oxen."

"So they are." The sleepy donkeys were quite dwarfed by the high wagon. Between the Cayds and myself Hoob would be a poor man. One cannot work land without beasts. "I have no money with which to recompense your generosity," I began.

The partially toothed grin vanished, and Hoob drew himself up. "In Your Majesty's service," he said proudly. "If in later times my name is once mentioned with yours in the plaiv I shall be satisfied." Then he grinned again. "Just send the beasts back, if you can."

After this gracious statement it would have been an affront for me to insist. So we set off. Silverhand, muffled in her cloak and hood, drove. Xalan and Rodis shared the wooden seat with her. Melayne and

I, who were more recognizable, burrowed into the sweet crackling hay behind. The fat donkeys pulled willingly but very slowly, and the wooden wheels creaked and jounced up the unpaved lane. When we came to a more traveled way Silverhand turned north; it would join up with the major road that runs from the smaller City gate along the northern shore of the strait.

"Sleep, Melayne," I urged, "if you're warm enough."

She yawned and lay back. Then she squirmed. "There's something hard here," she complained.

I reached behind her, deep into the hay, and dragged the object forth. It was a round covered basket. Inside was a knife, some cold roast pigeon cut up, barley rolls stuffed with nuts, sausage and sliced lotus root, pickled greens wrapped in leaf-bundles, and a bottle of brandy.

"How thoughtful" Xalan exclaimed. "I'm terribly hungry."

"Me too," Melayne said, passing him a roll.

"He didn't have to do that," I said, touched. "Some-day I must recompense this gift."

Silverhand bit into a pigeon-wing and said, "The blade should earn him the most gratitude. You keep it, Liras." It was not a kitchen-knife, but some memento of former wars, with a long leaf-shaped blade and a blue and white enameled hilt. But no one had honed it for years. I borrowed Silverhand's whetstone and ground it bright and sharp.

By the time the food was eaten—I stowed away the brandy for emergencies—we could see past the rocky City scarp eastward to the sea. A pale yellow glow on the horizon showed morning was near. The moist cold air drank up the new light. It seemed hours before the Sun actually rose. Quietly Rodis invoked the One: "Bless our endeavor, Fire of Life, and keep us under your eye today."

"Be it so," echoed Silverhand and Xalan. Melayne was asleep on my shoulder, and I pretended to sleep too. We were quits, the god and I. From now on I

intended to stay safe above in reality, where he could
not reach. A tug on that one underlying thread
would draw the entire tangle down on me in an
enmeshing mass. It was all linked, the deity and his
mythic realm and the Crown.

The main road was still empty and untraveled.
The hooves and wheels crunched cheerfully over
oyster-shell paving. "It would be sensible," Silverhand
said, "to find a place to spend the day. The road is
hilly. Even with rest and feed the donkeys will take
more than one day to get to Cliffhole."

"Your monastery isn't far," I said. Then I could
have bitten my tongue.

"That's too obvious a place to look for trouble-
makers," Xalan said quickly. "There's a small inn just
before the turnoff that shouldn't be too busy anymore."

Silverhand's back was stiff under her cloak, but
her voice betrayed nothing. "The fewer who know of
our route the better. We must find a lonely spot in
which to camp."

There was no lack of them. As the road swung
east, following the shore, houses and villages became
fewer. To our right the drop to the water grew
steeper. The cold waves boiled over rocky teeth and
died, hissing, on a narrow pebbly beach. The land to
the left was forested and full of cliffs and streams.

The problem was finding a place to hide the wagon.
At last Silverhand chose a ravine from which a sparkling creek flowed over a wide stony bed to tumble
over the cliff into the sea. With a great deal of
shouting, tugging bridles, and slapping with reins we
persuaded the donkeys to drag the wagon off the
road and up the creek bed. Melayne had to take the
reins while the rest of us helped push it uphill. The
water was no more than knee-deep but its cold made
us gasp. The wagon stuck fast in a pool just below
another narrow waterfall, high above the road. "We
can leave it here," Silverhand panted. "The wheels

are high enough to keep the hay out of the wet, and the water won't freeze."

"That's what you think," Xalan groaned. "My very knees are blue with cold, and I think my toes have fallen off inside my boots."

I carried Melayne to shore, feeling carefully at every step lest I stumble and drop her. Xalan splashed up with our bags, while Silverhand and Rodis unhitched the donkeys and led them after. "They'll have to eat hay," Silverhand worried. "If this takes too many days you won't have any left to hide in."

We wrung out our clothes and shook out our boots. Tall beeches and nettle trees arched above our hiding place, the bare boughs nearly touching over the chattering waterfall. Lichened boulders poked up through the deep drifts of leaves and prickly beechnut husks. We set an order for watches, rolled ourselves in our cloaks, and slept.

By midafternoon we were too cold and hungry to sleep any more. "Up here, at this time of day, a fire shouldn't be too noticeable," Silverhand decided. "Start one, and I'll find something to eat." She vanished almost soundlessly into the forest.

Xalan and I looked at each other. "You're a magus," I said. "How *does* one make fire?"

He blinked. "I'm a geomant, not a pirolurge. What do you ordinarily do?"

"I call a servant."

"So do I."

"You two!" Rodis exclaimed in disgust. "The milk's not dry on your lips!" She scuffed a clearing in the leaves and took some flints from her midwife's bag. I filched some wisps of hay from the donkeys, and she taught us how to kindle a merry little flame. We built it up with fallen branches and twigs. The warmth relaxed our stiff limbs, and the smell of woodsmoke made me think of bacon. By the time Silverhand returned we were all ravenous.

"What's for dinner?" I hailed her.

"Not so loud," she cautioned. "Rabbit." She held

up a coney which would have made a fine meal for one. Skinned, cooked and divided among five it was hardly a snack. "Hunting takes time," Silverhand pointed out, so we made the best of it with cheese and bread from the pack.

The donkeys were sullenly unwishful to wade out into the icy stream again. It was not very pleasant for us either; even after a full day of Sun the water still flowed numbingly cold. Again Melayne was the only one who could ride. Everyone else had to help ease the wagon down over the rocks. By the time we reached the main road I was too cold to sit still. "We'll walk for a while," I told Silverhand.

"There's certainly no danger the beasts will run too fast for you," she said, slapping the reins on their wet rumps. So Xalan and I trudged ahead and to one side, on the narrow grassy verge where the white lime-powder raised by the wheels would not stick to our wet clothes. A strong playful wind quickly dried our cloaks; though it felt chilly on our wet limbs I knew it was not all that cold. The brief Viridese winter was nearly over. The last of the day's sunlight was already warm on our damp backs.

"How did you like being a dishwasher?" I asked Xalan.

"It's hard work," said he. For a while we plodded on in silence. Then he said, "I was glad to have it, to keep me busy. Grand-uncle is dead."

"Ah, no!" I put out a sympathetic hand, but he averted his gaze, concentrating instead on plucking leaves from the brush we passed. "Did the Cayds put him to the sword, as he foretold?"

"No," Xalan said. "No, they remembered him from Ieor, and treated him with respect. But I suppose the stress, and the hardships of the siege, wore him out. He was found dead in his bed the morning after."

"I am sorry," I said. "He was the wisest and most loyal of magi; we shan't see his like again."

Xalan smiled faintly. "He's irreplaceable. I hope that means I don't have to be Master Magus."

"He named you his successor," I reminded him. A terrible dread was rising in my chest. "You don't think you ought to go back, and take up the office he left you?"

But Xalan is adept at talking his way out of trouble. "The Cayds have hardly settled in their rule yet," he pointed out. "Suppose they decide to start eradicating magery next week? And there's also the question of who's really Shan King. If King Mor isn't, then he doesn't rate a Master Magus. And if you can be Shan King in exile, surely I can be an exiled Master of Magery."

"That doesn't sound unreasonable," I conceded. The truth was I did not want to lose his company.

The road wound back and forth, following the cliff. There were few other travelers. The rocky northern lands support only vineyards. The trees in the hills give livelihood to woodcutters and charcoal-burners, while the marshy islands and shore-country produce only shellfish, and sea-grass and reeds to weave into hats and baskets. Piracy is rooted deep in the Cliffhole district. My great-grandfather had put paid at least to the more blatantly organized manifestations. Nowadays the inhabitants had nominal trades, and studiously referred to their sideline as "salvage work."

Near nightfall the road curved around a small headland. The donkeys lagged on the uphill pull, so Xalan and I were first to see the checkpoint ahead— five Cayds, halting and scrutinizing all traffic. We dashed back to warn Silverhand.

She squinted up at the gathering purple twilight. "Do you think they saw you?" she asked.

"Probably," I admitted. "The sunset was behind us."

"Then there's nothing for it but to brazen it out," she said. "You've still got that bruise. It's not likely they'll recognize your face."

I helped tuck Melayne well under the hay—no Cayd could fail to recognize her. Rodis also hid there. "I'm no fighter," she said, "and a midwife will start unfortunate associations in their minds." In her care we left Xalan's wand and mirror, and our weapons. I belted the gray linen robe over all my clothes. It came down past my knees, and the green boots underneath looked innocent enough.

"We mustn't arouse suspicion by delaying too long," Silverhand said as she clucked to the beasts. Xalan and I climbed into the wagon, and sat dangling our legs over the back.

"Look as ignorant as you can," Xalan whispered, scrubbing at his hair to make it dusty. I pulled the straw hat low over my forehead.

It seemed to take the wagon hours to rumble down the hill. My neck crawled with nerves as I stared resolutely back at the curving road. The hill was black against a yellow sunset. Fortresses of puffy cloud sailed high in the sky, their bottoms tinted orange by the light slanting past them. The hooves scraped, and the wheels crunched in rhythm with my pounding heart.

"All right," a deep voice boomed in atrocious Viridese. "Stop!"

We halted. The road here dipped in a bridge over a cleft that let another creek run down to the sea. Deepening her voice Silverhand complained, "Great Lord, we are very late! The beasts are weary, the sky grows dark, and we have yet a long way to go to reach our grandfather's steading."

"What do they say?" another Cayd asked in his own tongue.

"Limaot alone knows, or cares either! Here, you, out of the wagon." But Silverhand pretended not to understand, and he had to repeat in his vile accent, "Out!"

The wagon creaked as Silverhand climbed down. The bored Cayd who came around to the back could not even say so much; at his curt gesture Xalan and I slid obediently off the tailboard to stand with Silverhand against the hill. The foreigners towered over us, muttering in Caydish. "Right, you saw him, Ose." "He's tall, you said, these three are pretty runty." "They're all runty; I said he was tall for a Shan."

Abruptly a big hand knocked my hat off. I grinned feebly, not needing to pretend to look scared, as Ose stared doubtfully down into my face. He was tremendously tall, with long light-brown hair tied back with string and a matching light-brown beard with bread crumbs in it. For the first time in my life I was glad to be dirty. My eye and face were still a little swollen and discolored. "Curse the Warlord, this is a fool's errand," he grumbled in Caydish, and moved on to Xalan. As I bent to pick up my hat I glimpsed Xalan, his best wide-eyed innocent expression plastered over his face.

"Maybe there's something in the wagon," one of the Cayds said hopefully. "Aha, here's a bottle!" They took the flask of brandy from the seat and passed it around before Ose continued his inspection. Whether the liquor sharpened his wit, or whether the westering light brought out some quality in her face, Ose stooped to look more closely at Silverhand.

"That isn't the Witch-King," the youngest Cayd quavered. "The five of us wouldn't be much good against a witch."

"No, he's a she!" Ose announced. "It's a woman!"

We froze, not daring to reveal our comprehension. "I don't believe it," someone said.

"Look, I'll show you!" Before anyone could interrupt he grabbed the slack of Silverhand's coarse tunic. The linen tore down the front. But even as Ose began, "See, breasts!" a hard grasp closed round his wrist. Silverhand slammed one foot into his belly and as he sagged, vaulted over, using Ose's own weight to throw him back. He hit the stones edging the verge, staggered, and fell over. A choked cry was cut off sharply, as he smashed into the rocky sea below.

"They're mad! They've killed Ose!" the youngest exclaimed.

"No! It's the Witch-King!"

I darted to the wagon and fumbled in the hay for our weapons. As the Cayds reached to grab me Silverhand leaped on one. The killing light in her eye was terrible to see. I threw Xalan his wand, and tugged the stabber out of its sheath.

A dull crack came as Silverhand broke a Cayd's neck. With my back to the wagon I fenced clumsily with another. The unfamiliar blade slipped harmlessly off his leather armor when I cut; it was as much as I could do to dodge his axe. The lime dust rose and flung itself about as Xalan geomantically blinded another.

Leaving my assailant to Xalan I ducked underneath the high wagon box and skittered to the other side where Caydish boots were scuffling with Silverhand. This warrior had a javelin, and was quick enough to keep her at a distance. I grabbed a boot as it passed, and when the Cayd stumbled threw my sword to Silverhand. She pounced like a cat on a mouse, the blade already poised in her hand.

I crawled back out from under the wagon and took up Hoob's knife just in time to help Xalan. The narrow road was too easy to get bearings on, and the Cayd he had tried to blind trapped him against the cliff. I slashed with the knife between two plates of his back armor. But it pinched fast between them as the Cayd raised his axe. He swung around with a yell, wrenching the handle from my hand. A slice of woven straw hat went flying as the blade whistled right over my head and, losing my footing, I sat down hard. The return-stroke would slice my neck just as neatly.

But to my astonishment the Cayd slowly knelt down in the dust before me. Then he fell back against Xalan, and I saw the needle-like knife sticking out of his eye.

"Viris, what happened?" Xalan asked in awe. "Was it you?"

"No, it was Melayne." I scrambled to my feet and tugged the blade free. Melayne was standing in the wagon, her second knife ready between her fingers. For want of their supporting rods her braids had tumbled down around her neck and shoulders. Through all this fuss the donkeys stood, nearly asleep. "You were supposed to stay hidden," I remarked.

She scowled down at the horrid drip from the narrow blade I held. "Wipe it off for me, dear," she said. "I don't want to get our hay dirty." So I wiped it on the grass and handed it up to her.

"Nice work," Silverhand told Melayne. She had had no difficulty with the last Cayd. Now she knotted her torn blouse together with trembling fingers.

"Silverhand, are you all right?" I asked sharply.

She leaned on the tail-board as if all her strength were gone. Rodis hugged her bowed shoulders and Melayne glared at us. "Where's that brandy?" she demanded.

I reclaimed the stoneware flask from one of the fallen. For a moment the three women seemed united against us, the enemy. But then Silverhand breathed deeply and gave us a watery smile. "The whole experience was destructive," she confessed. "But I recover a little more, with every Cayd I kill. And speaking of which, one never knows when Caydish clothes might not be handy. We must strip the bodies."

"What if someone sees us?" I asked.

"It's nearly dark," she said, "and they'll just assume we're robbers."

"Well, we are," Xalan said gloomily. It was grisly work, made bearable only by the fact that there was little blood. Silverhand was a tidy killer. We tugged off their distinctive armor and outer garments, but the woolen shirts and breeches underneath smelt so odd even Silverhand agreed they were superfluous for our purposes. "Don't they wash?" Xalan asked.

'In the spring," Melayne replied from the wagon.

As each corpse was stripped she and Rodis tied the armor and clothing into bundles, and hid them in the hay. The bodies we threw, one by one, off the cliff into the sea. By the time this was done Silverhand was completely herself once more.

In a thicket nearby we found the Cayds' gear— valuables like coin or food, jumbled together in bags with eye-catching junk such as enameled Thumb-print tiles. "They didn't even steal a complete set, the dolts," Xalan complained.

We took everything, tidying the spot as best we could to confuse our enemies. Then we toasted our triumph in our recovered brandy.

"No hunting tonight," Silverhand rejoiced. "And if we drive all night, we'll get to Cliffhole tomorrow." Rodis slapped the donkeys with the reins, as the wagon lurched into motion again. Their slowness no longer mattered, since in the dark no pursuer could speed along the narrow winding road. We snuggled into the warm hay and made a fine late supper of the Cayds' provender.

Throughout the night we took turns at the reins, halting every now and then to feed and water the donkeys. The stars, unrivaled by moon or lamplight, glowed big as pearls and unnumbered as oysters in the sea. As it grew colder, we were glad of the Cayds' cloaks. The sea played tirelessly between the rocks on our right, while on the left twig and bough whis-pered together in the deep-riven valleys.

Warm and full-fed, with Melayne's sleeping head heavy against my shoulder. I drifted in and out of slumber on a tide of contentment. Though danger and grief lurked both before and behind, it seemed unimportant now. I had never seriously disbelieved in the world's goodness, I realized. The trust was worked into the foundation of my thinking, and I fell easily back into the old way. Only the inarticulate resentment remained, the residue from the holo-caust that had consumed my life: the unforgiving feeling that the deity had let us down once.

CHAPTER 13:

Cliffhole

The old moon rose late. In its light the ruins of the beacon-tower stuck up toothlike far ahead at the end of our road. The land ended in a lofty headland high above the waves. Innumerable sea-caverns give the district its name, undermining the rock so that the beacon was no longer safe. No one lived on top anymore, fighting wind and weather. The mazes below supply house and harbor, road and roof, to their inhabitants. To us, too—if they would take us in.

Though the ruin looked close the road dipped and wound about up to the final point. The weary donkeys were clumsy and slow. We reached it just at dawn. The new sun lit enamel-bright sea in every direction around us save one, the way we had come by. The rocky edges were seamed and fissured, ready to crumble back into the sea. A stiff wind sang past our ears and brought a wild smell of the ocean. Cliff-nesting terns, pure white with long pointed black tails that looked as if they had been dipped in ink, whistled to each other below. The lonely beauty of the spot overawed us. In a low voice I asked, "How do we inform the rebels we're here?"

"Word in the City has it there's a gong, somewhere in the ruin," Silverhand said. "The partisans have two leaders—a mighty fighter, who used to head the local pirates, and someone else, who stays always in the caves but is said to be unequaled in cunning and resource. The sound of the gong will bring somebody up to inspect us."

Glad to stretch our legs, we all climbed out of the

wagon. The ancient gray stones of the tower were polished by the wind. Some walls still reared proudly up, but the rest were only tumbled stones, embedded in the stunted yellow grass. There was no hope of building a fire. Everything even remotely useful had long been "salvaged," particularly the long timbers that had once supported the roofs. Shivering in the keen wind, we quartered the site.

Xalan found the gong, a disc of greenish copper suspended over what appeared to be a disused well. "It's not a well, but a chimney, a fissure down into the caves," Silverhand said. "They'll hear us, below." And she rapped the gong with the hilt of her sword.

Its piercing note rang in our back teeth, but nothing happened. "Let's go back and wait in the wagon," Melayne said. "I'm cold. Will your friends feed us breakfast?"

"I hope so," I said. For the first time I wondered if a pirate-lord would look kindly on a fugitive descendant of my great-grandfather. We crawled under the hay, out of the wind, and waited.

Rodis pinched me, and with a start I realized I must have fallen asleep. A tall Viridese in black leggings and tunic was climbing up from a seam in the southern cliff. With him came others, all armed with knives and swords. Only their captain swaggered up without, as if height and weight alone made him indomitable. I had never seen anyone less like a pirate; he looked more like a farm-hand, tall as I but much more thick-built, with a broad, cheery face like a ham. "I can see you're Shan," he greeted us. "We, of course. are resistors of the Caydish invasion. My name is Pol, my profession piracy and rebellion. Who are you?"

Silverhand jumped down from the wagon. "I am Silverhand, once commander of the Sisters of Mir-Hel."

His confident smile vanished, replaced by a look of respect. "We can certainly use you, Commander," he said politely. "No other Sisters have arrived here;

let's hope they've retreated to the western forests, like in the Tsorish war."

"They didn't," she said. "Call me Silverhand."

An uncomfortable pause followed this statement. Then Xalan introduced himself, adding, "I don't look it at the moment, but I'm a magus."

Elsewhere this might have gone down without comment. But Pol squinted doubtfully and asked, "Can you prove it?"

Xalan slid his wand out from under the hay. A gesture, and the gravelly soil crept up between the sparse roots of the grasses at his feet. Like an invasion of ants the bits of dirt began to crawl up Pol's unpolished shoe. "Enough!" he said, standing first on one foot and then the other. "We don't have but one magus. He's an herognomer, and always useful. I suppose you had to change your clothes to escape the Cayds? Well, he can probably lend you a suit of red."

The sharp black eyes swiveled to me. "You're a quiet one. That's good, because I'm talkative, and need quiet people to talk to. What's your name?"

I sat on the tailboard and swung my legs. "My name is Liras-ven Tsormelezok," I said slowly. "I am the Shan King."

Not an outlaw moved. Pol's mouth opened, but no sound came out. Like a small poisoned dart came the thought that a week ago my word had been law. Now I was reduced to begging for help, pleading my identity before bandits. "You don't believe me," I said, hiding my hurt.

"Well, no, I don't," Pol admitted. "If you're him, where's your Crystal Crown?"

Inwardly I winced. That was where the shoe pinched. "I can vouch for him." Silverhand put in.

"And I." Xalan came back to the wagon and stood beside me.

"The Cayds have the Crown," I said bravely. "But you'll admit only the Shan King would have *chun-hei* enough to come to you hoping for help in rescuing it from them."

Pol grinned. "We'll take you down to the caves," he said, "and sort this out. The Crown isn't the only touchstone of truth in Averidan."

"Well, I do have one more proof," I said. "You remember the Shan King's foreign wife? Here she is." And Melayne poked her bright head up over the hay-rack.

They gaped. Then the swords came out. "She's Caydish," Pol thundered. "We can't possibly reveal our secrets to a Cayd. Suppose she tells her family?"

"Then I'm not going," I said flatly.

"Oh, don't be such dolts," Melayne said in her perfect Viridese. She shook the hay out of her skirts and, with my help, stepped down. Her enormous bulk gave her the dignity of a ship in full sail. "I killed a Cayd, just last night. You think I ride in hay-wains, in the winter, so near my time, for amusement?"

"It's almost spring." Pol objected feebly with the proverb, "And kinship ties outlast bronzen bands."

"In Cayd," Melayne retorted, "the proverb calls sons a shield in his father's hand, but daughters a dagger in his foes'." The illogic, citing a Caydish saying in support of her loyalty to me, fuddled Pol even further. Conscientiously I kept my expression grave, but relaxed to enjoy Melayne's skill.

"She's in no condition to cause trouble," Rodis pointed out. "I'm a herbal and a midwife, by the way. To shut out a woman in this condition would be inhumane. And if you can truly prove Liras' rank the question will be moot."

"Well, we do have someone below who knew the Shan King in the City," Pol allowed. "And Silverhand's word should be good."

We had to leave the wagon in the charge of Pol's men. I gave them careful instructions on how to find Hoob's farm again, and let it go. Taking up our baggage we followed Pol. A rope ladder was fastened to bronze spikes at the top of the crevice. "Melayne can't climb far on this," I said.

"It's a short one," Pol assured us. "Once we're inside, there are stairs." And he climbed down nimble as a squirrel. The upper part of the rock slot opened on the seaward side, so that the Sun showed him clearly. But like a flea descending into a partly fastened shirt, he vanished into the shadowy depths. "You go first," Silverhand suggested, "in case Melayne has trouble with her footing. We'll follow."

Very carefully I helped her down the ladder. The sheltered rock held the Sun's warmth; then in the shadow the cool clammy smell of sea-wet rock enfolded us. As Pol had promised, it was a short descent, not more than twenty feet or so. At the bottom was a narrow stone platform. The light trickling down from above showed the first of a flight of wooden steps down. When we were all ready Pol took up a waiting lamp and led the way down.

The stair was narrow and rickety, half-rotted from the constant moisture. Since wood is hard to come by hereabouts, broken treads were repaired with chunks of log or bits of driftwood, slick with green mildew. Crude railings of slippery rope segments were pinned at intervals to the walls, first on one side and then the other, so that our hands had to grope unpleasantly along the dripping walls. "I'm getting tired," Melayne said. "These steps make my back ache."

"You can't stop now." Pol's voice echoed creepily up from below. "The stair runs from cliff-top to sea level. You can hear the waves." And as we descended the sound became clearer—the endless surge and ebb of water beating in the hidden heart of the hill.

Our descent ended in a long straight climb down to a silty strip of rock. Pol blew out the lamp, and in the sudden dark we could see the waves rushing in from the sunlit world outside through a high narrow cleft in the rock into the cave. A few dinghies and small craft were drawn up on the shingle below.

Behind, the cave ran away into several low archways. Through one a single rushlight winked at us.

As we walked up the natural rock path Melayne leaned heavily on my arm. "Liras, I don't feel well," she said.

"Oh, Viris." I glanced wildly back at Rodis, who nodded reassuringly at me.

"At least two days, I told you," she said.

"Not far now," Pol said encouragingly.

And indeed, through the smooth-worn arch was a wide twisting corridor carved by the sea. The sea-scoured unevennesses of the floor had been made good with sand. Opening to right and left were rock rooms of every size, from closets to halls. Some were plainly Ennelith's sole work, while others had been chipped or partitioned to more convenient dimensions. They bustled with people, like any ordinary village. Many chambers in this lower section were fitted out as shops, while others were used as homes. Xalan was quickly hailed and swept away by the local herognomer, who noticed his wand and mirror. "I'll catch up with you," he called back to us.

Melayne's step was unsteady. Her eyelashes cast a fragile shadow against the delicate curve of her cheek. Distractedly I said, "She can't go on."

"She doesn't have to," said Pol. "Here we are. We have rather a large Sodality here; Ennelith is powerful in these parts."

He pushed open a door on the right. Inside was a large suite hung in blue. Blue-robed women hurried up to support Melayne, assessing her condition with sharp, concerned eyes. "I'm the local Mistress of Ennelith's Sodality," a short plump one introduced herself. "And you must be the anxious father, I can tell by your face. Leave her to us."

"Leave her?" I clutched at Rodis. "You'll stay, won't you? She doesn't know anyone here, she'll be frightened without a familiar face."

"I'll stay," Rodis promised. "Don't be silly."

Silverhand took my elbow and drew me toward

the door, where Pol waited discreetly. "The Sodality manages all women's business," she soothed. "And how many healthy babes has Rodis eased into the world?"

My mouth no longer worked very well. "When will it be?"

She smiled. "You're asking me?"

Pol confided, "I've sired three, and my wife's gotten so deft, the babe slides out like a duck into water."

"The thing to do is keep busy," Silverhand interrupted, before Pol's clinical details could harrow me further. "Let's go and clear up this business of your identity. We can hardly expect Cliffhole to entertain an impostor."

I could not care much about it at all. Left to my own devices I would have crouched at the Sodality's door and listened. But Silverhand and Pol hauled me up the corridor. "Tell us about Cliffhole," Silverhand prompted him.

"Well, we've always used the caves for storage and what not," Pol began. "They make nice living quarters too, once you get up above water level. But since the Cayds came we've put our minds to organizing them. A steady water supply, a system of getting food—the idea is to become a center of resistance, a thorn in the Cayds' bottoms."

"I approve," Silverhand said.

In spite of myself I was becoming interested. "But what will harassment accomplish?" I asked. "Are you expecting the Cayds to give up and go home, or what?"

"We could always try to restore you to the throne," Silverhand said. "If we succeed in recovering the Crystal Crown we'll have both the right and a good chance to do it."

"The rule goes with the Crown," Pol agreed. He looked sideways at me. "When we prove your claim, I'll ask you how you ever let it slip out of your hands."

"It's complicated," I said gloomily. When the Master Magus had talked about passing on the Crown he had sounded so lucid. But he was dead, and now the argument was not only proven wrong, but had a rather craven air. Surely the proper thing to do was fight to regain my rule.

All this time we were walking deeper and higher into the cliff. This route must run more or less north, parallel to the ocean; every now and then on our right we glimpsed sunny windows and cracks. Once, where an entire chamber had crumbled away, a wide gap showed us curling waves and sharp rock below. Every hole and opening was fitted with wicker or canvas shutters. "So that ships at sea don't spot our lights at night," Pol said, grinning. I knew a favorite pirate trick was to lure ships to disaster on the treacherous shifting shoals by signaling with lamps.

The corridor was less busy here, plainly rising to its end. The rocky ceiling swung low, revealing its cracks and seams. The only rooms now were on the right, and those scarce. Around a corner the corridor ended in a final door. Pol tapped on it and, giving me another sidewise glance, went in.

Inside, the wide low chamber was full of light. Hairy yellow beards of sea-oats fringed the view out the window, showing that the rock above was giving way to earth. We were very near the top of the cliff, which had itself become less craggy. The room was simply furnished with a floor-cloth, some chairs, and a desk where a black-cloaked figure bent over a scroll.

"Here's some new stuff, my lady," Pol called. "Including one who says he's the Shan King."

The chair scraped on canvas over rock as the sitter rose and turned. "Liras-ven?"

I could not believe my eyes. "Mother?" I wanted to say, but a queer sinking sensation in the back of my skull made me dizzy and, to my own mortification, I fainted.

I came to myself with the pleasant sound of argu-

ment in my ears. "You haven't been feeding him,"
Mother accused, "and then to pop this kind of
surprise on him!"

"*I've* been feeding him right along," Silverhand
said defensively. "The Cayds starved him a few days.
And of course he's been wounded. But the surprise
is entirely Pol's management."

"Now how could I have known, my lady?" said Pol.
"He doesn't look like any Shan King, and he didn't
have the Crystal Crown, did he? Surely you realize I
didn't intend any disrespect."

I opened my eyes and sat up. "Mother?" But how
changed she was, all in black. Gray streaks I did not
remember were in her black hair. Her skin, bare of
paint for the first time in my memory, looked trans-
lucent. When I hugged her I was shocked at the
fragility of the bones under the thin flesh. "Mother,"
I wept, "however did you come here, of all places?"

"With the Sodality. Didn't you receive my messen-
gers?"

"No—didn't you hear about the siege?"

"Ah. I had indeed." She lowered herself stiffly
into her chair again, and added, "From your presence, and Silverhand's, I should judge the City has
fallen."

I counted on my fingers. "Yes, six days ago."

"Seven," Silverhand corrected. "You lost a day in
the dungeons."

"Your Majesty's come out of the dungeons?" Pol's
voice was stiff with respect.

"And that wound! Send someone for a bonesetter,
Pol," Mother said. "From the look of the bandage no
one has examined that hand in days."

"We traveled rough," I excused myself. I had discarded the sling to better descend the cliff.

While the bonesetter examined my hand Mother
and I caught up on each other's tidings. She listened,
outwardly unmoved, as in no particular order I told
of the siege, Siril's brief widowhood, our escape,
Melayne, and Yibor's melancholy end. But when I

mentioned Zofal's disappearance she said, "He is dead. I feel it."

"No body was ever found," Silverhand put in gently.

"We mourned you as dead too," I said. I did not myself believe it, having never known a world without Zofal.

"He was my first-born, and he is gone." Suddenly her lean old face became hard as flint. "What shall we do about it?"

There comes a time when a decision, never consciously considered, leaps forward into prominence out of the crowd of thoughts that had hidden it. The Master Magus had laid it upon me to surrender the Crown and die. I had done neither, but had let circumstance—in the persons of Silverhand and Melayne—sweep along. The tide of their will was so powerful I hardly needed to lift a finger. Now I decided to swim forward with the flood that had carried me so far. "We must get the Crown back," I said. "When I have it I have the right to rule. Besides, they'll destroy it else."

"Then we must gather news," Mother said. "They may already have done so. Pol and his men can fight. And I have helped them prepare Cliffhole better. But neither pirates nor old women are adept at learning secrets."

"I can help with that," Silverhand said. "As of our departure the Crystal Crown had not yet been smashed. Leave it to me, and the magi, to learn more."

After a midday meal we discussed ways and means. Spying was difficult when the foreigners spoke in their own tongue. Only Silverhand and of course Melayne were fluent in Caydish, although I could get by. We resolved to send Silverhand back to the City to stretch her ears. Any news she would write and leave in an agreed place and time, where Xalan could descry it. Meanwhile, he and the herognomer would keep their mirrors, in shifts, on Mor and Musenor, in case they revealed anything. The Cayds had not, as I had hoped, been careless around the mirrors and pools which made scrying easy. "That rat Bochas warned them," Silverhand said. So Pol's lone magus had not been able to learn much. But two magi would have enough power between them to override such difficulties.

Silverhand stretched, and yawned hugely. "I'll sleep a few hours," she announced, "and then start back. Without a wagon to slow me down I'll be in the City by tomorrow morning."

Pol and I were round-eyed at this exhibition of stamina, but Mother only nodded. "Keep your eye out in town for likely young maidens," she added. "It isn't too early to start rebuilding your Order."

"That's over," Silverhand said quietly. On the arms of her chair her knuckles showed white under their tan. "A Sister must be virgin."

"If you are not a Sister, then what are you?" Mother retorted vigorously. And it is true, that everyone in Averidan has a rank and position. "We certainly need more than one of you, whatever you choose to call yourself. If your Sisters are all slain then shall you be the last?"

I noted with fascination that Silverhand actually seemed shaken. It was unheard of. "You don't know what you ask," she said bitterly. "If it had been you—"

"I wouldn't give the Cayds the satisfaction of destroying my spirit as well," Mother finished for her. "Virginity is a state of mind as well as body."

Stung, Silverhand rose. "I'll think about it," she said, and banged the door.

For a moment no one spoke. Then I said, "I see how you can be useful to Pol. I'm Shan King, but I can't imagine saying that to her. Though it was necessary."

"Exactly," Mother said with satisfaction. "Help me up, Liras. My joints are stiffening since I've moved to the seashore. I want to call on the Sodality and inquire about my daughter-in-law. Will it be a grand-son or granddaughter, do you think?"

"Melayne!" I had forgotten all about her. Leaving Pol to help Mother down the corridor, I ran ahead. The Sodality's door was open, as usual. When I burst in nothing was changed—the blue hangings, the calm, blue-clad women. But Melayne was not in sight. "How is she?" I demanded.

An acolyte blocked my way as I made for the inner rooms. "As well as can be expected," she said firmly.

I dared not command her to stand aside. Ennelith is a very powerful goddess and, like her ocean do-main, rather tempery. An invasion of the private precincts would simply offend her, and I had es-tranged deities enough this season. It was infuriating to watch Mother hobble slowly across the room and be admitted.

I sat down to wait, fuming with frustration, and after some hesitation Pol sat down beside me on the bench. In Averidan there is no such thing as a for-mer King of the Shan. On the other hand, a Shan King without a Crown is also unthinkable, and no protocol exists to converse with one. There is hardly ever call for court manners in Cliffhole, and I could see Pol was at a loss. "How's the hand?" he asked at last.

I flexed it. The bonesetter had decided to let the wound breathe. A hard brown scab clung to my palm, and ran around the outside to the back. The thumb and two fingers worked; my fourth and lit-tlest finger would not obey me. The sinews had probably been cut. "It doesn't hurt much, anymore," I said.

"And your sword arm is still whole," he said. "A shield can be managed with three fingers."

I could not resist picking at the scab a little, and it did not bleed. "I'll live," I decided.

Mother reappeared, saying, "Don't do that, Liras, it'll scar. The birth will take awhile yet; you'll only get nervous, loitering about here. Pol will find you a suite suitable to your rank. You must rest, after your journey." Her masterful tone took me back to my youth. I allowed her to install me in relatively grand chambers near her own, with a low wide bed placed to look out of the low wide windows. Purple twilight lay over the restless ocean, and gulls patrolled the incoming tide. The sight of the bed reminded me how long the day had been. Sleep overtook me before I could ask when supper would be.

The early night meant I woke early next day. Word of my arrival had spread, and I found a set of proper pirate clothes laid out to replace my Caydish-and-peasant garb. The fashion in Cliffhole inclines to sober colors, suitable for night work. I put on the thick dark-blue trousers and the short quilted tunic, and hurried back down the corridors to the Sodality. There I found no tidings, for either good or ill. But Xalan was there. "I knew where you'd come," he greeted me. "I have strict orders from Lady Zilez, to take you out. We're to eat breakfast with Pol, who will show us the lay of the land."

So after a meal Pol led us to one of the dozens of bolt-holes out of Cliffhole. This one let us into a sandy cave almost completely full of ocean. "Use this particular cave only at low tide," he warned.

Outside was a gravel beach no wider than a table, which ran between the overhanging cliff and a foam-flecked sea studded with weedy rocks. Pol led us north, into the wind. Xalan's borrowed red robes snapped against his calves ahead of me, and my boots slipped over the coarse gravel and slick seaweed.

"Not so fast," I panted. "Where are we going?"

"Up the coast a bit," said Pol, "to the marsh inlets. Your mother has an idea about scouting good ambush spots."

"This whole district seems perfect for it," I replied. It was true. A dozen navies could wreck each other on the shoals and gray rocks in the sea. Ahead, the shore curved so that we could see a long way.

The fissured cliffs sank away into a lowland thickly grown with reeds and salt-marsh grasses. At the lowest point a finger of sea extended inland. Beyond, the shore rose up into another crumbly bluff. Averidan undulated in and out of the sea like a joyous dolphin. Two armies could chase their tails here forever.

When the cliff on our left was low enough Pol guided us up a crack, to see the view inland. It was a wild and desolate sight. The yellow marsh grasses spread deep inland along many narrow estuaries, while the stony ridges were furred in dark green scrub pine. From the look of it a giant could have pressed open handprints in a neat row all up the coast.

"You can see," Xalan said instructively, "that the City's harbor is of the same pattern as these little estuaries. Viris merely chose the biggest and the best to found the City in."

"Let's go back," I interrupted. "Melayne's been in labor for a full day. Something's wrong."

"Nothing's wrong," Xalan said firmly.

"That's right, and if there were you couldn't do anything about it," said Pol. "Your mother sent us out to look at ambushes, and that's what we're going to do. Otherwise, she'll take it out of our hides."

"You're conspiring against me," I complained, but followed them down into the marshes. The coastal folk are well-accustomed to obeying strong-minded women.

Pol halted at a place where the reeds and grass rustled higher than our heads on either side of an estuary. "Lady Zilez's idea is this," he explained. "That water's only about knee deep. We cut these reeds to a sharp point, like this." Chips and fiber flew under his whittling knife. "If we stick them into the muck like this—"

"A nasty surprise for someone wading across," Xalan finished for him. "How will you get the Cayds out here?"

"Oh, we'll get them to chase us. The planning is important; we have to map out all the booby-traps in advance so our own folk can keep out of them. And it would never do to rig up surprises for the oyster-men or reed-gatherers either. All the useful inlets must be let alone."

He produced a large parchment map in three colors. Xalan could sense the earth currents, and of course Pol knew the district perfectly. But I soon lost my bearings, as we splashed across mud-flats, thrust through the grasses, and labored up the bluffs. The other two cheerfully debated the relative merits of each pool and inlet, while I wondered whether Melayne was suffering very much. Lost, a little bored, and gnawed by anxiety, I looked around as Xalan and Pol tested the depth of the tenth estuary of the day.

This finger of water was brackish, being fed by a fresh-water rivulet. And far upstream some large animals of various colors were drinking from it. "What are those?" I asked, pointing.

Pol shaded his eyes. "I've seen them before, but I don't know," he said. "I'd wager a basket of scallops, though, that they're Caydish cattle of some sort. They were unheard of, until just this year."

"Done with you!" Happily I closed the bet, and then began to push upstream, squelching quietly through the reeds.

Behind me Xalan said, "Suppose it's tigers?"

"Nonsense," I said. "Don't you recognize them?" We were close enough now to see the long fringed necks reaching down to the water. "Those are the horses Zofal had released around here."

"So they are!" At that moment I startled a marsh snipe. The bird shrieked in alarm and flapped out almost from under my nose. The noise surprised me very much, and alarmed the horses. Heads tossed in alarm, eyes rolled white at us and, with a flurry of hooves that spattered us all with muddy water, they were gone.

Only one black mare hesitated, as some memory perhaps of salt or carrots lingered in her equine mind. Though I had no treat to offer I held out my empty hand, and saw with delight long colt legs wobbling behind the mother. Though it was very early in the season, the beasts were already multiplying.

Then the spell was broken. The mare whisked around and led her foal away into the grasses. "Some kind of antelope?" Pol guessed. "Are they edible?"

"Not in the slightest," I said severely. "You owe me some scallops, by the way. My brother brought these horses here for safe-keeping. You must warn everyone in Cliffhole that they are my property, and not to be hunted."

After this I insisted on returning to Cliffhole. A nasty apprehension griped in my stomach, as if I were in labor too. "It's your imagination," Xalan dismissed it.

But Pol, fatally, reminisced, "When my wife was in child-bed with her first, I had the most appalling belly-cramps. I don't see how women bear it. I was in a tavern at the time, trying to get drunk, and I fell right over onto the table, writhing like a gaffed eel."

A definite twinge in my middle made me wince. I doubled over, and mumbled, "We have to return, I feel it too."

"You and your wife," Xalan said indignantly to Pol.

When we got back Mother met us at the Sodality's suite. "This way, dear," she called, and directed me to a side room. My courage utterly failed me, but Xalan pushed me gently forward.

I tiptoed in. There was Melayne, quite flat underneath the quilt and apparently asleep. Beside her pallet was a rush cradle. A tiny pink face, no bigger than a clenched peony bud, lay swathed in linen quilts. The blood rang dizzily in my ears as I knelt. With one cautious finger I reached in to touch the crumpled-petal cheek. In tiny blind movements the miniature hands clutched, and a mouth no bigger than a comfit nuzzled my fingertip, trying to suck.

I laughed softly in delight. Melayne stirred at the sound, and I sat on the pallet to kiss her forehead. "How clever of you, dearest! It's beautiful. What is it, boy or girl?"

"A—a girl!" She pressed her face against me and wailed. Bewildered, I slid off onto the floor and held her. Alarmed by the sound, Mother called the Mistress. "I'm so ashamed," Melayne gulped.

"But she's perfectly lovely," Mother insisted, and quite rightly. Plucked from its wrappings the babe revealed itself red as an apple, with a quantity of thin black fuzz on its tiny fragile skull. Mother plopped her casually into my lap for inspection, and I froze, torn between delight and fear that she would wriggle off.

"The right number of fingers and toes and everything," the Mistress pointed out proudly. Ennelith always claims a share of the credit for every babe.

"But fathers yearn only for sons," Melayne said tearfully. "When my mother's first was female, my father had her beaten."

We all stared. A mild preference for one sex over the other is not unknown in Averidan, but violence is unthinkable. "That's terrible!" the Mistress exclaimed, genuinely shocked.

"*We* have a civilized realm, at least in these parts," Mother said. "No wonder your folk are barbarians, if the civil sex is so spurned!"

But Melayne looked only at me, staring up into my face to read my sincerity. Mother prodded me in the thigh with her toe, where Melayne could not see, and belatedly taking the hint I spoke up. "There's no change I would make at all, Melayne." I said. "She's so perfect, it's a pity to cover her in all those fancy clothes you brought."

Melayne borrowed my handkerchief and blew her nose. "Let me see her." But I did not have the nerve to pick her up—she looked so frail that my hands felt as large and clumsy as spades. Mother had to transfer my daughter to Melayne's arms.

"She's hungry," I observed.

"One moment," the Mistress said, and poured out a little wine for me. With one finger I let a drop fall onto the wee questing lips. "There, now the nipple."

"What's that for?" Melayne asked sleepily.

"It seals her to life," I said, draining the cup.

Melayne did not really understand, but comforted by the ritual of acceptance gave our child her first meal. Mother and the Mistress had other business that demanded attention, but I sat cross-legged beside the pallet, too happy to speak, and watched Melayne nurse our daughter. After so many changes, all terrible and unwelcome, this one only was balm.

CHAPTER 14:
To Regain the Crown

We named her Tarys-yan. Foreign-born Melayne had no generational syllable to reckon from, so we started at the beginning of the "count." Baby clothes were, as Melayne had foreseen, hard to come by. She dressed Tarys in the sumptuous little garments from her luggage. For a day or so I paraded proudly through Cliffhole's corridors, showing off the new Princess to everyone. In ordinary times there would be a dedication-offering at the Temple. Despite my difficulties with the One I found I did not want Tarys estranged as well. The blatant inconsistency of my feelings made me uncomfortable, but no Viridese has much difficulty holding two diametrically opposed beliefs at once. And since no offering was possible anyway I did not have to resolve it.

A great deal was happening in the City. The discovery of Melayne's complicity caused Mor to execute every Cayd who had guarded me, on the theory that the guilty should be scotched at any price. Curiously enough, they were dispatched by lapidation, rather than the beheading favored in Cayd. The occasion supplied Mor with further irritation—an unprecedented number of Shan participated in the execution. The subtle insult made Mor glare, but he had no ground for complaint. The unfortunates were crushed under so many tons of rock that when their bodies were excavated a week later, they had not dried out sufficiently, and attracted flies. No Viridese lost this further opportunity for wit and racial remarks.

Silverhand was the source of this news, but other-

223

wise sent only a terse note announcing her safe arrival. Xalan and the local herognomer scried without result for the Crystal Crown. "Either he's keeping it shut up somewhere," Xalan surmised one day in my chambers, "or they've already ground it to powder."

"If they have, and tell no one, we shall never know it," Mother said.

"No." I spoke positively. "I would know. The Crown still lives, I'm sure of it."

Xalan looked up from his mirror. "It's only an object; it can't live," he corrected, and I did not protest. I was the sole living wearer of the Crown; no one else could share my special knowledge. "It's a little early, but let me have a look at the slate."

Silverhand had rented a little attic room above a dockside tavern in the City. In its one window, every day at noon, she placed her report, written on a slate, for the magi to descry. "How odd," Xalan now reported. "There's a slate on the sill already, but Silverhand is sitting on the floor scribbling on another."

"How does she look?" Mother wanted to know.

"Same as ever. Are you ready to hear the slate?" I smoothed the wax on my tablet and poised the wooden stylus over it. Xalan read aloud slowly, and I wrote it down: "The Cayds find they cannot smash the Crystal Crown. They resolve to throw it in the sea."

"Is that true?" I ejaculated, letting my stylus fall.

"Siril Tsormelezok," Xalan continued, "told Musenor that the sea is very deep off the south shore near Ennelith-Ral. He and Mor leave this evening—that's all on this slate."

"Don't stop!" I exclaimed. "Go and scry over Silverhand's shoulder!"

"That's very rude," Xalan grumbled, but obeyed me. "She writes, 'Leave this evening with the Crown. Go and mark its fall, so that the shallows may be dredged after the Cayds leave'."

"What a thumping great lie!" Pol said with admiration. "How can Mor possibly believe that? Anyone with half an eye can see which shore is the shallow one. The shoals and long beaches on the south shore should tell the tale."

"But Mor doesn't have half an eye, not for the sea," Melayne reminded us. "None of us knows anything of the sea. Mor has no choice but to believe what he's told."

"The mystery is, why he didn't ask his tame traitor," I said. "Or anybody. Surely no one of sense would deliberately consult Siril."

"Your sister must be rising to the occasion," Mother said tartly. She had always credited Siril with far more brain than Zofal or I had done. "If they plan to travel at night they must intend secrecy and speed. Mor has realized he cannot advertise his intent to destroy the Crown. Now, suppose we waylaid them on this journey?"

"Silverhand said to mark the Crown's fall, and rescue it," I objected, "not attack them on the way."

Mother stared at me, astonished by my innocence. "If we kill them both," she explained patiently, "the Cayds will lose two leaders."

The difficulty was that in the dark the Cayds might easily slip past Pol and his men. After much argument we decided on a two-pronged rescue attempt. Pol would lead a disguised band of bravoes and attack Mor, if possible, on his way east. If they managed to waylay him and regain the Crystal Crown, all would be well. But Xalan and I would go to the southern shore, so that the Crown at least might be recovered if the Cayds happened to succeed. Pol could take another shot at Mor on his return trip.

Swiftly the plans were set in motion. Pol chose men who could plausibly fit into the suits of Caydish gear we had stolen. Transport had to be prepared for the hasty journey across the strait, and Mother pored over maps of the road between Ennelith-Ral and the City.

For my part, Pol directed me to one of the sea-caves. "Tou is considered the best smuggler alive," he informed me. "You'll like him; his epithet is 'the Lame Tiger.' "

"Why lame?" Xalan wanted to know.

"Well, his only handicap, which has cost him many a cargo—" But at that point Mother interrupted, with a list of likely ambush spots Pol would do well to keep in mind.

Leaving them to it we made our way down the caves to Tou's lair. Evidently Pol had warned him he would be needed, for he was readying his boat. Its name, the *Petrel*, was painted in light green on the dark-blue bows. Xalan and I tried not to stare. Tou was just like a pirate in plaiv—a short, ageless yet sea-gnarled person with a rolling limp, an enormous copper knife, and a leather hood stained with salt. His face was tanned by wind and wrinkled like a walnut. Though he must have known who I was he looked us over without much favor. "Going to Ennelith-Ral, are you?" he barked.

"Just off the point," I said. "We want to recover what the Cayds throw into the sea there."

The Lame Tiger spat green leaf-gum juice into the water. "Can't get you very close inshore," he grumped.

"We'll swim," I said bravely. The sea was wintry-cold. "We'll have to dive anyway for the Crown."

Tou did not condescend to express his approval, but grudgingly admitted, "I could be pushing off at sunset. Get you there by midnight."

"Good," I said. "We'll meet you here, a little before sunset then."

The question of what to bring was a nice one. Weapons, I thought, would be of little use, so Xalan left his wand. Melayne packed us a change of warm dry clothing, some food, and a little covered traveling brazier. We borrowed fishermen's clothing and hoods. I contributed a flask of strong spirit. When we met Tou at the appointed time he looked on all this dandified luggage with disgust. But he did allow, "I'd take a sip of that brandy."

"We're saving it for later," I explained, and he sniffed.

The sea-cavern's docks were of the most primitive sort, logs hammered into the bottom or rings bolted to the rock. Tou untied the *Petrel* and sat at the tiller folding a wad of leaves with one hand, while Xalan and I inexpertly pushed the boat off. We fell over each other in the wet scramble aboard; the Lame Tiger fixed us with a disdainful eye and waited silently for us to man the oars.

Slowly we pulled away from the faint lights of the caverns. The tide was still rather high, and we had to lie flat while the boat scraped through the low cave opening. The *Petrel*'s entrances and exits had to be carefully timed, for the opening must often be impassable.

Once in the open sea Tou stepped the mast. We helped him hoist the square black linen sail. A lurid sunset poured its rays across the wind-whipped ocean, and high close clouds skittered across the purple sky. "How will you steer in the dark without stars?" I asked. Tou pretended not to hear. The boat heeled over as we tacked. Hissing foam and taut sail gave the impression of urgent speed, but the *Petrel* did not actually progress very quickly. The little boat was plainly designed for the slow, clandestine labor of piracy. Even her name was traditionally piratical, for petrels skim the waves and follow ships.

Xalan and I crouched in the bows and pulled the cloaks close round our necks. "You're not subject to seasickness, are you?" Xalan asked, as the boat bucked over the waves.

"Of course not," I said too quickly. "Though Melayne is."

He grinned. "I'm only sick sometimes, in storms. Thank Viris the weather looks good."

As the night deepened, the wedge of sail became almost invisible behind us. Tou steered a compli-

cated course through the maze of shoals and rocks
that guard the strait. Due south was the other headland, but in the dark we could not see it and soon
lost our bearings. The steady rush of water and the
rocking boat lulled me to sleep.

It was after midnight when Xalan poked me awake.
"Here we are," he said. "How do you plan to work
this?"

I surveyed the situation. Tou had brought us quite
close before lowering sail. The clouds had blown
themselves away. The headland bulked directly before us, very much lower than the one that housed
Cliffhole. Around its blunt nose east and then south
was the great beach port of Ennelith-Ral. But here
there was no sign of life. Starlight silvered the tidal
flats that swept empty away. Only a single pinpoint
of light, on the beach at the foot of the cliff, showed
some fisherman awake. The tide was all the way out;
we could have waded ashore.

"I don't think," I said, "that Mor will go all the way
to the Holy City. For one thing, it hasn't fallen yet.
They'd hardly let a Cayd in, even if he said he
wanted to offer to the goddess."

"Also, there's no cliff in town," Xalan remembered.
"It's all beaches and flats."

"Yes. This is where it looks really deep, at least
when the tide's up. Mor will probably turn off the
main road around here. Let's watch the cliff for
him."

In silence Tou lowered the anchor, allowing plenty
of line for the rising tide. He folded another few
leaves into his mouth and chewed steadily. "I wonder if Pol found them," I mused.

"How will we know?"

"We'll wait until the next low tide tomorrow," I
said. "If the Cayds don't arrive by then we'll assume
Pol waylaid them."

"Then we'll be here for hours," Xalan yawned.
"Let's take the watch in turns. You can be first—I'm
terribly sleepy."

I was not sleepy at all. An exaltation filled me, the sense that Averidan's luck had turned at last—and mine with it. All during the bitter campaign we had been a copper short and a day late. But at last we had seized the initiative. Melayne and Silverhand had already foiled the best Mor could do. It was up to me to keep up the pressure.

Too slow to be perceived, the stars spun through the sky, and the tide trickled in. About halfway through the night I let Xalan take over; Tou refused to sleep and sat, endlessly chewing, with a watchful patience that we felt was entirely piratical. But by dawn I could not sleep anymore. Suspense made me restless. The boat was too small to allow stretching out comfortably, and a nail stuck out of the planking under my leg. Chilled from our long unmoving wait in the teeth of the wind, we huddled around the brazier. The fishrolls were unpacked, and I passed the brandy around.

The dawn crept in cool and slow over the water. Though the Sun's light and warmth were welcome, I felt we were conspicuous, the only craft visible in the strait. At my request Tou produced a shrimp seine, in very bad repair. Xalan and I held the poles and spread the net out in the shallow sparkling water. "We should have some fish in the boat," I worried. "We could have purchased some and brought them along."

"I don't sleep with fish," Xalan said firmly. "There's such a thing as too much verisimilitude."

All this time we were watching the southern shore. The cliff was not a high one, topped by a slope rather than a sheer drop. From the City to Ennelith-Ral is only a day's walk down the road. If the Cayds had left last night they should be here very soon. "We should have posted someone on the road," I fretted. "Or you could have brought your mirror."

"Hush! Look!" Xalan bent busily over the net, and peered up from under his borrowed hood. I pretended to watch a sea gull, and stared. Up on the sloping cliff were people. The tiny figures crept here and there among the rocks and scrub, like ants searching for a crumb—or like Cayds scouring an area for ambush.

They were muffled in hoods and cloaks, but their height betrayed them. "It's Musenor, over there near the drop," I hissed.

"Then that must be Mor up above, watching them," Xalan said. "See, by that pointed rock."

"And that must be the Crown, under his arm!" I leaped up and let the pole slip from my unheeding fingers. Fear and desire seemed to twine like invading vines up my gaze, until I felt Mor must sense it. Every drop of my being focused on the distant figure with the dark blob under its arm. My throne, my absolute rule over Averidan, was nothing. The Crown itself was far more vital than what it symbolized. For it I must kill or die.

Xalan jostled me and whispered, "Liras, fish!" I knelt and snatched up the pole. Very faintly we could hear the Cayds talking in their own tongue, though wind and surf prevented us from making out any words. A stray gust flipped Mor's hood back as he marched down the slope, and the morning light showed his red hair clearly.

My knuckles were white on the pole, and we made a sad hash of seining nonexistent shrimps. Xalan had taken the precaution of turning his back to the cliff, but he watched my face sharply. Our tension infected even Tou, who aimlessly coiled and recoiled the mooring rope.

When Mor reached the verge my shoulders ached with the suspense. For a moment he stood unmoving as he inspected sea and sky. Though he could hardly recognize me at this distance, I bent to shadow my face a little.

Then he raised his burden high above his head. It flew in a long arc far out to sea. The dark bundle undid itself in its tumbling fall, and for one instant the Crystal Crown glittered white in the sunlight.

Then it vanished with a splash into the water about two hundred paces south and east of us.

I leaped to my feet again, making the boat rock. I could almost imagine the Crown had screamed to me, its wearer, for help, as Tarys might have wailed, "Father!" in her fall. And I reacted as instinctively as if it were my child. With a splash I jumped over the side, chest-deep into the breathlessly cold water.

"Liras, what are you doing?" Xalan cried in alarm, and then clapped a hand over his mouth and glanced up at the cliff to see if he had been heard. The Cayds had seen too, and were shouting and searching for a path down the hill. Tou hauled up the anchor and unshipped the oars.

Ignoring them all I floundered through the icy surf. Submerged rocks and weed caught at my waterlogged boots. The cold drove into my limbs, sucking like leeches at the warmth of my blood. How could the Crown survive this? I kept my eyes fixed where it had vanished, in a terror lest I accidentally glance away and then lose the place forever.

When I splashed up to the spot, the Cayds had found a winding trail down the hill. Already Musenor was pounding on the door of the humble shack on the shore. I took a deep breath, and dived. My leather hood floated away. The cold made me gape, letting bitter salt water into my mouth. My eyes stung as I peered into the depths. All I could make out was pale sand and brown rocks. Seaweed waved in time with the sea-surge, and an oyster clapped its shell closed at my noisy approach. Spluttering, I stood up above the surface again. Had I marked the spot rightly?

The Cayds on the shore saw me clearly now, and yelled, "Look, it's only chest deep!" and "The Witch-King!" One had strung his bow, and now aimed a shaft at me. Others began to wade out into the water. I ducked again, this time groping with my hands as well as using my eyes. Almost immediately I felt smooth crystal under my fingertips. The Crown was there, invisible against the white sands.

I clutched it to my chest and kicked upward, shaking the water from my hair. When I had blinked my eyes clear I saw the *Petrel* quite close, with Tou at the oars. Xalan leaned over the prow to give me a hand. "You got it!" he cheered, beaming.

With his aid I scrambled into the boat. An arrow hit the side and bounced off. Tou spat green after it. "You two row," he barked, "while I raise sail." I dropped the Crown into the bottom of the boat, and we flung ourselves on the oars.

But even as the boat came around, the foremost Cayd was wading near. He must have been that rarity among his countrymen—a swimmer—for he had far outstripped his fellows. As he neared my side of the boat I unshipped my oar and swung it at his head. To my dismay he grabbed it and jerked, nearly dragging me overboard. When he pushed it sharply back, tearing it from my weakened left hand, he caught Xalan in the stomach with the handle. As his great hands clamped onto the gunwale the poor *Petrel* rocked like a toy.

Then with a creak of the pulleys the sail rose up the mast. The boat began to foam out into the strait. But still the Cayd hung on to the gunwale, glaring up at us from furious blue eyes as he tried to heave himself aboard.

Now I cursed our folly in not bringing a weapon. One oar was gone. I wrenched the other free and smashed at the Cayd's clutching hand. "Of all the gutless stunts!" Tou snarled, and instead slashed with his copper knife. With a gurgle the Cayd vanished, leaving behind two severed fingers that leaked red. Tou kicked them overboard on his way back to the tiller.

"A Tiger indeed!" Xalan panted, rubbing his bruised midriff. "I think I'll be seasick after all." But instead he accused, "I thought the plan was to mark its fall, and rescue it later. Now the Cayds know we've got it back."

"We might have lost our bearings," I explained, and picked the Crown up. It was shockingly cold to the touch. I turned it over, but found no mark of Mor's attempts to crush it, not even a scratch.

"Well? Aren't you going to try it on, to see if they've hurt it?"

I stared at the Crown and said nothing, but Xalan's question was answered in my own heart. As in dreams, where knowledge is never questioned but only accepted, I knew I should never dare to wear it again. The "Shan King" was brave, to entrust his self, his very personality, to the spirit it housed, but Liras Tsormelezok's courage did not suffice. When last the nightmare became reality I had nothing left to lose. But now? Melayne, and Tarys, and Mother, all had their claims on me, to say nothing of the entire burgeoning rebellion, which would fail without me to rally around. Furthermore, the Crown embodies both the sigil and the power of the Sun our ancestor. Since the One and I had parted company, wearing the Crown would be dishonest.

But having been dragged so far, my specious reasoning stood threadbare in its inconsistency. Though I was done with the god I could not quite suppress the knowledge that it could not be so simple as that. After all, was I not here, free and well, vastly better off than I had been in the dungeons? It was at best discourteous to accept favors without making thanks. And if I never again wore the Crown, what use was it to me? I recalled the fight at the Upper City gate; I had not needed the Crown then, to draw on the power that underlies the everyday veneer. Then I remembered I meant to stay clear of that realm, and the sky for an instant seemed dull, the sea lifeless. A world that was nothing but surface was not worth living in.

The whole business was far too confusing to mull over on a sea-tossed boat. I blinked, and saw that

Xalan was lifting the last of the fishrolls out of their sack. He took out the brandy-flask too, and tossed the empty sack over. "The Cayds probably got its casket," he said. I nodded agreement, and put the Crown inside.

"I'd take some of that," Tou remarked again, and this time I passed the bottle back.

"We're infinitely grateful for your help, Tou," I said. "You saved us, there."

"Not yet," he said tersely, and jerked a thumb over his shoulder. Past the angle of the sail we peered shoreward. A boat was putting out to sea, launched from the shanty's rickety dock. The terrified owner, menaced by Caydish swords, was at the helm. "An oysterman's craft," Tou said with contempt. "He'll not outrun us."

Unfortunately the wind was against us, and we had to tack. Our pursuers did not bother with sails. A half-dozen Cayds manned the oars of the oyster-tonger, and despite their ignorance of technique were driving the flat-bottomed craft along at a good clip. Slowly our lead lessened, and to my horror I saw the archer kneeling on the prow of the pursuing boat.

"He can't possibly hit," Xalan said nervously. "With both boats pitching like this—"

A black arrow flew between us and embedded itself to the fletches in the linen sail. The Lame Tiger took another gulp of brandy and roared, "We'll show them, the land-snails! No one knows the seas around these parts better than me!"

He leaned on the tiller and the *Petrel* came hard around. She skimmed at an angle past the oyster-craft, running before the wind straight out to sea. For one instant the archer had a point-blank shot at us, but we crouched low and he missed. Yelling with rage, Musenor and Mor wrestled with the unfamiliar tangle of sails and ropes. With the captive captain's help they raised sail, and foamed after us.

"They've got two sails," I said, peering back. "Will that offset their bigger load?"

"Watch this," Tou muttered to me in reply.

I looked forward, and my hair nearly rose on end. He was steering us straight for the shoals, which stuck like clawing fingers out of the surf. There were channels between them, cruelly complex in their twists and turns, shifting with every tide and storm. Hidden rocks made the passage even more perilous than it looked. And the tide was going out. The big ships always steered well to the north and west of this area. Only the lightest and most skilfully steered vessels could negotiate it at all, and then only at high tide. Tou barreled at it as if the *Petrel* truly had wings.

Too terrified to protest, Xalan and I clung to the gunwales. The wind whipped through our hair, buffeting the Petrel over the sunny surf like a crazed thing. Behind us the Cayds' boat came steadily, but not as fast as before. Its frantic owner was expostulating with his uncomprehending passengers.

For their part, the Cayds seemed nearly as paralyzed as we. Caydish navigation, such as it is, is confined to lakes and rivers. This careening race over rock-strewn ocean must have appeared suicidal. Only Musenor was able to shake his fist at us. Everyone else aboard was rapidly succumbing to seasickness— the tail wind brought the sound clearly to our ears. I could see why Melayne avoided sailing.

Our keel grated horribly as we scraped over a submerged sand bar. Just below the surface we could see fangs of rock skimming past. We whirled round a huge wet hump of stone close enough to touch it. The oyster-tonger was less lucky. With a splintering crash all the oars on one side were snapped as they sideswiped the rock. The retching Cayds were tossed about like dolls. For a moment all was confusion, and the craft swung sideways into the combers. Then a wave broke over the side, and pushed it onto the rocks. The Cayds screamed prayers as their boat broke into several pieces.

"Let's hope they drown," Xalan said with satisfaction.

"No, I'm sure the other Cayds have found a second boat by now," I said. "They'll be rescued. After all, that's the King of Cayd out there. Let's take this opportunity to make ourselves scarce."

Tou accordingly turned north to thread a course through the rocks and shallows. I looked back, past the sail. His red hair dripping wet, Mor stood knee-deep on a submerged shoal, staring after us. As clearly as if I were wearing the Crown I knew he was marking our direction. A sensible soldier would take care to leave no witnesses to guide pursuers. Furthermore, as Mother had noted, the deaths of Mor and Musenor would fracture the invasion. But we were weaponless, and also another impulse danced in my head—to put about, and fish the Cayds out of the sea. Only a pirate would leave anyone to drown. I was Shan King.

But then I remembered I myself sailed with a pirate now. Between the two impulses I did nothing, cheering myself with the reflection that if Ennelith wanted the Cayds she could easily send a sea drake for them.

The Sun was a high golden coin in the sky, and we had succeeded: the Crystal Crown was mine once more. "I can hardly believe it's true," I said to Xalan. "We did it!"

He clapped me on the back, grinning. "The experience has aged me terribly," he declared. "I never was so scared."

"What about you, Tou?" I called. "You weren't in the least bit nervous."

There was no reply. After a while, a little disturbed, I ducked aft under the sail. The Lame Tiger lolled against the tiller, his head rocking on his shoulders. I grasped his arm, and the heavy stoneware bottle clunked onto the planking. It was empty.

"Xalan!" I shouted. "Quick! Dash sea water in his face, or duck him! He's drunk all the brandy!"

"That must be the fault Pol meant to warn us of," Xalan said with a groan. "How else could so little spirit knock him out?" He held Tou by the belt and draped him over the side, sousing arms and head in the waves without result. "What about our course?"

"I don't know anything about these shoals," I said, taking the tiller. "But I think we're clear—do you see any rocks?"

Xalan did not. The high northern cliffs were plainly visible, so even I should be able to steer the Petrel back to Cliffhole.

Xalan rolled the dripping Lame Tiger into the bottom of the boat. "And I was going to suggest giving him a commendation, or something," I said dismally.

"It's a disappointment," Xalan agreed. "When they come to do your plaiv they'll have to omit this part."

Since the wind set from the west I had to work to make the northern shore. It was a nerve-wracking business for, though I could sail, both the sea and boat were unfamiliar. To a passenger our journey out had seemed slow. Now that I was captain the *Petrel* traveled so fast I could not relax a moment.

The terns were diving and whistling to each other as we approached the cliff. The tide was ebbing, and we probably could have entered Tou's cave. But we could not pick it out. Dozens of holes and caves showed black in the sunlit rock-face. We could hear everywhere the hollow sound of wave under stone. "Do you recognize our cave?" I asked.

"No, it was dark when we left."

"I never thought we'd have to get back alone," I said regretfully. "We'll have to pick the likeliest-looking one. I can't just stop the boat here, like reining in a horse. If we don't enter a cave, we'll have to turn."

"How about that big one," Xalan pointed. The indicated cave showed about two stories high, with a wide comfortable-looking mouth that I felt quite confident about steering through. We wouldn't even have to unstep the mast, a business neither of us felt certain of.

"All right," I said, and leaned on the tiller. The obedient Petrel swung around and nosed toward the

cave. Xalan went forward and leaned over the prow
to con the passage.

"It looks good," he reported. Then, "Wait! There's
no cave—"

With an appalling crunch, we hit. Xalan yelled as he
was jerked overboard. I waggled the tiller helplessly.
The *Petrel* was stuck, neat as an oyster on a fork, on
a hidden point of rock. Worse, a large hole had been
torn in its planking. The sea rushed in, rewetting my
feet and floating Tou's clothing around his inert
limbs. The wind pushed on the sail and ground us
farther onto the rock.

"Xalan!" I shouted.

"I'm here," he spluttered. "What happened?"

"We hit something. The *Petrel's* breaking apart.
Here, I'm going to push Tou overboard to you."

"You realize if I drop him he'll drown," Xalan said.

"I'll help you," I assured him. The strings of the
food sack knotted conveniently around my waist.
With the Crown safe, I heaved Tou up and over the
collapsing side. Then I followed him down. The
waves were icy cold, but the Lame Tiger showed no
signs of returning consciousness. "Take one arm," I
said, "and I'll take the other."

"Where are we going?" Xalan asked, treading water. "I saw, just before we hit—the cave's blind, just a
cup in the rock."

"We'll swim to the next," I said, gritting my teeth
so that they should not chatter. But it was easier said
than done. We each of us had only one arm to
paddle with. A fierce undertow dragged at us so that
it was as much as we could do to keep all our heads
above water. The situation was so unsatisfactory that
I gasped, "Suppose I hold Tou while you lift, and
bring help."

"I oughtn't leave you," Xalan protested.

"You want me to make it a command?" With numb
fingers I untied the sack from my middle. "Here
take this—carefully! Now I'm expendable. Go, and
hurry before I freeze."

Reluctantly Xalan released Tou and took the sack. He rose straight up, dripping, and fluttered away along the rock-face.

With Tou's entire limp weight to support, I fumbled over the slick sea-worn rock for a hand or foot-hold. But the narrow ledges I found crumbled under any weight. The only resting-place was the Petrel's wreckage. I shoved a plank under Tou, but it could not float me as well. And when I leaned on a separate plank Tou's limp form began to slide off his own. In the end I had to tread water beside him, holding his head onto the plank. Through the slap of the waves I could not tell if he was breathing, and my hands were too cold to feel his pulse.

For an endless time I fought the undertow and the waves, and tried not to think how attractive my dangling ankles must look to lurking sea drakes. Then came a shout. I cried weakly back, and a rowboat appeared around the spur. "Here you are!" the steersman remarked unnecessarily, and Xalan helped him haul us to safety.

"Are you frozen?" Xalan asked anxiously.

I rather thought so. My limbs had lost all feeling, and a cold pain squeezed my lungs so that I lay in the dinghy and gasped like a hooked fish. "Got caught in the Fool's Needle, did you," the steersman said with satisfaction. "There's many a guardsman and soldier tried that, and drowned for it, during the pirate wars. It only *looks* like a haven."

"What I've always wanted," I gasped. "To be like my great-grandfather."

Maddeningly, Tou roused from his drunken stupor at that very moment. "I'm wet!" he exclaimed. "And my boat—where's my *Petrel*? You land-snails have wrecked my beautiful *Petrel*!"

I couldn't help it, I shouted with laughter. Xalan glared at him, his mouth open, but for once was completely at a loss for words.

CHAPTER 15:
The Realm Beneath

When Mother learned we had spared the Cayds she was furious. "A tactical error we'll pay dearly for," she upbraided me bitterly. "Your father was just like that—an idiot."

It soon became plain she was right. The recapture of the Crystal Crown made Cliffhole's situation far more precarious. Mor had been embarrassed by my escape, and inconvenienced by the Crown's imperishable quality. No doubt he also knew of the insurrection based in Cliffhole—it could not be kept secret long, especially when Mor began conquest of the remaining coastal regions. But the three irritations, conjoined, were no longer pinpricks. They were become a deadly threat to his new rule. He would be ready to go to any lengths to deal with me—and he now knew the Crown and I were hiding in Cliffhole.

Squads of foreigners poured down the north road the very next day, blocking all traffic and scouring the countryside. Mor also mounted a sea assault. The Cayds were poor sailors, and had to trust the local seamen. But it was amazing what holding the fishermen's children hostage would do. With that unwilling help the Cayds systematically explored the caves from the sea.

These efforts were only partially successful. When it came to cave-fighting all the advantage lay with the Cliffholers. All the tricks that had annoyed my great-grandfather—the submerged chains, the cavern deadfalls, the passages that vanished and then reappeared, the tidal waters cunningly dammed and then released—I helped Pol use on the Cayds. The ambushes and booby-traps that Mother had ordered set up also took their toll. But I thought I recognized a terrible pattern. They had us cornered again, and were once more chipping away at our position. Cliffhole could stand, but not forever.

"Oh, I can't bear another siege," said Melayne about a fortnight after my return with the Crown. We were looking out Mother's windows at the eastern sea. The Cayds were outside in dinghies, trying a new trick—pouring linseed oil onto the incoming tide. When the oil-slick had been carried deep enough into the hill they touched it off. Several boats moored within were burnt, but the real peril was the black acrid smoke that swept through the caves. The long corridors with their many windows and gaps were as good as chimneys. The lower caves were temporarily uninhabitable.

As Melayne spoke, my thoughts crystallized into one clear idea. "We're losing the initiative again," I said. "We have to get out of this, or they'll kill everyone."

"Do you suggest giving up?" Mother demanded.

"No." By now I had learned to hold Tarys properly, and the tiny warm torso in my hands, so full of new life, clarified my thinking. "All our problems spring from the fact that Mor knows where I am," I said. "All you have to do is tell the Cayds I'm gone. Let them in, if you have to, to search the caves. I'll just vanish: go out to the marshes, catch a horse, and ride away. You can give me about two weeks' lead, before you surrender. They'll never pick up my trail then."

"But where will you go?"

I had no idea. "But it doesn't matter," I realized. "As soon as the Cayds start looking for me there, I'll come back." In a tiny cough, like a squeaking kitten, Tarys began to fuss. I passed her back to Melayne. Immediately my simple yet grand concept began to complicate. Melayne looked me straight in the eye and said, "I'm coming with you."

"But it'll only be for a month or so—"

"You promised!"

It was true. I shut my mouth on my protests, and then opened it to say, "But what about the baby?"

"We'll bring her with us."

"Impossible," Mother said decisively. "How can you haul a newborn all over Averidan? You're just nervous about the Cayds' progress, dear. But they can't always win. They shall never take Cliffhole. You'll be safe here forever."

"I said that myself, about the City," I remembered. "No—this time we'll win by cunning, not raw strength."

Very rarely did anyone ever question Mother's judgment. Now I could see her reminding herself I was Shan King. With deceptive mildness she turned to Melayne. "You must think," she urged. "How could you nurse my grandchild, galloping about the marshes? And marsh air is very unhealthy for babes. You're hardly over your labor, too. Whereas you'd be quite safe here. Now the babe is born I'm sure Mor will look kindly on her. Has he ever had a niece before?"

"Several," Melayne said, in her most mulish tone.

I grinned and left Mother to rehash all the arguments I had already worn out on Melayne's stubbornness. In the outer room Xalan was scrying on the Cayds for Pol. I went up to him and said, "I feel an attack of *chun-hei* coming on. We're leaving Cliffhole, and since Melayne's coming perhaps you'd like to also."

"Certainly," Xalan said absently, without looking up from his glass. Then he glanced up, startled. "What did I just agree to?"

"Too late," I said jubilantly, and went out into the smoky corridor to start packing.

The very next day I sneaked out of Cliffhole into the marshes, armed with rope, salt, bread, and apples. With these lures it was easy to capture four horses. Zofal had intended this to be only temporary, so all our stock roamed the marshlands. Now I chose only the geldings. The mares could be left to bear more foals. Since they were already more or less tame, and recognized me, I took very little time. But the two pirate lads I had brought along to help were awed at this uncanny mastery over beasts. "That's why he's Shan King," I overheard one whispering to the other. "He's a hero, he can do things no other can."

We tethered them at the back of a beach-cave on the eastern shore which the Cayds had already unsuccessfully searched. That night under cover of darkness we loaded them with our baggage. Melayne brought all the baby's clothes. I had our own garments, with the Crystal Crown rolled up in the center of the luggage-roll, and Xalan packed food. The extra horse carried blankets and camping gear. For lack of proper tack the beasts were bridled with ropes and saddled with blankets.

Though by then it was very late the Cliffholers turned out to see us off—of course their work had accustomed them to irregular hours. Mother was last to arrive, hobbling stiffly over the rocks on Pol's arm.

"I have a gift for you, my son," she said in ringing tones. Pol passed it to her, and she to me: a sword in a plain leather sheath. I slid it out and saw it was the very model of a Viridese blade, wide and leaf-shaped, with a central rib worked in the bronze and two edges like razors. The hilt was ivory, carved to represent two sturgeons lunging for a sardonyx berry.

"It's beautiful, Mother," I said. "Thank you!"

"Use it well," she commanded, "on our enemies."

I held it out and spoke loudly enough for all to hear. "On this edge I vow that someday I shall return, and win my kingdom back again." The waves broke hissing on the beach, as if to underscore my sincerity. Then I spoiled the heroic effect by saying, "I'll soon be back. Pol, I count on you to take care of Mother until then."

"Haven't I been?" Pol said indignantly.

It was too cold and damp for Mother to stand
about, so with a final embrace I took my leave. The
lamps were extinguished, the canvas blinds rolled
back, and I mounted and guided my horse out of
the cave. It had to wade over the sand bar, but the
water came only up to its knees. We turned north.
The gravelly beach was just wide enough, between
cliff and sea, for the laden beasts.

A new mildness sweetened the midnight breeze.
With amazement I calculated it must have turned
Ynbas during our Cliffhole stay. Spring was already
here. Yet the war had only begun in autumn. It ought
to have been a century ago; certainly enough had happened. I felt quite elderly with the rush of events.

We rode at an easy pace along the shore until
dawn. By then the land had sunk into marsh. We
waded the shallow inlet, then turned left to conceal
our trail among the trackless grasses.

"How eerie!" Melayne complained. The rustling
reeds that closed around us were utterly foreign to
her. Each horse-hoof sank deep into the soft mud,
and came up with a sticky sound to leave water in
the bottom of the depression. Sea snipe, modest in
their gray-brown feathers, broke from their nests
almost at our feet, circling above us with shrill piping
shrieks until we passed and they could alight again.

All this I remembered. But the warmth had brought
out the first gnats of the season. The marshland
resonated now with the hum of new-awakened insects,
hungry for their first meal. They leaped happily on
us, no doubt thanking their gods for this unexpected
bounty so early in the year. We slapped and cursed,
and Melayne had to bundle Tarys up like laundry,
for the gnats liked tender baby skin. "How shall we
camp in this?" she demanded, brushing the insects
away. "We'll be eaten alive."

"There's higher ground ahead," I said. But it took
us several hours to reach it, because we had to cross
the entire valley. Our only consolation was that any
pursuer would be quite thrown off.

We halted at a rough stone hut, obviously one of the seasonal dwellings used by reed-cutters. It nestled into the northern side of the ridge we had just crossed, more a cave with an outer annex than a proper house. Twisted pine trees anchored the sandy soil, and a sea breeze swept away the gnats. From the woven-cane door we could see east over the wilderness of salt marsh to the sea. In these untraveled parts it was not worth the trouble to set a watch. Instead I trusted to the sea-snipe to warn us of any approach.

Melayne sat just inside to nurse the babe, while Xalan and I gathered pine boughs and lit a fire, proudly exhibiting to each other our new-learned skills. "Where are we going?" Xalan asked.

"There are fishing villages all up and down the coast," I said. "Suppose we find one with a decent inn?" Mother had helped me convert Melayne's jewelry into coin, so we could afford it.

"But then I'll have to hide all day," Melayne objected from within. "Word of a traveller with a Caydish wife would soon spread. Why can't we stay here?"

"It's a little lonely," Xalan said. "How should we hear, if anything happened?"

"Well, we can try it a few days anyway," I decided. For the first time in years I had no duties, no need to hurry anywhere. The sensation was so unusual, I wanted to enjoy it. "No doubt we can find a village to buy food in tomorrow."

So the next day, after lunch, Xalan and I made our way to the nearest village. We did not know the paths through the marshes, but it was easy to guide ourselves by the distant blue smudge of smoke from the cook-fires. Xalan wore not his eye-catching magian red but the simple dress of a reed-gatherer. In my borrowed yellow tunic I had assumed the rank of a very minor noble. My sword and full purse would otherwise excite undue nterest, perhaps even robbery. A peasant rarely carries large sums or weapons, and it's known that ill-gotten goods are fair game for anyone strong enough to steal them away.

The village was a humble one, no more than eight whitewashed wattle-and-daub huts clustered around the inlet. Thick grass thatches lowered over the walls and gave the settlement the shaggy look of ungroomed ponies. We strolled down the one sandy street to the harbor. Most of the boats were out fishing, but a few had returned early. One fisherman silently displayed a basketful of sardines and two medium-sized bass. His equally silent wife scrubbed an octopus to tenderness against a nearby rock. I bargained for a bass. While I waited for it to be hung on a grass string, another craft appeared at the mouth of the inlet. The fisherman and his wife turned to look, by which we knew it was a stranger's. Curious, Xalan loitered on the beach as the boat foamed a little nearer, while I counted out copper coins.

"Sweet Viris, look!" Xalan shouted and pointed. I stared out to sea and grew cold all over. A tall red-headed figure was just visible in the boat near the steersman. "The Cayds!"

"What an ill chance!" I gasped. But there was no time to worry about that now. We turned and ran through the village, the fish flopping annoyingly at my back. "Once on horseback we can outrun them." I panted.

In our anxiety we nearly lost our way in the tall grass. We raced up the hill to the stone hut. Melayne had just undone her braids. Comb in hand, she said, "Don't be too noisy; Tarys is asleep."

"Your kinsmen are here!" I exclaimed. "We saw them from the village!"

"They must be putting in for water," she said placidly. "We can see them coming for a long way from here. Suppose we broil that fish while we wait and see?"

Nervously Xalan set about scaling and cleaning the fish, while I watched the shore. Sure enough, the snipe began to rise and circle fretfully around a distrubance in the high grass. "Wrap the fish in leaves," I told him. "I'll saddle the horses. Melayne, get the baby."

The sleepy infant fretted as we rode away. Melayne had contrived a Caydish-style sling out of an old blanket, which held the child to her breast and left her arms free. "We'll circle north, through the hills," I said. "The next village will be safe." Few betraying birds lived in the pines, so we slipped away, as I had hoped, unnoticed. The wary tension of the hunted beast beat in our blood; Melayne clutched Tarys close to her, and I kept turning to scan the forest. We rode a weary way west and then north, beating our way through pine-scrub and myrtles before turning back toward the sea again. When another settlement became visible on the shore we circled it, to halt on an overlooking ridge and examine its harbor.

"That's a big boat out there, for a fishing town," Xalan noted.

With despair I saw the glint of westering light on metal on the debarking passengers. "This is incredible," I said. "How can they know we're here? It can't be coincidence." Then a horrid idea occurred to me. "Could a magus be scrying upon us?"

"It's impossible," Xalan assured me.

"Why?" I demanded.

He could supply no reason. With a jerk of the reins I turned my mount away and kicked it into a canter downhill. Only Xalan could test the accuracy of my guess, and he would need a quiet spot, secure from interruption or violence from the Cayds.

We thundered north up the beach until the ridge began to fall away beside us. I pulled up where huge gray rocks crumbled from a cliff into the sand. Melayne's horse nearly overran me, I leaped off so quickly, and had to halt in a stinging spray of grit. "Look in your mirror, Xalan," I commanded. "Will you be able to detect a watcher?"

"Certainly," he said. "Mirrors attract scries, you know."

The Sun was low on the western hills, and Xalan had to crouch in the long shadows cast by the rocks to see properly. While he uncovered his glass I climbed up onto a house-sized crag to keep watch. The first thing I noticed was Melayne gathering driftwood, the baby still tied on her back. "We're not camping here, Melayne," I called.

"I know," she replied. "but I want to cook this fish."

"Can't you wait?" I fretted.

"I'm hungry," she said. "Nursing a baby requires regular meals."

Only gulls moved on the shore, wading out as each wave retreated to search among the pebbles for edible jetsam. Occasionally one or two would take wing, tracing lazy circles on the purpling sky before alighting again. But for me the sea and sky were full of eyes. Not only the magi's mirrors, but that other patient presence was harrying me. I could not escape the nagging sensation that I was being driven to something.

I slid down to the sand again and loitered behind Xalan's tense hunched back, now and again peeking over his shoulder. "What do you see?" I asked at last.

"Locally?" Xalan's voice was remote. "Cayds have put in at every hamlet from here to Cliffhole. You were right, it's not a coincidence."

"How did they learn where we are?" I pressed.

"Mmm, let me cast about." Suddenly his tone sharpened. "The magi! The Order is scrying us!"

"I knew it!" But the satisfaction was bitter in my mouth.

Ignoring me Xalan berated his mirror—or rather, the magi on the other side. "How dare you collaborate with the foreigners!" he cried. His audience obviously made their own demands in reply, for he continued, "But I'm with the Shan King, Liras Tsormelezok. Look at his face, if you don't believe me." I felt a blush rising to my face at the thought of dozens of unseen magi peering into my countenance.

After another pause he objected, "But Mor doesn't have the Crystal Crown. Liras still has it." He glanced away to me. "Didn't you tell everyone, that the Cayds planned to smash the Crown?"

I cast my mind back to that frantic final day of my reign. "Why yes, I'm sure I told the magi. At least—" Suddenly I remembered. I had told Xorlev, counting on him to pass the word along. But he had died. "Silverhand knows, and she's in the City," I told Xalan. "Let them consult her."

"If they can find her! They don't believe us, Liras. Mor told everyone he would don the Crown soon, and it never occurred to them to doubt his word!"

"Let him try!" I fumed. "Those gullible savants— here, tell them they can descry the Crown. I've got it right here."

I ran to the driftwood log where we had tied the horses. But as I untied my bundle I saw sails on the horizon. "They're coming!" I shouted. "Melayne!"

Xalan swore as he shoved his mirror back into its case. "You should have sent me back, to become Master Magus," he said in despair. "They have magi on board. How can we escape a foe who can see where we're going?"

"The sea," I declared. "Remember, once you told me to cross ocean, to escape scrying. We'll find a ship and sail away. Mounted, we can still outrun anything on sea or land. This is where Zofal's hobby proves its worth." I helped Melayne, the babe still tied on her back, into the saddle. "What is that?"

"Roast fish," she said, pushing a twig skewer into my hand. "Eat it while it's hot."

Distracted, I slid the white piping-hot flesh off into my mouth and gulped it down. "Hurry!" Xalan begged. The sails were still only white flakes on the evening-blue sea as we galloped off.

Once the Sun set we had a temporary respite. The waning moon cast little light. So long as we lit no fire the mirrors could not descry us. Nor could the Cayds find us. Unfortunately, it was also difficult to make out our way, and we dared not leave the beach to perhaps become mired in the marsh. We rode for hours in the dark, putting our foes as far behind us as we could. Then, exhausted, we hitched the horses before a cleft in the rocks, and huddled within under all our blankets. Nothing could be cooked, so we nibbled dried fruits and old bread. The cold, and the chilly roar of the surf, kept sleep away.

"That fish was supper," Melayne said, taking credit for herself. "If I had listened to you we would have had to eat it raw."

"Don't let's talk about it," begged Xalan, who in the excitement had not gotten any.

In the cold blue light before dawn, as soon as we could make out our path, we moved on. We had debated whether to go ahead, or back. Returning to the previous village would mean a known journey of a definite length. On the other hand, though we did not know how far it was to the next harbor, possibly the Cayds had not arrived there yet. "A possible enemy's less dangerous than a certain one," I decided. So we continued north.

It was perhaps an error. In mid-morning we rounded a spur of rock. On the other side was a deep narrow bay, straddled by quite a large village. At the harbor's head no less than three docks bustled with boats and shipping, and at the longest a big merchanter was tied up. But nearer yet, drawn up on the beach, was a fishing trawler. At the sight of us an incredible number of Caydish warriors swarmed out onto the shingle.

Weapons ready, a dozen of them spread across the narrow beach to block us. "Don't slow down!" I shouted. I dragged my sword out of its scabbard and dug my heels hard into my horse's side so that it surged ahead of Xalan's. A Viridese line, even behind spears and shields, might have wavered. The Cayds, however, did not seem troubled by imaginings of the damage pounding hooves and a mounted swordsman could do.

I barreled at the thinnest point on their line. The gelding untrained for this sort of encounter, tried to shy off, but I refused to let it turn, and slapped at its

rump with my hat. At the last possible instant, when
I was close enough to count the hairs in his nostrils,
one Cayd shouted and threw himself aside. I hacked
downward at the other soldier, on my right. The
blade stuck fast in a Caydish helmet, nearly dragging
out of my hand. I slowed down, and tugged it free
so wildly I almost slashed Xalan's head off as he
whisked past us. The pack horse he led trampled
someone into the sand. Another Cayd grabbed my
ankle. But Melayne thundered by on that side of me,
and swept him aside. My frantic horse reared and
tried to break away again, maddened by the smell of
blood. I gave it its head, and let it tear down the
beach after the others.

The stunned Cayds gathered themselves up and
ran shouting after us. Meanwhile, their boat put out
to sea, the thrashing oars propelling it swiftly across
the narrow bay to cut us off.

"Where to?" Xalan shouted, as we whirled past the
first huts.

"The dock! The ship!" If we could get out to sea
the scryers could be foiled, the Cayds thrown off our
trail. The merchanter had looked tidy and ship-shape,
quite ready to sail. Of course her captain might have
other plans. It would be wrong—an act of piracy, in
fact—to forcibly take her over. But I was past worrying about such scruples now. It was more important
to stay alive, stay ahead.

From the beach the biggest pier ran a good way
out into the bay, giving even the heaviest ships depth.
We halted there, scattering the fish-vendors and dockside cats. "Get aboard," I gasped. "Xalan, haggle for
our passage. Melayne has money. Highjack the entire craft, if you have to." The hooves on the planking boomed like drums as they galloped up the pier.

I patted my mount's sweaty neck, and turned it to
block the pier. Xalan would need time—time to bribe
or coerce the captain and his crew, time to haul up
the anchor, untie the lines, raise the sails. Only I
could buy him that time.

My new sword balanced beautifully in my hand, and I also had Hoob's knife. I slowed my breathing, listening for the sound of running boots. Caydish footwear was never meant for work in salt water or sand. Now as my foes galloped into the harbor square I noticed some were limping, and at least one had entirely shed his leggings and boots.

"Foot-rot, is it?" I taunted them in my indifferent Caydish. "Shall I call on my powers, and heat the sands red-hot?"

Even with the power of the Crystal Crown I could do no such thing. But for an instant the Cayds faltered, glancing nervously down at the sand. In that moment I kicked my reluctant horse hard, making it dash forward among the foe. A trained warhorse would have trampled them. Instead my gentler beast trod on toes. I lay about with my sword, not striking to kill but merely maiming as many as I could. Shieldless as I was, my only defense was terror.

In a plaiv that would have sufficed. But since I was in a real fight, the Cayds soon banded together. One huge fellow engaged my sword, while his fellows hacked at my horse's legs. The animal screamed, a cry against human cruelty so terrible that my heart rose into my mouth. Suddenly the beast lurched onto its knees and, losing my purchase on the blanket-saddle, I fell off.

I rolled clear. The Cayds did not realize my thrashing mount was now harmless, and with howls of triumph hastened to chop its throat. It was an excellent chance to run up the pier. But, brushing the sand out of my face, I saw my luggage roll, still strapped behind the saddle. And the Crystal Crown was rolled in the center.

I almost turned away. The labor of defeating so many, to win the Crown yet again, seemed too much to bear. Since I never intended to wear it again, was it really worth dying for? But the habit of courage was upon me, and I hesitated too long. The Cayds turned toward me again and it was plain I would have to kill them all, or be killed myself.

For a moment anger filled me, the same bitter fury that had scalded me in the Temple after our final pathetic sortie. Too late now I saw the snare I was being forced into. There was only one way a single fighter could prevail against a dozen: by shifting the battleground to that other realm, where forlorn hopes come off and seven die at one blow. It came now as a wonder to me, that I had ever hoped to be free of it. When I had recounted my escape to Xalan he had truthfully remarked, "It would make a delightful plaiv." How could I have failed to note that all this time, while I congratulated myself upon my liberty, I had been winding myself ever deeper in the subtlest of nets? Though I had broken with that underlying reality, it had not broken with me.

But then my heart changed, and I saw the humor of my situation. In breaking a colt one begins gently, with a halter and many tidbits of fruit or bread. But one day the trainer offers an apple, and then throws the saddle on. I smiled to remember the startled expression the young horses had worn. My gyrations to elude the inevitable probably looked no less foolish.

"Witch!" the bravest Cayd accused, to work up his fellows' courage. "We'll give you something to grin about!"

I laughed at him, and for the first time deliberately dived deep into that other world. And a new rage possessed me, not a bitter private ire but the calm, white-hot anger of a King. The hunger and grief and labor of my folk; the destruction of our way of life; the crops burnt and people slain and land stolen—all these grievances lent my arm strength. And all my personal woes—the loss of kin, the fear that I defeated but never could quite oust, my cat, my two fingers—all these memories surged up in my chest in a scorching black tide, not quenching like water but like brandy igniting a hotter flame. The Cayds owed me some harvest, after this terrible sea-

son of sowing, and like an energetic farmer with his
scythe I swung my sword. It was good, after the long
sieges and retreats, to hack and slash, to dye the pale
sands scarlet. My foes, backed only by Mor's cold
commands, could not stand against me. They melted
away before the searing heat of my power, for I was
truly invincible here.

"Liras! Liras!" The voice was familiar. My hot rage
ebbed a little, and I saw Xalan waving anxiously
from the poop deck of the ship. "They're all dead!
Let's go!"

Startled, I looked around. The sand around me
was churned up and black with blood. Foundered
here and there were the remains of my foes, resem-
bling nothing so much as badly slaughtered pigs. A
horrible resemblance clicked into my mind: the Temple courtyard as I had seen it last. Had I really
created this gruesome echo? In the dream it had
been that other who could be cruel. Now my gorge
rose as I realized it was I alone. The Crystal Crown
had not created a Shan King. I, both good and evil
together, was Shan King. If I had not so strenuously
doubted myself the Crown would never have been
able to brush me aside.

"Liras!" Xalan wailed despairingly. "More Cayds
are coming!" The cut-off group from the boat had
landed, and were hurrying through the village on
the other side of the harbor. Staggering with a sudden weariness I went to the carcass of my horse and
slashed the luggage roll free. My hands left sticky
red prints on the blanket, and my yellow clothes
were new-dyed in red.

I trotted as fast as I could up the endless pier.
Xalan had done his work with surprising speed. The
anchor was up, and all the moorings were clear but
one, which a sailor stood ready near. Coaxing a last
effort from my trembling legs, I leaped the narrow
gap between pier and rail. I half-fell, panting, off
the rail onto the deck. Pulleys creaked and glazed
linen strained to cup the breeze. We were safe.

"Are you hurt?" Melayne demanded. She tugged at my shoulder, and I helped her by rolling over.

"No. Don't touch me, I'll come off on you." Obscurely, I was ashamed of my blood-steeped state. I sat stiffly up. The brisk wind off the marshes was drying the stains into my outfit. All the square and triangular ribbed sails were being hoisted by sailors in neat gray tunics. The surging deck was scrubbed bare and clean, and the two-story poop spread a protective shadow over us. I stared at it, dumbfounded.

The owners of merchant ships are usually a most prosaic set, busy wagering their investment of ship and men against Ennelith's capriciousness. Viridese ships tend to be well-supplied with good-luck bells and charms against storms, though otherwise plain. But the upper story of this particular poop was painted: bands of green curlicues roiled around the walls like fighting snakes, interspersed with wide undulating stripes of bright blue and red. No bar of the rail edging the narrow balcony was painted the same color. And while one upper cabin door was painted in concentric ovals of relatively modest white and brown, the other smote the eye in a stupefying angular scheme of vivid yellow, orange, purple, and black.

I tore my gaze from this incredible display up to the poop deck. Xalan dandled the baby, and waved at me to come up with his free arm. Beside him was a wide sturdy figure draped in billowing white. In delight I shouted, "Sandcomber!"

I hurried up the two slanting ladders to the deck, and grasped his dark-skinned hands. "I hardly dared credit young Xalan here," he declared in his oddly accented Viridese. "But here you are, Shan Liras King. How you've altered!"

"You haven't, not a bit," I babbled happily. "You've always saved me in the nick of time. Have you met Melayne, my wife? We would have perished back there, but for you. Where are you going? We'll go with you. However did you come here, of all places? I hope you weren't inconvenienced on our behalf."

Sandcomber stroked his short fluffy white beard and selected the most important item from this torrent of questions. "I've made a most lugubrious visit to the northern lands—an empty realm; do not, I advise, go out of your way to tour it—and have just laded the ship for my homeward voyage."

"Good." The deck was fitted with wooden benches, and I sat, breathless, on the nearest. Melayne curled up beside me on the cushions and took the baby from Xalan. "I hope a few extra passengers won't throw off your provisioning. We must leave the country."

His round face beamed down at me, so affable one would never think he had been abruptly afflicted with four hungry long-term guests. "Hah! And the last I saw you, you were at the pinnacle of fortune, newly a king—with some help from me—of a mighty realm," he recalled with a deep chuckle of satisfaction. "In such a brief time, you've made Averidan too hot to hold you! I owe you a boon anyway, but the account of your grievous and speedy fall from power will amply compensate for your passage to my homeland."

"Anything I can do—" I began to acknowledge gratefully.

But Xalan interrupted. "This may be a minor point," he said, "but where exactly *is* your homeland?"

"Far in the south," Sandcomber boomed in dramatic tones. "Perhaps you remember, I mentioned this was the farthest I have ever journeyed? How your folk reckon long sailing distances I do not know. But when I made my way here it was a year's voyage."

"A *year!*" Flabbergasted, I fell back against the cushions. I had not believed the world was so big.

Xalan's jaw dropped, a reaction which made Sandcomber bellow with amusement. Melayne turned on me like a tigress. "I'm not sailing anywhere for a year!" she cried. "I get seasick!"